WITHDRAWN
UTSA LIBRARIES

THE TORCH AND OTHER TALES

by
EDEN PHILLPOTTS

Short Story Index Reprint Series

 BOOKS FOR LIBRARIES PRESS
FREEPORT, NEW YORK

First Published 1929
Reprinted 1971

INTERNATIONAL STANDARD BOOK NUMBER:
0-8369-3782-1

LIBRARY OF CONGRESS CATALOG CARD NUMBER:
71-144167

PRINTED IN THE UNITED STATES OF AMERICA

CONTENTS

		PAGE
I.	'SANTA CLAUS'	11
II.	THE RETURNED NATIVE	39
III.	JOHN AND JANE	47
IV.	THE OLD SOLDIER	67
V.	WHEN FOX WAS FERRYMAN	85
VI.	MOTHER'S MISFORTUNE	99
VII.	STEADFAST SAMUEL	121
VIII.	THE HOUND'S POOL	141
IX.	THE PRICE OF MILLY BASSETT	159
X.	THE AMBER HEART	177
XI.	THE WISE WOMAN OF WALNA	197
XII.	THE TORCH	213
XIII.	'SPIDER'	233
XIV.	THE WOODSTOCK	253
XV.	THE NIGHT-HAWK	273

No. I
'SANTA CLAUS'

No. I

'SANTA CLAUS'

NOBODY knew where Teddy Pegram came from or why the man ordained to settle down in Little Silver. He had no relations round about and couldn't, or wouldn't, tell his new neighbours what had brought him along. But he bided a bit with Mrs. Ford, the policeman's wife, as a lodger, and then, when he'd sized up the place and found it suited him, he took a tumble-down, four-room cottage at the back-side of the village and worked upon it himself and soon had the place to his liking. A most handy little man he was and could turn his skill in many directions. And he'd do odd jobs for the neighbours and show a good bit of kindness to the children. He lived alone and looked after himself, for he could cook and sew like a woman—at least like the clever ones. In fact there didn't seem nothing he couldn't do. And his knowledge extended above crafts, for he'd got a bit of learning also and he'd talk with Johns at the shop-of-all-sorts about business, or with Samual Mutters, the chemist, about patent medicines, or with butcher or baker concerning their jobs, or with policemen about crime, and be worth attending to on any subject.

His pleasure, however, was sporting, and not until he'd dwelt among us a good bit did a measure of doubt in that matter creep into our praise of the man.

Round about fifty he might have been—a clean-shaved, active chap, five feet three inches high, and always bursting with energy. He had grizzled hair and a blue chin and eyes so bright and black as shoe-buttons. A hard mouth and lips always pursed up over his yellow teeth; but though it looked a cruel sort of mouth, nought cruel ever came out of it save in the matter of politics. He was a red radical and didn't go to church, yet against that you could set his all-round good-will and friendship and his uncommon knack of lending a hand to anybody in his power to serve. But he was up against the Government, and would talk so fierce of a night sometimes at the 'Barley Sheaf' that Ned Chown, the landlord, who was a true blue, didn't think so well on Mr. Pegram as the most of us. Friends he made, but hadn't much use for the women, though he declared himself as not against them. He was a bachelor-minded man by nature, and yet, what ain't so common in that sort, he liked childer and often had a halfpenny in his pocket for one of his pets.

Mrs. Ford, however, he regarded as a great and trustworthy friend, and her husband also, for, from the time he lodged with them, they all agreed uncommon well, and Joseph Ford, the policeman, was high in his praises of Teddy from the first. He happened to be a very radical thinker himself, did Joseph, but, as became his calling, put law and order first; and you felt that the newcomer agreed on that matter and didn't want to do anything contrary to the constitution, but just advance the welfare of the under-dog by proper means; so Joseph said there was no fault in the man and praised his opinions.

In truth Teddy Pegram appeared to be a very great stickler for the law and held it in high respect—so he always declared—and reckoned that those who put themselves within the reach of it deserved all they got. He might say doubtful things to Joseph Ford's ear now and again, but nought the policeman could fairly quarrel with, because both Joseph and Minnie, his wife, owed Teddy a bit by now, and, doting on their little son as they did, felt a bit weak to the man in that quarter.

Their only child was six years old, and the amazing beauty of young Joey Ford made him many friends beside Mr. Pegram. He was one of they children that look too good and too beautiful for this world, and you feel that, by rights, they did ought to grow a pair of wings and fly away to heaven. And for that matter, old Jane Marks, who was famous for seeing and pointing out the dark side of all human hopes, warned Minnie more'n once against putting her whole trust in the beautiful boy,

"To my eye there's early death looking out of his eyes," Jane Marks would say. "Such blue eyes belong to the sky, Minnie, and there's more to it than his angel face, because the child's so parlous good that it ain't straining truth to say the Old Adam be left out of him. And granted that, this vale of tears is no place for such a boy. Heaven's his home," Mrs. Marks would say, "and so you must fortify yourself for an early loss."

Minnie didn't worry, however, because her son was a strong lad and sturdy as well as lovely. He'd gotten his father's fine shape and his mother's gentle heart, and though good as gold, he weren't a Mary-boy, as we say—one of them gentle, frightened childer who can't let go their mother's apron. That sort, if they grow up, turn into indoor man-servants and ain't very powerful as a rule in their bodies or intellects; but Joey was a brave young lad enough and had already fixed on his father's profession for his own.

And Teddy Pegram took most powerful to him and made him many a game and many a clever toy. He'd walk with the child to the woods sometimes and teach him the ways of birds and beasts and show him how to catch 'em; for Ted was a rare sportsman and deeply skilled in all the branches of it. And 'twas his bent in that direction led to the extraordinary affair of this tale; though it was a good year before the crash came and for a long time no cloud arose to darken his steadfast friendship with the Fords. You might say they was more than friends, for Teddy explained to the young couple that he stood alone in the world, without chick or child of his own, and felt very wishful to have some special interest in his fellow creatures.

"I followed the sea," he told them once, "and that's why I'm so handy all round. But my passion be sporting, and now, having earned a little competence, I've retired from the ocean and don't want to hear nor yet see it no more. And you folk suit me and I suit you, so I'll put you first, and if all goes well in the time to come, I dare say your lad, if not yourselves, will be the gainers."

They was very pleased, of course, and Minnie showed it by fussing over the man a bit and looking after his linen now and then and doing such chores for him as he'd let her do; but he was very independent and, finding he weren't over anxious for her and her husband to be in his house, though always very willing to come to hers, she gave over her attempts to befriend him in that direction. Little Joey, however, was always welcome and he'd often drop in on the old sailor and never in vain. Teddy was fond of sporting dogs and he'd got a lurcher bitch from somewhere, and when she bore a litter, six weeks before Christmas, he had the thought to give Joey the best of the bunch. When they was a fortnight old, he drowned all but one, and on Christmas Eve, after the child was to bed and asleep, he took the little dog over and stopped and had a drink and explained his purpose.

'Twas strange to 'em to hear the hard-faced, grim-looking chap talk so tender of their only one; but they liked it well enough and fell in with his wish. He'd promised to eat his Christmas dinner along with them and Joey; but the pup was to come as a rare surprise next morning, and though Minnie Ford didn't much hold with a young dog about her spick and span home, she couldn't withstand the little silky creature, nor yet Teddy's wish to pleasure the child.

"You do this, Minnie," he said, for he called the family by their Christian names by now. "You keep the dog till dawn and then you put him in the stocking, what's hanging at the foot of Joey's bed, along with your own gifts afore you call him. Then first thing he sees when he rises up to grab his toys will be the little dog atop of all the rest."

Which Minnie promised to do and did do, and Joey toddled over the minute after he'd swallowed his breakfast to tell Mr. Pegram how 'Santa Claus' had sent him the wonderfullest little dinky dog ever was seen.

"I'm the Santa Claus that sent it, my lovely cherub," said Teddy, kissing his beautiful face; and 'Santa Claus' he was to Joey from that day forward. It pleased the man well to be so called, and he got the nickname in Joseph Ford's house and became 'Santa Claus' to all of 'em.

"There's much in a name," said Teddy, "and more in that one than you may guess. For I was mate of a ship so called once on a time and had some of my best voyages in her."

The friendship tightened after that Christmas and it weren't till many a long month later and the fall of another year that anything happened to strain it.

They had all got to be so friendly as you please and then in the 'Barley Sheaf' one day, Joseph Ford heard Ned Chown laughing with a customer or two, and, afore they knew it, he picked up a word. He didn't let 'em guess he'd heard, however, but ordered his beer and spoke of something else, which they was very willing to do; for Joseph happened to be a mighty smart officer, and secret subjects sometimes got mentioned that weren't meant for his ear.

It happened that poaching was in the air a good bit just then, for the big Oakshott covers ran half a mile from Little Silver and there had been a lot more trouble than usual that winter and the old head-keeper dismissed and a younger and sterner man engaged from up North. But the robbery went on and there's no doubt a lot of pheasants slipped away to an unknown market. Joseph Ford was so keen as the game-keepers to lay the rogues by the heels, for the police had heard a few hard words from the Lord of the Manor on the subject; but the general opinion ran that some clever rascals from far ways off in the South Hams were responsible; while the new keeper from Yorkshire, who had a large experience of poachers' tricks, said most steadfast that in his judgment it was local men with the advantages of being on the spot. They raked the poulterers in three market towns round about, but all gave a very good and straight account of their birds; and the mystery interested us a lot, for, of course, Little Silver had its doubtful customers like every other place.

And what Joseph Ford had heard, with a smothered laugh or two, was the name of his fast friend, Teddy Pegram, along with the disappearance of the Oakshott game. He gave no sign, but it hit him with a good bit of force, because he'd marked one or two things himself that made him restless, and he knew Teddy didn't pretend any great sorrow to think the pheasants were being stole. The man loved sport, and farmers round about let him shoot their rabbits and partridges also; but he knew very well pheasants were different, though he always argued against

B

all game laws. So Joseph counted to give Teddy a word in season on the quiet, and he done so.

"I heard your name whispered in the public-house a few nights agone," he said, "and I didn't like it too well, Pegram, because they named it along with this here poaching. They little thought I'd heard, of course, and I didn't undeceive 'em, but—there 'tis—and I'd avoid the appearance of evil if I was you and bide in on moony nights, which we know very well you do not."

The other showed much surprise to hear such a thing. He was playing along with Joey and the little dog at the time, and teaching the puppy to learn tricks. The creature was full of brains, as mongrels are apt to be, and Joey loved it dearly, and loved the giver only less. He'd called it 'Choc,' because the puppy loved chocolates so well as Joey himself, and the dog had grown to be his dearest treasure.

Well, Teddy gave over his games now and stood up and showed a great deal of annoyance. His bead-black eyes flashed and his jaw stood out, as it always did when he was vexed.

"Too bad!" he said, "and if I knew who the man was, I'd have him up for libel I reckon. I may or may not agree about the damn birds, but I wouldn't have made a policeman my fast friend in this place if I weren't a straight man, and I'm a good bit surprised, Joseph, that you thought it worth your while to name such a thing to me. And I'll go out of a moony night when and where I please so long as it's a free country. So now then!"

He sulked a bit and didn't come to see the Fords for a week, though Joey was over often enough to see him, and Joseph felt rather interested to mark how the little man had taken it. But then 'Santa Claus' made friends again and came into Sunday supper and brought a pheasant along with him!

He made a lot of fun about it and pretended as he'd shot it in the coverts over night; and presently he told Joseph that, if he wanted to run him in, he'd best to go to Mercer's at Newton Abbot first and find out if he'd bought it all decent and in order, or if he had not. So the matter dropped, and all was firm friends again till the blow fell.

Poaching went on, and Joseph noted that Teddy was apt to be from home a bit and would often go away for a day or two. And the new head-keeper, who was sleepless on the job, traced where a car had come across one of the drives in Oakshott's by night, for the wheels had scored the grass; and where the thing had stood was a dead bird the blackguards had overlooked.

The pheasant had been shot roosting and an air-gun was the weapon, for they found the slug in it.

And the next thing was that just afore the end of the season, Joseph Ford set out to lend a hand with the job on his own, unknown to anybody but the head-keeper. He worked out of his business hours and off the regular policeman's beats, and the keeper, who now felt pretty sure one of his own under-men was in it, and he'd got treachery to deal with, put Joseph up to a secret plan. Oakshott's is a huge place and the six keepers kept there couldn't be everywhere; but an unknown seventh man might steal a march on the rogues and lie hid when 'twas given out the others were somewhere else. And that was done by Joseph, with a very startling result.

The season had near reached an end, when on a quiet moonlight night in January, Joseph kept his third secret watch at the edge of the North Wood. He'd got there at dusk, being off duty at the time, and there he bided; and then, just after moonrise, he saw a dog slip past him within ten yards, and he knew the dog very well, and his heart sank.

Behind the lurcher came her master, and Teddy, with something in his hand that glinted, popped by, silent as a ghost and was gone into the covers.

But Joseph knew he'd be bound to come out on the high road, same way he went in, so he bided there and an hour passed and then twenty minutes more, and meantime the policeman heard the purr of a motor and saw a small car without lights draw up on the dark side of the lane twenty yards off. There was only one man in it and Joseph felt glad there weren't more. He chanced Pegram for a minute then and nipped out on the driver just as he was lighting a cigarette. He proved to be a young fellow from so far off as Torquay, and he didn't put up no fight whatever, feeling no fear on his own account. He was working for wages and doing what he was told, and he caved in at once and obeyed the policeman's orders, that worse might not overtake him. So he sat tight and waited, and then Teddy Pegram and his dog and his air-gun crept out of the woods with a load of ten birds. They roosted in the spruce firs, you understand, and 'twas as easy to slay them as blackbeetles, for Teddy's eyes, helped by the moon, marked 'em above his head quick enough.

Then Joseph Ford walked out from behind the car and the little man saw his games were ended, for Ford was a very powerful chap and could have eaten him if he'd wanted to do so.

But Teddy used his tongue for all it was worth, though at first he didn't guess he was up against it.

"Lucky 'twas you," he said. "If it had been your mate, I'd have met with a difficulty. Very smart, Joseph! You've bowled me out all right, so we'll cry quits and least said soonest mended."

But the policeman wasn't in no mood like that.

"Come, Pegram," he answered. "I'd sooner have took any man on earth but you, and you've put me in a cruel fix, and that's all there is to it. Give me that air-gun and get in the car and say nought if you please."

T'other had a lot to say, however. They talked for ten minutes, but the poacher couldn't move the policeman, though he appealed to his friendship and so on. Then Joseph saw a look that he never had seen afore in the little man's eyes and was startled, but not afeared. For a minute Teddy glared like a devil in the moonlight, and an awful evil expression fairly flooded his face.

"Think twice," he said. "For God's sake think twice, Ford, afore you do this. There's a lot more to me than you know—a lot I've thought to overcome—suffering, misery, curses, disgrace. But if you take me to the 'cooler' to-night—hear me on my oath: you'll be sorry as long as you live, for I'm built that way."

"I am sorry already," answered Joseph, "I'm as sorry as any living man can be, and 'tis a bitter cruel thing for me that you've forced this upon me. I warned you—most serious I done so—and what more could I do? You've none to thank for this but yourself and you well know it. But my duty's my duty, and I don't break my policeman's oath for you, or any man living."

"You ain't on duty to-night, however," replied Teddy.

"A policeman's always on duty," said Ford, "and 'tis vain to threat or argue. I've got no choice."

But the other did argue still, and when he saw he was done, he threatened also and said hard, terrible words. They went in one of Joseph's ears and out of the other, of course, and he only wanted to get a painful job out of hand by now. So he cut it short, and in another minute pretty well lifted Teddy into the car and bade the driver carry 'em to Little Silver.

Pegram said no more after that, but a fiend glared out of his eyes as he stared on the other, and Joseph, though he'd seen some hard cases, said afterwards that he never wanted to look on such a wicked face again.

But the look was dead when they got to the police-station, and Ford tumbled his man into a cell, then handed the pheasants over to the Inspector and made his report.

There was a good deal of stir about it and some applause for the policeman when the Justices gave Teddy two months' hard labour. And that was that. But what you may call the interesting part of the affair happened after, for when the two months was up, instead of selling his house and taking himself off to practise his games elsewhere, if Teddy Pegram didn't return to Little Silver, meek as Moses, and a reformed character!

Poor Joey, when he heard his dearest friend was in trouble, had wept a lot of tears and took on very bad and even said hard things to his father for catching 'Santa Claus' and sending him to prison. But he'd got resigned to his loss, for two months is a long time in a child's mind. And he'd walk every day to look at Pegram's house and pet the poacher's dog. 'Twas thought the creature ought to be shot, and the head-keeper at Oakshott's, who knew the cleverness of the animal, was strong for it; but humanity be full of strange twists and the Squire himself it was who ordered the cur should live and be tended.

"Let the dog be there to welcome him back," said the Squire

in his easy way. "The dog's done nothing but his duty and done it mighty well by all accounts."

He was pleased, you see, because he'd got to the bottom of the mystery, and he had a great trustful faith in human nature and hoped that Teddy would turn from his bad ways after a taste of klink. And it certainly looked as if the good man was right.

Little Joey would often take 'Choc' to see his mother on her chain at Teddy's house while the man was put away. And he'd carry the poor creature a tidy bone also when he could get one. And how long that two months was to the lurcher, who shall say? But one fine morning Pegram was back again, and he welcomed the child same as he'd already welcomed his dog, and Joey went back full of great joy to say as his friend was home once more and terrible pleased to see him. Which interested Joseph and Minnie Ford a good bit, for they guessed that they'd made a bitter and dangerous enemy in that quarter and little thought to see the man again. Yet he'd come back and, more wonderful still, afore he'd been home a week, he made bold to step in one night and shake their hands and say 'twas a very nice thing to be home in his own den a free man! They felt mazed to see him among 'em, so cheerful and full of talk as if he'd been away for a holiday. And Joseph wondered a lot and felt it on the tip of his tongue to name the past and express friendly hopes for the future. But he didn't, and it weren't till he saw 'Santa Claus' down to the gate on his way home, that the little chap spoke.

"Say nought and try to forget," he said. "You done your duty and that's all the best and worst of us can do. Be my friend, for I've got but few."

Then he was gone, and Joseph woke to a surer trust in humanity and felt our common nature crying to him to believe it; while his own policeman's nature warned him to do no such thing. He talked far into the night with his wife; but she was all for believing.

"Us be Christians," said Minnie, "and well we know how the Lord works. He's come to right thinking by chastisement, and his heart's softened and never will I believe a man as loves the little ones like him be so very bad. He's paid for what he done and, if he wants to forget and forgive, 'tis everybody's place to do the same."

"That sounds all right," granted Joseph. "And who be I to say he's not a repentant man? But—you didn't see his face, with ten devils staring out of his eyes, when I took him."

"Us'll watch and pray for him," answered Minnie. "My heart tells me the poor man won't fall again."

And they left it at that and Minnie prayed and Joseph watched; and the woman triumphed over her husband a good bit as time went on, for Teddy Pegram never looked back so far as could be seen, until, little by little, even Joseph felt that his spell in the jug had changed Teddy to a member of society a good bit out of the common.

His friends reckoned that, when another autumn came, the strain would be too much and the old poacher might be found to fall; but, as Ned Chown pointed out, it weren't very likely as Pegram would fall again in the same place.

"If he was minded to fall, he'd sling his hook and go and fall somewhere else, where he weren't known," he said, and indeed Teddy had made the same remark himself. He stuck to lawful sport and went his quiet way, until that happened which looked as though he might soon be minded to flit.

In the fall he sold his cottage to Ned Chown, who owned a few little dwellings already and was a great believer in the virtue of house property; but Pegram only let the inn-keeper have it on one condition and that was that he should be allowed to go on living in it while he chose to do so. He explained to Joseph Ford that he never meant to leave Little Silver; but that he was very poor and a thought pressed for money, and glad to have the value of the house in his pocket again.

So another year passed over 'em all, and the end of the strange business of 'Santa Claus' came on another Christmas Eve, when he dropped in to see the Fords and express his friendship and good wishes. They'd quite slipped back into the old, kindly understanding, and Joseph felt long since convinced that his stern dealing had been the salvation of the man—a fact Teddy himself often declared, without shame. They cared for him a lot by now, and Minnie never tired of singing his praises, and the child never felt a day well spent if his friend didn't come into it.

Joey was in bed and asleep before Pegram called in his character of 'Santa Claus'; but he'd not forgot his gift and produced a fine box of sweets, to be put on top of the child's stocking along with a Christmas card. He looked in on sleeping Joey also and smiled to see the child in the land of dreams with his dog asleep beside him. And then he gave Minnie a gift also—a piece of very fine cloth to make herself a gown. And he promised to come and eat his Christmas dinner along with them, which Joseph insisted he should do. Ford was on night duty at the time and he left the house with the old poacher and saw him to his own home, while good words passed between them. Then young Ford went to his beat and wondered as he walked at such a fine reformation, and felt proud of himself to think he'd had a hand in it. Yet, though seldom it came uppermost in his thoughts, by some chance, the ancient, awful look on Teddy's face rose to his mind that Christmas Eve. Joseph had a theory, sure founded on Scripture, and he stoutly believed that the poacher had harboured a devil in him in the past.

"Yet now without a doubt it has been cast out," thought Joseph, "and no man will ever see it look out of his eyes no more, because it have gone, thank God."

His duty done he went home to rest; but the man's sleep was broken just after peep-o'-day by the awfullest scream ever he heard.

His child it was. Joey slept in a little room alongside his parents and, of course, Minnie was up to him like a flash of lightning, with Joseph after her. He said at a later time that 'Santa Claus' had got in his dreams and he had suffered all night from a great uneasiness; but he was sleeping sound enough when, just after six o'clock, the child screamed and screamed again. And still he screamed when his mother got to him and his father followed after, stopping only to light a candle.

'SANTA CLAUS' 25

Poor Joey was out of bed with his mother's arms round him when his father got there; and on the bed lay Teddy's box of sweets scattered over the cover-lid, with the Christmas stocking dragged up also, but its contents not yet explored. The sweeties came first, and Joey had opened them and now he screamed and pointed and screamed again, but for the moment couldn't speak. He pointed into one corner of his little cubby-hole, and then the tears came flooding his cheeks and he stopped screaming and clung to his mother and wept as if his heart would break.

Ford, policeman-like, saw it all instanter, and a curtain seemed to lift off his soul, and there glared the eyes of 'Santa Claus' into his mind's eyes. In a second he put two and two together and understood why, deep in his brain that night, had hidden such a feeling of stark care.

"Have you touched they sweets?" he asked, shaking the little boy to make him attend. "Speak for your life, Joey! Have you ate one?"

Still the child couldn't collect himself. He screamed again when his father shook him, and it was clear some fearful thing had overtook him; but his grief didn't rise from no pain of body, and in truth the answer to Joseph's question lay before his eyes, if he'd but understood the truth. No scream would Joey have screamed, nor tear shed, if he'd helped himself from the box; but 'twas a case when a big heart saved a little body, for Joey had put another creature before himself and the first sweetie out of the gift had went to his pup. 'Twas chocolates 'Santa Claus' had left, and when the dog's jaws closed upon his little master's gift, he gave one jump and leapt off the bed and was stone dead in three seconds before the child got to him.

All that the parents presently learned from the shaking babe, and the moment Joseph grasped the truth, he left his wife to praise God and got on his clothes and ran without ceasing to Teddy Pegram's house. And in no Christmas temper did he run neither, for he'd have well liked, in his fury, to rob the hangman of a job. The size of the intended crime swept over him in all its horror as he measured the past and remembered all that the poacher had said and done ; and his feet very near gave under him to think of what a fellow creature can harbour hid from every other human eye.

But he wasn't overmuch surprised to find Teddy Pegram didn't answer the door, nor yet to discover the place was all unlocked. He doubted not that his awful enemy had departed overnight, and it came out presently that the last at Little Silver to see Pegram was Ford himself on the previous evening.

So he left it at that, then, and went home and joined his wife in blessing the Maker for His mercy and calming the sorrows and terrors of their little lad.

An unrestful Christmas for the local police, and the countryside was soon busy over Teddy Pegram, while next day the box of chocolates received attention and was found so full of venom as the poisoner could pack 'em.

A nine days' wonder and no more, for though the police was so placed they could soon learn a lot they didn't know about the would-be murderer, the wretch himself escaped 'em that time. But a very interesting thing threw light, and when Teddy's cottage came to be hunted over, though not a stick offered to show who he might be, or where he might have sped, some fingerprints was took by the police and they got a good picture off an empty bottle in a cupboard and another off a frying-pan. And so it got to be understood that 'Santa Claus' was a famous criminal, who had come to Little Silver straight from seven years of penal servitude for manslaughter and had a record so long as from Newgate to Princetown. And he was sixty-three years old, or so they thought.

They traced him back to London and lost him there ; but five years afterwards Hiram Linklater, for that was his famous name, swung in earnest for murder of a woman in the Peak of Derbyshire. Always for rural districts he was and a great one for the wonders of nature. He told the chaplain of his adventures at Little Silver, and expressed penitence afore he dropped. He also said that nothing in his whole career had given him more pleasure than to hear how his Christmas Eve effort down in Devonshire had miscarried after all. And he pointed out how, by the will of God, his own gift to the little boy had saved him !

And he was said to have made a brave end; which no doubt ain't as difficult as people imagine.

'Tis the like of Hiram Linklater I reckon, as keep up the sentiment of approval for capital punishment; because even in the softest head, it must be granted that a baby-poisoner is the sort that's better under the earth than on it.

No. II
THE RETURNED NATIVE

No. II

THE RETURNED NATIVE

OF course, every human being did ought to be interesting to their fellow creatures, and yet, such is the weakness of human nature, that we all know folk so cruel dull in mind and body that an instinct rises in us to flee from 'em at sight and never go where there's a chance of running across 'em. It ain't Christian, but everybody knows such deadly characters none the less, and you might say without straining charity, that Mrs. Pedlar was such a one.

Being a widow she had that triumphant fact to show how somebody had found her interesting enough to wed, and there's no doubt, by God's all-seeing goodness, the dull people do find each other out and comfort one another.

Jane Pedlar couldn't have been particular dreadful to Noah Pedlar else he wouldn't have married her and stopped with her, for they was thirty years wed before he dropped, and though she was too dull to have any childer, or ever larn to cook a mutton chop so as a man could eat it with pleasure, yet she held him. He didn't leave much money, because he never earned much, yet he did a pretty good stroke for Jane before he died, and got his employer, Farmer Bewes, to let Jane bide safe in her cottage for her lifetime.

There weren't nothing written between master and man; but Nicholas Bewes, who owned the place, came to see Noah Pedlar on his death-bed, and when Noah put up a petition for Mrs. Pedler to be allowed to bide rent free to her end, Bewes, who was a bit on the sentimental side and minded that the old chap had worked for him and his father before him for more than half a century, promised that Jane might have the use of the house for her life.

Noah Pedlar had never rose to be farmer's right-hand man

or anything like that. He was a humble creature, faithful unto death, but no use away from hedge-tacking and such rough jobs; yet he'd done his duty according to his limits, however narrow they might be, and so he got his way on his death-bed, and, in the sudden surprise that such a landmark as Noah was going home, Farmer Bewes gave his promise.

But that was twenty year agone, and Nicholas Bewes had grown oldish himself now, and Jane was thought to be nearer eighty than seventy by her neighbours. Friends she had not, except for Mrs. Cobley; but there's no doubt, though a much younger woman, Mary Cobley had a sort of feeling for Jane; and there was Milly Boon also—Jane's orphan niece, who lived along with her and kept house for her. She was a good friend too.

The adventure began, you may say, when a returned native came back to Little Silver, and 'twas Mary Cobley's son Jack who did so.

He'd gone to sea when he was fifteen, but kept in touch with his folk and left the sea and found work in the West Indies and bided there for five-and-twenty years. And now he came back, brown as a berry and ugly as need be. At forty you might say Jack Cobley couldn't be beat for plainness; and yet, after all, I've seen better-looking men that was uglier, if you understand me, because, though his countenance put you in mind of an old church gargoyle, yet it was kindly and benevolent in its hideousness, and he had good, trustful eyes; and, to the thinking mind, a man's expression matters more than the shape of his mouth or the cut of his nose.

Jack hadn't much to say about his adventures, for he was a very quiet man and better liked to list than talk; but he didn't make no splash when he came back and he was content to settle with his mother and till her little vegetable patch.

He'd stand a drink at the 'Man and Horse' public-house and, if he felt himself among friends, he'd open out a bit and tell stories of the land where he had lived and worked; but he proved to be the retiring sort and hadn't got anything to say about money. In fact, it didn't seem to be a subject that interested him over much and there was nothing in his apparel, or manner of life, or general outlook that seemed to show as he'd done very well in foreign parts.

So the people came to the natural conclusion that if he'd made any sort of pile, it was a small one, while some folk went to extremes and reckoned that Jack had come back to his mother without a bean, and was content to live on her and share her annuity. Because Mrs. Cobley, though her husband left little beyond his cottage, which was his own, took one hundred and fifty pounds per annum for life under the will of the last lady of the Manor of Little Silver.

Mary had served her ladyship as maid for fifteen years before she took Cobley, and she was a tower of strength to that important woman and had come to be generously remembered according.

So Jack was a mystery, in a manner of speaking. He bought himself a horse, and a good one, and was very fond of riding round about over the moor and joining in a meet of foxhounds sometimes; but that was his only pleasure; and his mother, when a woman here and there asked if her son was minded to wed, would answer that she'd never heard him unfold his feelings on that matter, and reckoned he'd got no intentions towards the women.

" He's so much impressed by his own ugliness," Mary Cobley would tell them, " that he never would rise to the thought of axing a female to take him; though I tell the man that the better sort of woman ain't prone to pick a husband, like a bird picks a cherry, for the outside."

Which was true, of course, for modesty might be said to be Jack's strong suit, and he couldn't abear the thought of inflicting his ugly mug on a nice young woman, which was the only sort of woman he felt he'd got any use for.

Then, after he'd been home six months, he found his parent in tears one night, and she explained the fatal situation that had arose with respect to her neighbour, Mrs. Pedlar.

" Poor Jane be up against it," she said. " Things have come to a climax in that quarter at last and, by all accounts, she's got to leave her lifelong home. And God judge Nicholas Bewes, for he's doing a thing that will put him on the wrong side of the Books."

Well, Jack had called on Mrs. Pedlar, of course, her being his mother's friend; but, like most other people, he'd found the poor woman parlous uninteresting. Her niece, however, was different, for in Milly Boon the folk granted you could find nought but beauty and good temper, and remarkable patience for a young woman. She was a lovely piece, with pretty gold hair and high complexion, and grey, bright eyes. Her mouth was rose-red and tolerable small, but always ready for a smile, and she was a slim, active creature, a towser for work, yet full of the joy of life and ready enough for a mite of pleasure if it came her way.

A good few courted her, but she had no eye for 'em, though civil to all; but now a desperate man was in the market, and he showed such a lot of determination over her and was so cruel set upon Milly that folk said he'd be bound to have his way—and why not?

'Twas Farmer Bewes—his son Richard—who wanted afore all else to have Milly to wife, and it looked right and reasonable, because he was the handsomest man in Little Silver, or ten miles round for that matter; and folk agreed they would make a mighty fine pair. Dicky was a flaxen chap, too, and shaved clean and had a beautiful face without a doubt. He stood six feet two inches, and was finely put together. But there was a black mark against him where the women were concerned, and he'd done a few things he didn't ought; because girls went silly over him.

An only child was Richard, and the apple of his father's eye, and spoilt from his cradlehood by both parents; and so, when he wanted Milly Boon, they didn't see why not, though she was a pauper, because his father felt that it might be a good thing for Dick to wed a wife and settle down.

But it takes two to a job of that sort, and Milly hung fire, much to the misery of young Bewes. He spared no pains in his courting, and told her how she was making an old man of him before his time and robbing him of his sleep, and his appetite, and his wish to live and so on; but she knew very well indeed he'd said all that and a lot more to other maidens, and she felt, deep down in her nature, he wasn't the right one for her, despite his fine appearance and education. For he was a clever man and had been taught knowledge at a Secondary School.

So things stood when Mary Cobley broke her sad tale to her son, while he sat and sucked his pipe and listened on a winter evening, with the wind puffing the peat smoke from the fire into the room off and again.

" 'Tis like this," she said. " Farmer's hard up, or so he says, and wants to sell Mrs. Pedlar's cottage over her head. But there's one way out and only one. Of course, Bewes be a lot too crafty to put it in words; but he's let it soak into Jane's mind very clever that if Milly Boon was to see her way to take Richard Bewes, then all would be well; but if she cannot rise to it, he's cruel afraid he must sell."

" And why for should Milly Boon take Richard Bewes ? " asked Jack.

" First, because he loves her with all his heart, I believe, and it would be a natural thing, them being the finest young man and woman in the place; and second, because everything points for it," declared Mrs. Cobley. " I wouldn't go so far as to say Milly wouldn't have come to it herself given patience in the man, for he's a fine, ornamental chap and would make a husband for a woman to be proud of. Besides, Milly has got nought but herself to offer. She's dependent on Jane for the clothes on her back, so Bewes would be a lot higher than she might ever have hoped to rise. She ain't the only pebble on the beach even as a good-looker."

" She can't take him if she don't love him, however," said Jack.

But Mrs. Cobley didn't set much store on that.

" Oh, yes, she could," the old woman replied. " Where there's respect, love often follows. And there's Jane to be remembered. Jane's been a good aunt to Milly and, in my opinion, the girl ought to see her duty and her pleasure go together, and wed young Bewes."

" And, if she don't ? " asked Mr. Cobley.

" Then Jane's in the street and it will be her death, because at her age you can't transplant her. You hook her out of that nice little house and she'll wilt away like a flower and very soon die of it."

Jack said no more, for he seldom wasted words, but he turned the matter over in his mind and took occasion to see Jane Pedlar a few days after and find out if what his mother had said was true.

"Because, ma'am," he said; "such things sound a thought contrary to religion and justice in my mind."

"They be," admitted Jane. "They be clean contrary to justice and religion both; but justice and religion are got so weak in Little Silver, that nothing don't surprise me."

Well, Jack was all for caution, and he said but little. He ordained, however, to look into the problem on his mother's account, and no better man could have done it. His first thought was whether farmer might not be reasonable.

"Maybe the maiden's only holding off the young man as maidens will, and be the right one for him after all," he said.

"Maybe 'tis so," his mother replied, "but meantime poor dear Jane Pedlar be suffering far too much for an old woman."

So Jack, he takes occasion to have a sight of young Bewes. They met riding to hounds together, and though Richard Bewes counted himself a good many sizes bigger and more important than the returned native, he was affable and friendly and rather pleased Jack by his opinions and his good sportsmanship.

But Cobley knew very well there's a sort of men very sporting in the open among their neighbours and very much the reverse when they are out of sight; and he also knew there's a sort very frank and honest to their fellow men, but very much the reverse to their fellow women. So he just took stock and had speech with Richard off and on and heard the gossip and figured up Dick pretty well.

"I see the manner of man he is," he told Mrs. Cobley, "and I judge that if he had a strong and sensible partner—a woman with her head screwed on the right way—she could handle him all right and keep him decent and straight. But she must be a woman of character who will win his respect and keep his affection —a woman who'll love him very well and serve him faithfully, but stand no messing about, nor any sort of nonsense. So the question rises, be Milly Boon that sort of woman?"

His mother didn't know.

"She's a lovely creature," said Mary, " and a good woman and faithful to her aunt, and that's all I know about her."

" Then, for your sake, I'll look deeper into it," Jack promised, and done so according.

He went in for a dish of tea once and again, much to Mrs. Pedlar's astonishment, for 'twas a novelty to have a male come in her house ; but Jack took it all very pleasant and heard her wrongs and condoled with her sufferings and much hoped that things might get themselves righted and Farmer Bewes be honest and keep his promise to the dead.

And meantime, he took stock of Milly Boon, and, after his first amazement at her beauty and her lovely voice, and beseeching eyes, he studied her character. And, after due thought, he came to the conclusion that, though in his opinion a very beautiful nature belonged to Milly, and she was not only lovely, but of a gracious and gentle spirit, yet he couldn't feel she was built to get the whip-hand of a man like Dicky Bewes.

He was properly sorry for all parties that it had to be so, but after a bit of study and thought over Milly he concluded she was in her right not to take young Bewes, because no such match would be like to pay her in the long run.

" She wants a very different man from Dicky," he told his mother, " and though, such is her fine character, I'm sure she'd like to do all in her power for Mrs. Pedlar, yet to ask her to put a rope round her neck and douse her light for evermore, married to a man she couldn't love, be a thought out of reason in my view."

And Mrs. Cobley said perhaps it might be.

There was a fortnight to run yet before Nicholas Bewes launched his thunderbolt on Mrs. Pedlar and bade her be gone, and during them days two men were very busy—one for himself and t'other for other people.

Dicky Bewes, he fought to wear down Milly and bring her into his arms, and Jack Cobley, he went into calculations and took stock of the cottage in dispute and finally came to conclusions with himself on the subject. He felt that if only a personable man could come along and win the girl's affection, 'twould put her in a strong position, for he was jealous on her account by now and wished her well; but nobody round about troubled to court Milly Boon after the people knew that Dick Bewes was making the running, for they felt he'd win her sure enough if he had patience to hold on.

So, as there was none else to hope for as might come forward and save the situation for Jane Pedlar, Jack resolved that he was called upon for the task.

He larned the market value of the cottage and then, three days afore the thunderbolt was timed to fall, he went up over to Nicholas Bewes and had a tell with the man.

For two mortal hours did they sit together smoking their pipes, and turning over the situation, and Bewes was bound to grant, when Jack was gone, that the chap possessed a lot of sound sense, though mouth-speech weren't his strong point, and it took him a deal of time to make his meaning clear. But none the less he could do so, when a listener was content not to hurry him, and Nicholas Bewes listened very patient, the more willingly because what Jack had to say interested him a lot.

He was a thought put about first, however, because Cobley didn't mince words.

"'Tis like this, if I may say so," he began. "Your son's wishful to marry Milly Boon—a good bit against her will, by all accounts; but you be on his side, naturally, and want to see him happy, so you've put a loaded pistol to old Mrs. Pedlar's head and told her if her niece don't take your boy, she's got to quit her home."

Bewes stared.

"What business might that be of yours, Jack Cobley?" he asked, and the visitor explained.

"On the face of it, none," he said; "but I wouldn't have come afore you only to say I disapproved, because you'd say my opinion didn't matter a damn. So I've come because I'm wishful to be in it and let you know my right so to be. There's the cottage and there's your son, and if you think that Milly Boon be the right one for your Richard, then I'm not saying a little judicious pressure ain't reasonable. But, to pleasure my mother, who's very addicted to old Mrs. Pedlar, I've looked into that question and, to say it kindly, I may tell you that Milly Boon is not suited to your Richard."

"You've a right to your opinion," answered Bewes; "and I've an equal right not to care one damn for your opinion as you say."

"Just so," admitted Jack. "Not for a moment do my opinion in itself matter to anybody, Farmer; but if I'm so positive sure that I'm right, then it becomes a duty to voice myself, though no man likes voicing himself less than me. And, because I'm so sure, after due consideration of the pair of 'em, I be come afore you to make suggestions."

"Perhaps you want her yourself, Jack?" suggested Nicholas, pulling his grey beard and shutting one eye.

"Me!" laughed Cobley, much amused. "Do a toad want a bird of Paradise? No, no. She's a lovely piece, and she's got a kindly nature; but she's the humble, gentle sort, and what your son wants, if he's going to be a successful husband and not a failure, is a woman who'll be his equal in strength of character and hold her own. He's wilful, to say it kindly, and he's fond of the girls, and no doubt, with such a handsome face as his, he finds they be easy prey. You know him better than I do and you very well know if he's to be worthy of you and Little Silver he must have a strong partner to guide him right."

Nicholas laughed.

"You've given a lot of thought to it, I see," he said.

"Nothing to do else for the minute," answered Jack. "And I'm not saying a word against your Richard. He's pleased with himself and he sits a horse so amazing fine that it's a treat to look at him, because I understand such things; but being of a mind that Milly Boon ain't the perfect partner for him, I'm here—in friendship. Mind you, I wouldn't have thrust in if I hadn't happened to find out the girl's got no use for him. If she wanted him, 'twould be different and I should have kept my mouth shut, of course; but she do not, and if she takes him it will be for one reason only—to save her aunt. And that ain't going to lay the foundation of a happy marriage—is it? So I've ordained to chip in. And even so, I wouldn't have done it if I hadn't a firm propostion to make."

"What proposition can you make, Jack?" asked Mr. Bewes, loading his pipe again. "My son be sure as death he's found the right one at last, and he may be so right in his opinion as you. And, be it as it will, how are you going to come between me and Dicky?"

"If your own conscience don't, I cannot," allowed the other. "But, it's like this. Supposing, first, you grant as an honest man it would be an ugly thing to sacrifice a harmless woman to your boy's passion. Then you say, if I ain't going to gain no political advantage out of leaving Mrs. Pedlar rent-free in a valuable house, where do I come in?

"Well, you rich men are pushed as often for money as the poor ones. I know that, and a man may have fifty thousand behind him and yet be bothered for a couple of hundred. And so I say this. Let any match between Dick and Milly go forward clean and not dirty. If they be meant for each other, let him win her fair, as a decent man wants to win a woman, or not at all. That won't do him no hurt. And, meantime, since it may be a thorn in your side having Mrs. Pedlar there, I'll buy the house. There's nothing on your conscience that can forbid you to sell, and you can leave the old woman's fate to me."

Mr. Bewes didn't answer very quick. He looked at Jack and his mind moved fast, though his tongue did not.

At length, however, he spoke. He'd felt surprised to hear Jack was a moneyed man, for the general conclusion ran that he'd come back with nought; then, being hopeful, Mr. Bewes jumped to the other extreme and guessed perhaps that Cobley was rich after all and keeping his savings hid.

"Of course," he said, "I've thought of that, and there's more than one would make me a price to-morrow if I felt minded to sell."

"I'm sure there is," answered Jack. "It's a very handy little property if it was attended to."

"And more than an acre of good ground to it."

"Just over an acre—ground that be run to waste for years, but could be made good."

"And what would you feel like paying, Jack, if I was to see your point about my boy?" asked Bewes.

"You do see that point, master," answered Cobley, "because you're clever and straight, else you wouldn't stand where you do. When you was young, you wouldn't have drove no woman into a corner for love, nor yet married her on a sacrifice. And I dare swear, if Dicky saw it like that, he'd be a lot too proud to carry on, but start again and start fair. As to what I'll pay, if you're a seller, the price lies with you."

"I've thought to auction it," answered Mr. Bewes, which was true, because he had done so

Jack nodded.

"I'd like none the less to buy it at a fair figure and save you the trouble. You'll be knowing, I expect, what would satisfy you in money down."

Then they talked for another solid hour, farmer trying to get Jack to name a price so as he might run it up, and Jacky determined not to do so.

In despair, at last, Nicholas said 'twas Cobley's for seven hundred pounds, well knowing the price ran about three hundred too high. In fact, Jack told him so; and then Bewes fetched his whisky bottle and they went at it again; and then they closed, and a good bit to farmer's astonishment, Cobley fetched a chequebook out of his pocket and wrote a cheque on the spot as though to the manner born.

Four hundred and seventy-five pounds he paid, and as Nicholas Bewes confessed to Jack, 'twas only the money in his pocket put enough iron into him to stand up to his son, afterwards.

But what Nicholas might have to say to Richard didn't trouble Cobley over much. He got his receipt and Bewes promised the deed should be drawn when he saw his lawyer to Moreton next market-day."

So they parted tolerable good friends, and it was understood between 'em that Jack should tell Mrs. Pedlar how things stood at his own time and nobody should be told who the purchaser was.

It happened, however, that he did not tell Jane after all, for, going down from Bewes in the red of the sunset, Jack fell in with Milly Boon, whose gait was set for the farm. He passed her a good evening, then marked a world of woe in her face and the smudge of tears upon it, clear to see in the last of the light, so he bade her stand a moment and tell him why for she was going up the hill.

" 'Tis private business, Mr. Cobley," she said, making to pass on ; but he heard by the flutter in her speech she'd been weeping, and in his slow way held her back while he thought it out. He was got to know her tolerable well by now, so he commanded her to bide and listen.

" You don't pass, Milly," he said, " till you tell me why for you be going."

" To have tea along with Mrs. Bewes," she answered.

He didn't believe that, however.

" 'Tis too late for tea," he said. " You'll be going up to tell Bewes you'll take his son if he'll let your aunt bide."

She didn't answer.

" So you can just turn round again and march home," went on Jack, " because the case is altered. 'Twas a very fine thought and worthy of you in a manner of speaking, Milly ; but you can console yourself with your good intentions now ; because, in a word, the house is sold, and it don't belong to farmer no more."

She stared and shook, and he touched her elbow and turned her back to the village.

" Go home and tell Mrs. Pedlar the house be sold," ordered Jack. " And you tell her also I've heard of the man that's bought it. She won't be called to do nought but stop there rent-free as before ; and the man's pleased with his property and will work up the garden for his own purposes and mend the leaks and put on some fresh paint come spring."

Milly was too staggered to grasp it all at once, and by the time she began to see the blessed thing that was happening, Jack had gone.

So she went home light-foot with her sorrows beginning to fade and her heart beating happy again. And Mrs. Pedlar praised her God far into the night, though 'twas a full week before she could grasp the truth and wake care-free of a morning.

But she heard nought of the purchaser, and the mystery grew, because Mrs. Cobley heard nought either ; and then there come a nice open sort of morning with just a promise of another spring in the air, and when Milly looked out of her chicket window, who should she see in their ruinous cabbage patch but Jack with his tools going leisurely to work to clean the dirty ground.

She told her aunt, and they talked a bit and come to a conclusion afore they asked him in to have a bite of breakfast.

" 'Tis clear he's jobbing for the owner," said Jane Pedlar. " No doubt he'll very soon put a different face on the ground, such an orderly man as him, and such a lover of the soil; but I'm sorry in a way."

" Why for ? " asked her niece. " A nicer man than Mr. Cobley don't walk."

" A very nice man indeed if it wasn't for his face," admitted the old woman, " and I've got to like even his face, because of his gentle and doggy eyes; but I'm sorry, because this shows only too clear the general opinion touching Mr. Cobley is the right one."

" And what's the general opinion ? " inquired Milly.

" That he's come home so poor as he went off," answered Jane Pedlar. " Because if he'd saved a little money he wouldn't be doing rough work for another man."

Milly saw the force of that and said no more at the time.

And then Cobley spoke to his mother one night and owned to a gathering dejection.

" I like to see a job through," he said, " and I'm casting around pretty far and wide for a man that might be good enough for that girl. She's a beautiful and simple character, in my opinion, and her heart's as fine as her face; but it won't do for her to get a fellow who is reckless and too fond of himself. She must have the right one, who puts her first, and though there's a few decent chaps in the running, now they know Dicky Bewes is down and out, yet I wouldn't say there's just the chap anybody would choose for her."

Well, Mrs. Cobley looked at him with a good bit of astonishment, for such modesty she couldn't believe ever dwelt in a male. She knew, under promise of secrecy, that Jack was a tolerable rich man; but he'd bade her not breathe the fact.

And Mary Cobley knew something else also, which she couldn't very well tell her son till now, so she'd kept her secret; but when she heard as he was busy finding somebody as might be good enough for Milly Boon, the woman in her broke loose and she said a thing she'd never said afore.

"Of all zanies, you be the biggest in the parish," said Mrs. Cobley; "and however you had the wits to win a fortune and make hard-headed men in the West Indies believe in you, I'm gormed if I know, Jack!"

He was put about at that.

"Would you say as I didn't ought to meddle in her affairs no more?" he asked. "You see, I've comed to feel very kindly to the lovely creature, and I'd work my fingers to the bone to find the man worthy of her; but if I'm too pushing——"

"Pushing!" she said. "God's light! You be a lot too retreating, Jack, and always was. Because you've got a face full of character, unlike other men's, why for should you suppose 'twas a bug-a-boo to frighten the woman? Don't your heart look out of your eyes, you silly man? How old are you?"

"Forty," answered Jack.

"And she's twenty-five, ain't she?"

"Who?" asked Jack.

"You did out to be put in an asylum, though, my son," said Mrs. Cobley. "Milly Boon is the woman I'm aiming at, and it may or may not interest you to larn that she loves you better than anything on earth—you—you she loves, you gert tomfool!"

Jack looked as if he'd been struck by lightning and his pipe fell out of his mouth and broke on the hearth.

"'Tis most any odds you're mistook," he said, with a voice that showed what a shock he'd suffered. "Such things be contrary to nature."

"Nought's contrary to nature where a woman's concerned," answered Mrs. Cobley as one who knew. "They be higher than nature, and a young woman in love defies all things but her Maker—if not Him."

"I'll see," said Jack; and he went to see instanter.

Mrs. Pedlar was keeping her bed for the moment with a tissick to the tubes, and when the man got there he found Milly busy over the ancient woman's supper. And, as he told her, he was glad she happed to be alone, though sorry for the reason.

And then in his direct, queer way he said :

"What's this I hear tell from my mother, Milly ? She says you be got to love me ? "

And something in his great, hungry eyes, and the very words in his question made it so plain as need be to Milly Boon that Jack was more than glad to hear the news. And she went up to him and kissed him ; and then he very near throttled her.

'Twas a most happy and restful affair altogether ; and when, about two hours after, poor Mrs. Pedlar croaked out over their heads for her soup, and axed Milly where she was got to be, the maiden cried out :

" I be in Jack Cobley's arms, Aunt Jane, and 'tis him owns the house, and us be going to get married direckly minute ! "

No. III
JOHN AND JANE

No. III

JOHN AND JANE

If you be built on a grand scale, there's always people to feel the greatness, and though, when you hap to be a knave, their respect is a bit one-sided, still there it is: greatness will be granted.

In the case of John Warner, he weren't a knave, but his greatness, so to call it, took the form of such a complete and wondrous selfishness that you was bound to own a touch of genius in the masterful way he bent all things to his purpose and came out top over his neighbours. The man was an only son, and what might have been chastened in his youth was fostered by a silly mother, who fell in love with his fine appearance and never denied him a pleasure she could grant. And his father weren't no wiser, so when, at five-and-twenty, he found himself an orphan and Wych Elm Farm his own, lock, stock, and barrel, young John Warner come to his kingdom with a steadfast determination to get the best he could for himself out of life and make it run to his own pattern so far as unsleeping wit of man could do.

He married a pretty woman with a bit of money and he altered a good few of his father's ways and used Jane Slowcombe's dowry to buy up a hundred acres alongside his own. The land had been neglected and wanted patience and cash; but where his lasting interests were concerned, John never lacked for one, nor stinted the other. He was a clever man and a charming man, and his cleverness and his charm appeared in many ways. Over the steel hand of sleepless selfishness John drew the velvet glove of good manners and nice speech. He created the false idea that he never wanted to do more than give and take in the properest spirit you could wish. He spoke the comfortablest words ever a farmer did speak to his fellow-creatures, and many a man was lost afore he knew it when doing business with John Warner, and never realised, till it came to the turn, how a bargain which sounded so well had somehow gone against him after all.

Of course, John prospered exceeding, for amongst his other gifts, he weren't afraid of work. He knew his business very well indeed, and always understood that it was worth his while to take pains with a beginner and paid him in the long run so to do. People felt a good bit interested in him, and though they knew there was a lot to hate in the man, yet they couldn't give a name to it exactly. When a fallen foe was furious and bearded John and shook a fist in his face, as sometimes happened, he'd look the picture of sorrow and amazement and express his undying regrets. But he never went back on nothing, and near though he might sail to the wind, none ever had a handle by which to drag him before the Law. 'Twas just the very genius of selfishness that sped him on his way victorious every time.

He never took no hand in public affairs, nor offered for the Borough Council, nor nothing like that. He might have been a useful man in Little Silver, where we didn't boast more brains than we needed, nor yet enough; but John Warner said he weren't one of the clever ones and felt very satisfied with them that were, and applauded such men as did a bit of work for nothing out of their public spirit. For praise, though cheap, is always welcome, and he had a great art to be generous with what cost him nothing.

He'd pay a man a thought above his market value if he judged him worth it, and he often said that on a farm like Wych Elm, where everything was carried out on the highest grade of farming, 'twas money in any young man's pocket to come to him at all. And nobody could deny that either. And he never meddled in his neighbour's affairs, or offered advice, or unfavourably criticised anything that happened outside his own boundaries.

One daughter only John Warner had, and that was all his family, and her mother struck the first stroke against his happiness and content, for she died and left him a widower at five-and-forty. She fell in a consumption, much to his regret, after they'd been wedded fifteen years; and their girl was called Jane after her, and 'twas noted that though sprung of such handsome parents, Jane didn't favour either but promised to be a very homely woman—a promise she fulfilled.

Her father trained her most industrious to be his right hand, and she grew up with a lively admiration for him and his opinions. Farming interested her a lot, and men mildly interested her; but among the hopeful young blades with an eye on the future who offered to keep company and so on, there was none Jane saw who promised to be a patch on her parent, and after his worldly wisdom and grasp of life and shrewd sense, she found the boys of her own age no better than birds in a hedge. Indeed she had no use for any among 'em, but made John Warner her god, as he meant she should do; for, as she waxed in strength and wits, he felt her a strong right hand. In fact, he took no small pains to identify her with himself for his own convenience, and secretly determined she shouldn't wed if he could help it. Little by little he poisoned her mind against matrimony, praised the independent women and showed how such were better off every way, with no husband and family to fret their lives and spoil their freedom.

Jane was one, or two-and-twenty by now—a pale, small-eyed maiden with a fine, strong body and a great appetite for manual work. There was no taint from her mother in her and she lived out of doors for choice and loved a hard job. She'd pile the dry-built, granite walls with any man, and do so much as him in a day; and folk, looking on her, foretold that she'd be rich beyond dreams, but never know how to get a pennyworth of pleasure out of all her money.

But Jane's one and only idol was her father, and for him she would have done anything in her power. She counted on him being good to live for ever, along of his cautious habits, and she'd give over all thought of any change in the home when the crash came and the even ripple of their lives was broke for her by a very unexpected happening.

Because, much to his own astonishment, John Warner found his mind dwelling on a wife once more—the last thing as ever he expected to happen to him. Indeed the discovery flustered the man not a little, and he set himself to consider such an upheaval most careful and weigh it, as he weighed everything, in the scales of his own future comfort and success. He was a calculating man in all things, and yet it came over him gradual and sure that Mrs. Bascombe had got something to her which made a most forcible appeal and awakened fires he thought were gone out for ever when his wife died. As for Nelly Bascombe, she was a widow and kept a shop-of-all-sorts in Little Silver and did well thereat, and Bascombe had been dead two years when his discovery dropped like a bolt out of a clear sky on John Warner.

It vexed him a bit at first and he put it away, after considering what an upstore a second wife would make in the snug and well-ordered scheme of his existence; but there it was and Nelly wouldn't be put away. So John examined the facts and came to the interesting conclusion that, in a manner of speaking, his own daughter was responsible for his fix. Because, being such a wintry fashion of female, she made all others of the sex shine by contrast, and her father guessed it was just her manly, hard, bustling way that showed up the feminine softness and charming voice and general appealing qualities of Nelly Bascombe.

Nelly was a tall, fine woman of forty years old. Her hair was thick and dark, her eyes a wondrous big pair and so grey as the mist, and her voice to poor Jane's was like a blackbird against a guinea-fowl. Farmer, he dropped in the shop pretty often to pass the time of day and measure her up; and for her part, being a man-loving sort of woman, who had lost a good husband, but didn't see no very stark cause why she shouldn't find another, she discovered after a bit what was lurking in the farmer's mind. Then, like the rest of the parish, she wondered, for 'twas never thought that such an own-self man as Warner, and one so well suited by his daughter, would spoil his peace with another wife.

But nobody's cleverer to hide his nature than a lover, and Warner found himself burrowing into Nelly's life a bit and sizing up her character, though full of caution not to commit himself; and she was very near as clever as him, and got to weigh up his points, good and bad, and to feel along with such a man that life might be pleasant enough for a nature like hers. For she was a good manager with a saving disposition. She liked John's handsome appearance and reckoned the fifteen year between 'em would work to suit her. And, more than that, she hated her business, because a shop-of-all-sorts have got a smell to it like nothing else on earth, and Nelly found it cast her spirits down a bit as it always had done. She made no secret of this, and John Warner presently got to see she was friendly disposed towards him and might easily be had for the asking if he asked right. He took his time, however, and sounded Jane, where he well knew the pinch would come.

He gleaned her opinion casual on the subject of a woman here and there, and he found Jane thought well enough of Mrs. Bascombe, whose shop was useful and her prices well within reason. But it was a long time before he made up his mind, the problem being whether to tell Jane of the thing he was minded to do before he done it, or take the step first and break it to her after. In the end he reckoned it safer to do the deed and announce it as an accomplished fact; because he very well knew that she would take it a good bit to heart and hate with all her might any other female reigning at Wych Elm but herself.

And meanwhile, all unknown to farmer, Jane chanced to be having a bit of very mild amusement with a male on her own account.

Martin Ball was known as 'the busy man of Little Silver,' and none but had a good word for him. He was a yellow-whiskered, stout, red-faced and blue-eyed chap with enough energy to drive a steamship. The folk marvelled how he found time for all he undertook. He was Portreeve of the district— an ancient title without much to it nowadays—and he was huckster to a dozen farms for Okehampton Market. He also kept bees and coneys and ran a market-garden of two acres. He served on the Parish Council and he was vicar's warden. And numberless other small chores with money to 'em he also undertook and performed most successful. And then, at forty-two years of age, though not before, he began to feel a wife might be worked into his life with advantage, and only regretted the needful time to find and court the woman.

And even so, but for the temper of his old aunt, Mary Ball, who kept house for him, he would have been content to carry on single-handed.

He knew the Warners very well and Jane had always made a

great impression on him by reason of her fearless ways and great powers and passionate love of work ; and though he came to see very soon that work was her only passion, beyond her devoted attachment to her father, yet he couldn't but mark that such a woman would be worth a gold-mine to any man who weren't disposed to put womanly qualities first. Of love he knew less than one of his working bees, but maybe had a dim vision at the back of his mind about it, which showed him clear enough that with Jane Warner, love-making could never amount to much. He measured the one against t'other, however, and felt upon the whole that such a woman would be a tower of strength if she could only be got away from her parent.

And so he showed her how he was a good bit interested, and had speech with her, off and on, and made it pretty clear in his scant leisure that she could come to him if she was minded. It pleased her a good bit to find such a remarkable man as Ball had found time to think upon her, and she also liked his opinions and his valiant hunger for hard work. She'd even let herself think of him for five minutes sometimes before she went to sleep of a night, and what there was of woman in her felt a mild satisfaction to know there lived a man on earth she'd got the power to interest. Marriage was far outside her scheme, of course ; but there's a lot that wouldn't marry for a fortune, yet feel a good bit uplifted to know they might do so and that a male exists who thinks 'em worth while.

So Jane praised Martin Ball and let him see, as far as her nature allowed, that she thought well of him and his opinions and manner of life ; and he began to believe he might get her.

He touched it very light indeed to John Warner one day when they met coming home on horse-back, and then he found himself up against a rock, for when he hinted that Warner would be losing his wonderful daughter some time, the farmer told him that was the very last thing on earth could ever happen.

"Never," said John Warner. "The likes of her be her father's child to her boots. I'm her life, Ball, and there's no thought of marriage in her, nor never will be so long as I'm aboveground. She ain't that sort anyhow, and I'm glad of it."

He wanted it both ways, you see. In his grand powers of

selfishness, John had planned to have Nelly for wife by now, and he'd also planned to keep his daughter, well knowing that no wife would do a quarter of what Jane did, or be so valuable on a business basis. Jane for business and Nelly Bascombe for pleasure was his idea.

And then John offered for Mrs. Bascombe, after making it clear to her that he was going to do so and finding the running good. He put it in his masterly language and said that he'd be her willing slave, and hinted how, when he was gathered home, the farm would be her own for life and so on ; and while knowing very well that John weren't going to be her slave or nothing like that, Mrs. Bascombe reckoned the adventure about worth while, having took a fancy to him and longing most furious to escape the shop-of-all-sorts. And so she said " Yes," though hiding a doubt all the time, and Warner, who hated to have any trouble hanging over him, swore he was a blessed and a fortunate man, kissed her on the lips, and went home instanter to tell Jane the news. He broke it when supper was done and they sat alone—her darning and him mixing his ' nightcap,' which was a drop of Hollands, a lump of sugar and a squeeze of lemon in hot water.

" I've got glad news for you, Jane," he said. " Long I've felt 'twas a cheerless life for you without another woman to share your days on a footing of affection and friendship and—more for your sake than my own—I've ordained to wed again. Not till I heard you praise her did I allow my thoughts to dwell on Mrs. Bascombe, but getting better acquaint, I found her all you said, and more. A woman of very fine character—so fearless and just such a touzer for work as yourself, and, in a word, seeing that you did ought to have a fellow-woman to share your labours and lighten your load, I approached her and she's took me. And I thank God for it, because you and her will be my right and left hand henceforward ; and the three of us be like to pull amazing well together. 'Tis a great advancement for Wych Elm in my judgment, and I will that the advantage shall be first of all for you."

She heard him out with her little eyes on his face and her darning dropped and her jaw dropped also, as if she'd been struck dead. But he expected something like that, because he very well knew Jane would hate the news and make a rare upstore about it. He was all for a short battle and very wishful to go to bed the conqueror. But he did not. Jane hadn't got his mellow flow of words, nor yet his charming touches when he wanted his way over a job; but she shared a good bit of his brain-power and she grasped at this fatal moment, with the future sagging under her feet, that she'd never be able to put up no fight nor hold her own that night. In fact, she knew, as we all do, that you can't do yourself justice after you've been knocked all ends up by a thunderbolt. But she kept her nerve and her wits and looked at him and shut her mouth and put up her work in her workbasket.

"Good night, father," she said. "Us'll talk about it to-morrow, if you please."

Then she rose up and went straight to her chamber.

He was sorry for himself, though not at all surprised; and he finished his liquor, locked the house and retired. An hour had passed before he went to bed, and he listened at Jane's door and ordained that if by evil chance he heard her weeping he'd go in and say comforting words and play the loving father and advance his own purpose at the same time. But Jane weren't weeping; she was snoring, and John Warner nodded and went on. He couldn't help admiring her, however, even at that moment.

"She's saving all her powers for to-morrow," thought Jane's parent; and she was. She slept according to her custom, like a dormouse, and woke refreshed to put up the fight of her life. They got to it after breakfast, when the house-place was empty, and Warner soon found that, if he were to have his will, 'twould be needful to call on Heaven to help him.

Jane didn't waste no time, and if her father had astonished her, she had quite so fine a surprise for him after she'd thought it all over and collected herself.

"'Tis in a nutshell," she said. "All my life I've put you afore everything on earth but my Maker, and I was minded so to continue. I've been everything any daughter ever was to a father, and you have stood to me for my waking and sleeping thought ever since I could think at all. And now you want me to go under in my home and see another take my place. Well, dad, that's your look-out, of course, and if you think Mrs. Bascombe will be more useful to you than me, then take her. But I'll say here and now, please, that if you be going to marry, I shall leave Wych Elm for good and all, because I couldn't endure for another woman to be over me and closer to your interests than what I am. Never, never could I endure it. Is that quite clear ? "

He looked at her and filled his tobacco pipe while he done so.

" So clear as can be, Jane," he said. " 'Tis like your fine courage and affection to feel so. But I make bold to believe you haven't weighed this come-along-of-it same as I have, and find yourself getting up in the air too soon. I could no more see Wych Elm without you than I could see myself without you, and the affection I feel for Mrs. Bascombe is on a different footing altogether. Love of a wife and love of a daughter don't clash at all. They be different things, and she would no more come between me and you and our lifelong devotion than love of man would come between you and me."

He flowed on like that, so clever as need be, and she listened with a face that didn't show a spark of the thought behind it. But he failed to move her an inch, because, unknown to him, she'd got a fine trump card up her sleeve, of course.

He saw presently that he wasn't making no progress and sighed a good bit and turned on a pathetic note, which he had at command, and blew his nose once or twice ; but these little touches didn't move Jane, so he ventured to ask her what her future ideas might be away from Wych Elm, if such a fearful thing was thinkable.

" God, He knows," said John Warner, " as I never thought to be up against life like this, and find myself called to choose by you, who was the apple of my very eye, between a wife and an only child ; but since you can have the heart to come between me and a natural affection towards Mrs. Bascombe, may I venture to ask, dear Jane, what your own plans might be if you could bring yourself to do such a deed as to leave me ? "

" That's easy," she answered. " If your love for me was not strong enough to conquer your love for Nelly Bascombe, then

I'm very much afraid, father, my love for you might go down in its turn, before my feelings for another man. In a word, dad, if I felt I wasn't the queen of your home no more, I should turn my attention to being queen of another."

He stared at that.

"Never heard anything more interesting, dear child," he said. "'Tis a wonderful picture to see you reigning away from Wych Elm. But though I'm sure there's a dozen men would thank their stars for such a wife as you, I can't but feel in these hard times that few struggling bachelors would be equal even to such a rare woman, unless it was in her power to bring 'em something besides her fine self."

She smiled at that and rather expected it.

"I thought you'd remind me how it stood and I was a pauper if you so willed," she replied. "But we needn't go into figures, because the man I'm aiming at knows you very well, and he'll quite understand that if he was to get me away from you, there won't be no flags flying when I go to him, nor yet any marriage portion. He ain't what you might call a struggling bachelor, however, but a pretty snug man by general accounts."

"And who might he be, I wonder?" asked John; because in his heart he didn't believe for a moment there was any such a man in the world; and when Jane declined to name Martin Ball, her father was more than ever convinced that she was bluffing.

"We will suffer a month to pass, Jane," he told her. "Let a full month go by for us to see where we stand and get the situation clear in our minds. Certain it is that nought that could happen will ever cloud my undying affection for you, and I well know I'm the light also to which your fine daughterly devotions turn. So let this high matter be dead between us till four weeks have slipped by."

"Like your sense to suggest it," she answered.

And the subject weren't named again between 'em till somebody else named it.

But meantime John didn't hesitate to take the affair in strict secrecy to the woman who had promised to wed him; and when the engagement was known, of course, Martin Ball struck while the iron was hot and felt a great bound of hope that Jane would now look upon him with very different eyes. And even while he hoped, his spirit sank a bit now and again in her company. But he put the weak side away and told himself that love was at best a fleeting passion.

Jane didn't say much to him herself, because in truth she would have a thousand times sooner bided at Wych Elm with her parent than wed the busy man of Little Silver ; but Martin screwed himself to the pinch and urged her to let there be a double wedding. He found her very evasive, however, for hope hadn't died in Jane, and she knew by a good few signs her father was hating the thought of losing her. The idea of Jane away from Wych Elm caused him a lot of deep inconvenience, and Nelly Bascombe seemingly weren't so much on his side as he had hoped. Of course the woman well knew that life at Wych Elm would be far more unrestful with Jane than without her, and so she rather took the maiden's view and tried to make John see it might be better if his girl was to leave 'em. And this she did because it happened, after a week had passed, she knew a lot more about the truth than Mr. Warner could. He still clung to the hope that Jane was lying and that no man wanted her ; and even if such man existed, John, well understanding that his daughter was not the sort to fill the male eye in herself, doubted not that the lover would soon cry off if he heard Jane's prospects were gone. He voiced this great truth to Nelly Bascombe, and he'd have been a good bit surprised to know that on the very day he did so, she reported his intentions word for word to the man most interested. Because, when the situation unfolded, Martin Ball had gone to Mrs. Bascombe in hope to get some useful aid from her.

They were acquaint, because Nelly sold Ball's honey in her shop, but more than that Martin didn't know of the woman. She had a good name for sense, however, and when he heard that she had taken Warner, he saw what her power must now be in that quarter and asked for a tell in private. Which she was agreeable to give him, and in truth they saw each other a good few times and traversed over the situation most careful.

Nelly had a way to understand men and she listened to Martin and liked the frank fashion he faced life. He was honest as the day, though fretting a bit because Jane Warner wouldn't say

"Yes" and be done with it. He'd wanted to go to her father, too, and let John know his hopes; but that Jane wouldn't allow at this stage of the affair.

"In fact, she won't let me whisper a word," said Martin to Mrs. Bascombe, "and 'tis treason to her in a way my coming to you at all; but I feel terrible sure you can help, and it looks as if it would be all right and regular and suit everybody if she was to take me and leave the coast clear for you when you wed her parent."

"It does look like that to a plain sight," admitted Nelly, "but in truth things be very different. And for your confidence, in strict secrecy, I can give you mine. Warner don't want her to go. He badly wants me and her both, while, for her part, she don't want to go and hates the thought; but, so far, she's determined to do so if I come."

"That ain't love, however," argued Mr. Ball.

"It ain't," admitted Nelly Bascombe, "and you mustn't fox yourself to think she'll come to you for love. A good helper she'd be to any man in her own way; but she belongs to the order of women who can't love very grand as a wife. She do love as a daughter can love a father, however, and it's very clear to me that John Warner is her life in a manner of speaking. On the other hand, it would upset her existence to the very roots if I went to Wych Elm at farmer's right hand, where naturally I should be."

Mr. Ball listened and nodded, and his blue eyes rested upon Mrs. Bascombe's grey ones.

"You throw a great light," he said. "In a word, there was deeper reasons far than any growing affection for me that have made her so on-coming of late?"

"God forbid as I should suggest such a thing as that," answered Nelly. "You're a sort of man to please any woman, if I may say so; but I'm only telling you what lies in her mind. And I'll say more in fairness to the both of you. Her father don't believe there is a man after her at all. Jane's just sitting on the fence, in fact, and waiting to see if she can't shake him off me. And if I'm turned down, then you'll be turned down. 'Tis rather amusing in a way."

"It may be, but I ain't much one for a joke," he confessed, and then went on. " Though too busy for love-making and all that, yet I've got my pride, Mrs. Bascombe, and I shouldn't like to be taken as a last resort—amusing though it might be."

" No man would," she answered. " And I hope I'm wrong. She may be turning to you for your qualities. She may be coming for affection after all, knowing you'd prove a very fine husband."

" I would," declared Mr. Ball. " I can tell you, without self-conceit or any such thing, that where I loved I'd stick, and the woman as shared my life would share my all. There's a lot in me only hid because nothing have yet happened to draw it out. I'm busy and I'm wishful to do my little bit of work in the world for other people ; but if I was married, my home would be a find thought to me, and my wife would be first always and her comfort and happiness a lot more to me than my own. ' My home ' I call it, but it have long been borne in upon me that a home is a hollow word with nought in it but an aunt such as Mary Ball. It may be like blowing my own trumpet, and I wouldn't say it save in an understanding ear ; but I do think Jane Warner would find I was good enough."

" She certainly would," admitted Nelly ; and deep in her heart, such was her powers of perspection, she couldn't help contrasting Martin's simple nature and open praise of himself with John Warner's cleverer speechifying and far more downy and secret mind.

After that Ball and the widow met a good few times unknown to the farmer and his daughter, and there's no doubt that the more Martin saw of Mrs. Bascombe, the more impressed he felt with her good sense. They couldn't advance each other's interests, however, for all Nelly was able to tell him amounted to nothing. John revealed to her that Jane hadn't taken no steps to relieve the situation, but that she still asserted that she'd got a man up her sleeve ; while all Martin could say was that Jane held off and marked time and wouldn't decide for or against.

" At the end of a month," explained Nelly. " John Warner is to get on to Jane again. He's death on her stopping at Wych Elm ; but she's given no sign that she will stop if I come. I may also tell you that she's been to see me on the subject and given it as her opinion I'll be doing a very rash act to go to Wych Elm. She says I'll live to find out a lot about her wonderful father as might surprise me painfully."

"And for her part to me," replied Martin Ball, "she says I'm still in her mind as a husband, but there's a good bit to consider and I mustn't name the thing again till she do. In a word, she's still tore in half between her father and me. And I don't like it too well, because, little though I know of love, I feel a screw's loose somewhere still."

Nelly looked at Martin, in doubt whether to tell him something more, or not. But her woman's mind decided to tell him.

"And another curious fact," she said, "I do believe, at the bottom of his mind, which is deep as a well, her father's torn in half between me and her also!"

His blue eyes goggled at that.

"God's goodness!" he cried. "He knows what love is surely—even if she don't. You must be dreaming, woman."

"No," she answered. "You don't dream much at forty years old. He thinks to hide it—my John does—so to call him. But I see it very plain indeed. He knows what amazing gifts his daughter have got, and he knows she's vital to Wych Elm; but he don't know what gifts I have got to put against 'em, and so I do believe that deep out of sight he's weighing her parts against mine."

"That ain't love, however," vowed Martin.

"'Tis one love weighed against another," she told him. "A man over fifty don't love like a boy."

"The depths of human nature!" cried Mr. Ball. "I never thought that such things could be. It looks to me, Mrs. Bascombe, as if—— However, I'm too loyal to say it. But you do give one ideas."

"Like father like daughter, I shouldn't wonder," she said thoughtfully.

"Just the same dark fear as was in my mind," he confessed.

He left her then in a mizmaze of deep reflections; but he didn't go until they'd ordained to meet again. A considerable lot more of each other they did see afore the fateful month was done, and the more easily they came together because John Warner began to be very much occupied with Jane at this season. The fourth week had very near sped and still she remained firm; while behind the scenes, when he did see her, John found no help from Nelly Bascombe. In fact he marked that she'd got to grow rather impatient on the subject and didn't appear to be so interested in her fate, or yet his, as formerly.

So things came to a climax mighty fast, and while Warner, who didn't know what it was to be beat where his own comfort was concerned, kept on remorseless at Jane, she hardened her heart more and more against him and finally took the plunge and told Martin Ball as she'd wed when he pleased. He hadn't seen her much for ten days owing to press of business, and when she made up her mind, 'twas she had to write and bid him go walking with her. But he agreed at once so to do and came at the appointed evening hour. And then, afore she had time to speak, he cried out as he'd got a bit of cheerful news for her.

"And I've got a bit of cheerful news for you," said Jane Warner, though not in a very cheerful tone of voice. And then, in a dreary sort of way, she broke her decision.

"Father's going to marry the woman at the shop-of-all-sorts, as you know," explained Jane; "and if him, why not me? And, be it as it will, you've said so oft you could do with me that——"

She stopped to let him praise God and bless her and fall on her neck; but, a good bit to her astonishment, Martin didn't show no joy at all—far from it. He was silent as the grave, for a minute, and then he only axed a question that didn't seem to bear much on the subject.

"Your father haven't seen Mrs. Bascombe to-day, then?" he said.

"Not for a week have he seen her, I believe; but he's been a good bit occupied and worried. He was going to sup with her to-night," answered Jane. "And that's why for I asked you to meet me, Martin."

"What a world!" mused Mr. Ball; and he bided silent so long that the woman grew hot.

"You don't appear to have heard me," she told him pretty sharp, and then he spoke.

"I heard you only too well," he replied. "If my memory serves me, it's exactly three weeks now since last I offered for you, Jane, and your answer was a thought frosty. In fact, you dared me to name the subject again until you might be pleased to."

"Well, and now I do name it," she told him.

"Why, if I may ask?" he said.

'Twas her turn to be silent now. Of course she saw in a moment that things had gone wrong, and she instantly guessed, knowing her father, that 'twas he had made up a deep plot against her behind her back and called the man off her.

So sure felt she that she named it.

"This be father's work," she said. "You've changed your mind, Ball."

"Minds have been changed," he admitted, "and not only mine. But make no mistake, Jane. This has got nothing whatever to do with your father so far as I'm concerned. You've been frank, as you always are, and I'll be the same. And if Mr. Warner be taking a snack with Nelly this evening he'll make good every word I'm telling you. In fact I dare say what you have now got to pretend is bad news, Jane, be really very much the opposite. There's only one person is called to suffer to-night so far as I know, and that's John Warner. And even he may not suffer so much as he did ought. He put Mrs. Bascombe afore you, and so you ordained to keep your threat and leave him. And you come to me to take you and make good your threat."

"You didn't ought to put it like that—it ain't decent," she said. But she knew, of course, she'd lost the man.

"It don't matter now," he replied, "because human nature overthrows decency and delights in surprises—decent and otherwise. What has happened is this. Me and Nelly Bascombe was equally interested in your family, and along of that common interest and seeing a lot of each other and unfolding our opinions, we got equally interested in one another. And then nature cut the knot, Jane, and, in a word, I darned soon found I liked Nelly Bascombe a lot better than ever I liked you, if you'll excuse my saying so; and, what was a lot more to the purpose, she discovered how she liked me oceans deeper than she liked your father."

"My goodness!" cried Miss Warner. "That's the brightest news I've heard this longful time, you blessed man! Oh, Martin, can you get her away from father? I'll love you in real earnest—to my dying day I will—if you can!"

She sparkled out like that and amazed him yet again.

"I *have* got her away," he said. "And that's what Mr. Warner's going to hear from Nelly to-night, so brace yourself against he comes home."

And that's what John Warner did hear, of course, put in woman's nice language, when he went to sup with his intended. First he was terrible amused to learn that Ball had come courting Nelly because, when he thought on Jane, it looked as if he had been right and she was only putting up a fancied lover to fright him. In fact, he beamed upon Mrs. Bascombe so far, for it looked as though everything was coming his way as usual after all.

But he stopped beaming when she went on and explained that she was forty and Martin Ball forty-two, and that she'd come to feel Providence had planned everything, and how, only too bitter sure, she felt that Martin was her proper partner, and that John would find his good daughter a far more lasting consolation and support than ever she could hope to be at her best.

John Warner had never been known to use a crooked word, and he didn't then. He made no fuss nor yet uproar, for he was a wonder at never wasting an ounce of energy on a lost cause. He only asked one question:

"Are you dead sure of what you're saying, Nelly?" he inquired, looking in her eyes; and she answered that, though cruel grieved to give such a man a pang, she was yet convinced to the roots of her being it must be so.

Then she wept, and he said 'twas vain to work up any excitement on the subject, and that he doubted not it would be all much the same a hundred years hence. And she granted that he was right as usual.

So he left her, and Martin Ball waited, hid behind the hedge,

E

to see him go; and Jane was home before him. Then John told his daughter word for word all that had happened at the shop-of-all-sorts; and he wasn't blind to the joy that looked out of her little eyes. She didn't even say she was sorry for him, but just answered as straight as he had and confessed how she'd offered herself within the hour to Martin Ball and found that his views were very much altered and he didn't want her no more.

"And God knows best, father," finished up Jane.

"So it's generally believed," he answered. "And nobody can prove it ain't true. For my part, you was always balanced in my mind very tender against that changeable woman, and nought but a hair turned the balance her way. 'Tis a strange experience for me not to have my will, and I feel disgraced in a manner of speaking; but, if I've lost her, I've gained you, seemingly. And I shan't squeak about it, nor yet go courting no more; and I'll venture to bet, dear Jane, you won't neither."

"Never—never," she swore to him. "I hate every man on earth but you, dad."

She closed his eyes and tied up his chin twenty years after, and when she reigned at Wych Elm, she found but one difficulty —to get the rising generation of men to bide under her rule and carry on.

No. IV
THE OLD SOLDIER

No. IV

THE OLD SOLDIER

A WOMAN may be just as big a fool at sour seventy as she was at sweet seventeen. In fact, you can say about 'em, that a woman's always a woman, so long as the breath bides in her body; and my sister, Mary, weren't any exception to the rule. You see, there was only us two, and when my parents died, I married, and took on Brownberry Farm and my sister, who shared and shared alike with me, took over our other farm, by the name of Little Sherberton, t'other side the Dart. A very good farmer, too, she was—knew as much as I did about things, by which I mean sheep and cattle; while she was still cleverer at crops, and I never rose oats like she did at Little Sherberton, nor lifted such heavy turnips as what she did.

Mary explained it very simply.

"You'm just so clever as me," she said, "but you'm not so generous. You ain't got my powers of looking forward, and you hate to part with money in your pocket for the sake of money that's to be there. In a word, you're narrow-minded, and don't spend enough on manure, Rupert; and till you put it on thicker and ban't feared of paying for lime, you'll never get a root fit to put before a decent sheep."

There was truth in it I do believe, for I was always a bit prone, like my father before me, to starve the land, against my reason. You'd think that was absurd, and yet you'll hardly find a man, even among the upper educated people, who haven't got his little weak spots like that, and don't do some things that he knows be silly, even while he's doing 'em. They cast him down at the moment; and he'll even make resolves to be more open-handed, or more close-fisted, as the case may be, but the weakness lies in your nature, and you could no more cure me from being small-minded with my manure than you could have cured Mary from shivering to her spine every time she saw a single magpie, or spilled the salt.

A very impulsive woman, and yet, as you may say, a very keen and clever one in many respects. I don't think she ever wanted to marry and certainly I can call home no adventures in the way of courting that fell to her lot. And yet a pleasant woman, though not comely. In fact, without unkindness, she might have been called a terribly ugly woman. Yellow as a guinea, with gingery hair, yellow eyes, and no figure to save her. You would have thought her property might have drawn an adventurer or two, for Little Sherberton was a tenement farm and Mary's very own; but nobody came along, or if they did, they only looked and passed by; and though Mary had no objection to men in general, she didn't encourage them. But in her case, without a doubt, they'd have needed all the encouragement she could give 'em, besides the property, to have a dash at her.

So she bided a spinster woman, and took very kindly to my childer, who would run up over to her when they could, for they loved her. And by the same token, my second daughter, by the name of Daisy, was drowned in Dart, poor little maid, trying to go up to her aunt. My wife had whipped her for naughtiness, and the child—only ten she was—went off to get comfort from Mary and fell in the river with none to save her. So I've paid my toll to Dart, you see, like many another man in these parts.

Well, my sister, same as a good many other terrible ugly women, got better to look at as she grew older; and after she was sixty, her hair turned white and she filled out a bit. Her voice was always a pleasant thing about her. It reflected her nature, which was kindly, though excitable. But her people never left her. She'd got a hind and his wife—Noah and Jane Sweet by name; and he was head man; and his son, Shem Sweet, came next—thirty year old he was; and besides them was Nelly Pearn, dairymaid, and two other men and a boy.

Then came along the Old Soldier to Little Sherberton; and he never left it again till five year ago, when he went out feet first.

To this day I couldn't tell you much about him. His character defied me. I don't know whether he was good, or bad, or just neither, like most of us. But on the whole I should be inclined to say he was good. He was cast in a lofty mould and had a wide experience of the seamy side of life. I proved him a liar here and there, and he proved me a fool, but neither of us shamed the other in that matter, for I said (and still say) that I'd sooner be a fool then a rascal; while he, though he denied being a rascal, said that he'd sooner be the biggest knave on earth than a fool. He argued that any self-respecting creature ought to feel the same, and he had an opinion to which he always held very stoutly, that the fools made far more trouble in the world than the knaves. He went further than that, and said if there were no fools, there wouldn't be no knaves. But there I didn't hold with him; for a man be born a fool by the will of God, and I never can see 'tis anything to be shamed about; whereas no man need be a knave, if he goes to the Lord and Father of us all in a proper spirit, and prays for grace to withstand the temptations of the world, the flesh, and the Dowl.

Bob Battle he called himself, and he knocked at the door of Little Sherberton on a winter night, and asked to see Mary, and would not be put off by any less person. So she saw him, and heard how he had been tramping through Holne and stopped for a drink and sang a song to the people in the bar. It happened that Mr. Churchward, the innkeeper, wanted a message took to my sister about some geese, and none would go for fear of snow, so the tramp, for Bob was no better, said that he would go, if they'd put him in the way and give him a shilling. And Churchward trusted him, because he said that he reminded him of his dead brother. Though that wasn't nothing in his favour, seeing what Henry Churchward had been in life.

However, Bob earned his money and came along, and Mary saw him and took him in, and let him shake the snow off himself and eat and drink. Then began the famous blizzard, and I've often thought old Bob must have known it was coming. At any rate there was no choice but to let him stop, for it would have been death to turn him out again. So he stopped, and when the bad weather was over, he wouldn't go. There's no doubt my sister always liked the man in a way ; but women like a man in such a lot of different ways that none could have told exactly how, or why, she set store on him. For that matter she couldn't herself. Indeed I axed her straight out and she tried to explain and failed. It wasn't his outer man, for he had a face like a rat, with a great, ragged, grey moustache, thicker on one side than t'other, and eyebrows like anybody else's whiskers. And one eyelid was down, though he could see all right with the eye under it. Round in the back he was and growing bald on the top ; but what hair he had was long, and he never would cut it, because he said it kept his neck warm.

He had his history pat, of course, though how much truth there was to it we shall never know in this world. He was an old soldier, and had been shot in the right foot in India along with Lord Roberts in the Chitral campaign. Then he'd left the service and messed up his pension—so he said. I don't know how. Anyway he didn't get none. He showed a medal, however, which had been won by him, or somebody else ; but it hadn't got no name on it. He was a great talker and his manners were far ahead of anything Mary had met with. He'd think nothing of putting a chair for her, or anything like that ; and while he was storm-bound, he earned his keep and more, for he was very handy over a lot of little things, and clever with hosses and so on, and not only would he keep 'em amused of a night with his songs and adventures ; but he'd do the accounts, or anything with figures, and he showed my sister how, in a good few ways she was spending money to poor purpose. He turned out to be a very clean man and very well behaved. He didn't make trouble, but was all the other way, and when the snow thawed, he was as busy as a bee helping the men round about the farm. He made his head save his heels, too, and was full of devices and inventions.

So when I got over after the worst was past, to see how they'd come through it, there was Bob Battle working with the others ; and when I looked him up and down and said: " Who be you then ? " he explained, and told me how Mary had took him in out of the storm and let him lie in the linhay ; and how Noah had given him a suit of old clothes, and how much he was beholden to them all. And they all had a good word for the man, and Mary fairly simpered, so I thought, when she talked about him. There was no immediate mention of his going, and when I asked my sister about it, she said:

"Plenty of time. No doubt he'll get about his business in a day or two."

But, of course, he hadn't no business to get about, and though he talked in a vague sort of way concerning his home in Exeter and a brother up to Salisbury, it was all rubbish as he afterwards admitted. He was a tramp, and nothing more, and the life at Little Sherberton and the good food and the warm lying at nights, evidently took his fancy. So he stuck to it, and such was his natural cleverness and his power of being in the right place at the right moment that from the first nobody wished him away. He was always talking of going, and it was always next Monday morning that he meant to start: but the time went by and Bob Battle didn't. A very cunning man and must have been in farming some time of his life, for he knew a lot, and all worth knowing, and I'm not going to deny that he was useful to me as well as to my sister.

She was as good as a play with Bob, and me and my wife, and another married party here and there, often died of laughing to hear her talk about him. Because the way that an unmarried female regards the male is fearful and wonderful to the knowing mind.

Mary spoke of him as if she'd invented him, and knew his works, like a clockmaker knows a clock. He interested her something tremendous, and got to be her only subject presently.

"Mr. Battle was the very man for a farmer like me," she said once, "and I'm sure I thank God's goodness for sending him along. He's a proper bailiff about the place, and that clever with the men that nobody quarrels with him. Of course he does nothing without consulting me; but he's never mistaken, and apart from the worldly side of Mr. Battle, there's the religious side."

I hadn't heard about that and didn't expect to, for Mary, though a good straight woman, as wouldn't have robbed a lamb of its milk, or done a crooked act for untold money, wasn't religious in the church-going or Bible-reading sense, same as me and my wife were. In fact she never went to church, save for a wedding or a funeral; but it appeared that Mr. Battle set a good bit of store by it, and when she asked him, if he thought so much of it, why he didn't go, he said it was only his unfortunate state of poverty and his clothes and boots that kept him away.

"Not that the Lord minds," said Bob, "but the church-goers do, and a pair of pants like mine ain't welcomed, except by the Salvationists; and I don't hold with that body."

So he got a suit of flame new clothes out of her and a new hat into the bargain; and then I said that he'd soon be a goner. But I was wrong, for he stopped and went down to Huccaby Chapel for holy service twice a Sunday; and what's more he kept it up. And then, if you please, my sister went with him one day; and coming to it with all the charm of novelty, she took to it very kindly and got to be a right down church-goer, much to my satisfaction I'm sure. And her up home five-and-sixty years old at the time!

To sum up, Bob stayed. She offered him wages and he took them. Twenty-five shillings a week and his keep he got out of her after the lambing season, for with the sheep he proved a fair wonder same as he done with everything else. And nothing was a trouble. For a fortnight the man never slept, save a nod now and again in the house on wheels, where he dwelt in the valley among the ewes. And old shepherds, with all the will to flout him, was tongue-tied afore the man, because of his excellent skill and far-reaching knowledge.

Mary called him "my bailiff," and was terrible proud of him; and he accepted the position, and always addressed her as "Ma'am" afore the hands, though "Miss Blake" in private. And in fulness of time, he called her "Miss Mary." The first time he went so far as that, she came running to me all in a twitter; but I could see she liked it at heart. She got to trust him a lot, and though I warned her more than once, it weren't easy to say anything against a man like Battle—as steady as you please, never market-merry, and always ready for church on Sundays.

When I got to know him pretty well, I put it to him plain. One August day it was, when we were going up to Princetown on our ponies to hear tell about the coming fair.

"What's your game, Bob?" I asked the man. "I'm not

against you," I said, " and I'm not for you. But you was blowed out of a snow storm remember, and we've only got your word for it that you're a respectable man."

" I never said I was respectable," he answered me, " but since you ask, I'll be plain with you, Rupert Blake. 'Tis true I was a soldier and done my duty and fought under Lord Roberts. But I didn't like it, and hated being wounded and was glad to quit. And after that I kept a shop of all sorts on Salisbury Plain, till I lost all my little money. Then I took up farm labourer's work for a good few years, and tried to get in along with the people at a farm. But they wouldn't promise me nothing certain for my old age, so I left them and padded the country a bit. And I liked tramping, owing to the variety. And I found I could sing well enough to get a bed and supper most times ; and for three years I kept at it and saw my native country : towns in winter it was, and villages in summer. I was on my way to Plymouth when I dropped into Holne, and Mr. Churchward offered me a bob if I'd travel to Little Sherberton. And when I arrived there, and saw how it was, I made up my mind that it would serve my turn very nice. Then I set out to satisfy your sister and please her every way I could, because I'm too old now for the road, and would sooner ride than walk, and sooner sleep in a bed than under a haystack."

" You fell into a proper soft thing," I said ; but he wouldn't allow that.

" No," he answered. " 'Tis a good billet ; but nothing to make a fuss about. Of course for ninety-nine men out of a hundred, it would be a godsend and above their highest hopes or deserts ; but I'm the hundredth man—a man of very rare gifts and understanding, and full of accomplishments gathered from the ends of the world. I'm not saying it ain't a good home and a happy one ; but I'm free to tell you that the luck ain't all on one side ; and for your sister to fall in with me in her declining years was a very fortunate thing for her ; and I don't think that Miss Blake would deny it if you was to ask her."

" In fact you reckon yourself a proper angel in the house," I said in my comical tone of voice. But he didn't see nothing very funny in that.

"So I do," he said. "It was always my intention to settle down and be somebody's right hand man some day; and if it hadn't been your sister, it would have been some other body. I'm built like that," he added. "I never did much good for myself, owing to my inquiring mind and great interest in other people; but I've done good for others more than once, and shall again."

"And what about the church-going?" I asked him. "Is that all 'my eye and Betty Martin,' or do you go because you like going?"

"'Tis a good thing for the women to go to church," he answered, "and your sister is all the better for it, and has often thanked me for putting her in the way."

"'Twas more than I could do, though I've often been at her," I told the man, admiring his determined character.

And then came the beginning of the real fun, when Mary turned up at Brownberry after dark one night in a proper tantara, with her eyes rolling and her bosom heaving like the waves of the sea. She'd come over Dart, by the stepping stones—a tricky road for an old woman even by daylight, but a fair marvel at night.

"God's my judge!" began Mary, dropping in the chair by the fire. "God's my judge, Rupert, and Susan, but he's offered marriage!"

"Bob!" I said; and yet I weren't so surprised as I pretended to be. And my wife didn't even pretend.

"I've seen it coming this longful time, Mary," she declared. "And why not?"

"Why not? I wonder at you, Susan!" my sister answered, all in a flame. "To think of an old woman like me—with white hair and a foot in the grave!"

"You ain't got a foot in the grave!" answered Susan. "In fact you be peart as a wagtail on both feet—else you'd never have come over they slipper-stones in the dark so clever. And your hair's only white by a trick of nature, and sixty-five ain't old on Dartmoor."

"Nor yet anywhere else," I said. "The females don't throw up the sponge in their early forties nowadays, like they used to do. In fact far from it. Didn't I see Squire Bellamy's lady riding astride to hounds but yesterday week, in male trousers and a tight coat—and her forty-six if a day? You're none too old for him, if that was all."

"But it ain't all," answered Mary. "Why, he offered me his brains to help out mine, and his strong right arm for me to lean upon! And he swears to goodness that he never offered marriage before—because he never found the woman worthy of it—and so on; and all to me! Me—a spinster from my youth up and never a thought of a man! And now, of course, I'll be a laughing-stock to Dartymoor, and a figure of fun for every thoughtless fool to snigger at."

"You couldn't help his doing it," I said. " 'Tis a free country."

"And more could he help it, seemingly," she answered. "Any way he swore he was driven to speak. In fact he have had the thing in his prayers for a fortnight. 'Tis a most ondacent, plaguey prank for love to play; for surely at our time of life, we ought to be dead to such things?"

"A man's never dead to such things—especially a man that's been a soldier, or a sailor," I told my sister; and Susan said the same, and assured Mary that there was nothing whatever ondacent to it, silly though it might be.

Then Mary fired up in her turn and said there wasn't nothing whatever silly to it that she could see. In fact quite the contrary, and she dared Susan to use the word about her, or Mr. Battle either. And she rattled on in her violent and excited way and was on the verge of the hystericals now and again. And for my life I couldn't tell if she was pleased as Punch about it, or in a proper tearing rage. I don't think she knew herself how she felt.

We poured some sloe gin into her and calmed her down, and then my eldest son took her home; and when he came back, he said that Bob Battle had gone to bed.

"I looked in where he sleeps," said my son, "and Bob was in his shirt, quite calm and composed, saying his prayers."

"Trust him for being calm and composed," I said. "None ever saw him otherwise. He's a ruler of men for certain, but whether he's a ruler of women remains to be seen—for that's a higher branch of larning, as we all know."

Next day I went over and had a tell with Bob, and he said it weren't so much my business as I appeared to think.

"There's no doubt it flurried us both a lot," he told me. "To you, as an old married man, 'tis nothing; but for us, bachelor and spinster as we are, it was a great adventure. But these things will out and I'm sorry she took it so much to heart. 'Twas the surprise, I reckon—and me green at the game. However, she'll get over it—give her time."

He didn't offer no apology nor nothing like that.

"Well," I said—in two minds what to say—"she've made it clear what her feelings were, so I'll ask you not to let it occur again."

"She made it clear her feelings were very much upheaved," answered Bob; "but she didn't make it clear what her feelings were; because she didn't say 'yes' and she didn't say 'no.'"

"You don't understand nothing about women," I replied to him, "so you can take it from me that 'tis no good trying no more. She's far too old in her own opinion. In a word you shocked her. She was shaking like an aspen leaf when she ran over to me."

Bob Battle nodded.

"I may have been carried away and forced it on to her too violent, or I may have put it wrong," he said. "'Tis an interesting subject; but we'd better let it rest."

So nothing more was heard of that affair at the time; though Bob stopped on, and Mary never once alluded to the thing afterwards. In fact, it was sinking to a nine days' wonder with us, when blessed if she didn't fly over once more—this time in the middle of a January afternoon.

"He's done it again!" she shouted out to me, where I stood shifting muck in the yard. "He's offered himself again, Rupert! What's the world coming to?"

This time she had put on her bonnet and cloak and, Dart being in spate, she'd got on her pony and ridden round by the bridge.

She was excited, and her lip bivered like a baby's. To get sense out of her was beyond us, and after she'd talked very wildly for two hours and gone home again, my wife and me compared notes about her state ; and my wife said that Mary wasn't displeased at heart, but rather proud about it than not ; while I felt the contrary, and believed the man was getting on her nerves.

" 'Tis very bad for her having this sort of thing going on, if 'tis to become chronic," I said. " And if Bob was a self-respecting man, as he claims to be, he wouldn't do it. I'm a good bit surprised at him."

" She'd send him going if she didn't like it," declared Susan, and I reminded her that my sister had actually talked of doing so. But it died down again, and Bob held on, and I had speech with Noah Sweet and his wife ; and they said that Mary was just as usual and Bob as busy as a bee.

However, my sister spoke of it off and on, and when I asked her if the man persecuted her, and if she wanted my help to thrust him out once for all, she answered thus :

" You can't call it persecution," she told me, " but often he says of a night, speaking in general like, that an Englishman never knows when he's beat, and things like that ; and when he went to Plymouth, he spent a month of his money and bought me a ring, with a proper precious blue stone in it for my sixty-sixth birthday. And nothing will do but I wear it on my rheumatic finger. In fact you can't be even with the man, and I feel like a bird afore a snake."

All the same she wouldn't let me speak a word to him. She wept a bit, and then she began to laugh and, in fact, went on about it like a giglet wench of twenty-five. But my firm impression continued to be that she was suffering and growing feared of Battle, and would soon be in the doctor's hands for her nerves, if something weren't done.

I troubled a good bit and tried to get a definite view out of her, but I failed. Then I had a go at Bob too ; but for the first time since I had known him, he was a bit short and sharp like, and what I had to say didn't interest him in the least. In fact he told me in so many words to mind my own business and leave him to mind his.

Then another busy spring kept us apart a good bit, till one

evening Noah Sweet came up, all on his own, with a bit of startling news.

"I wasn't listening," he said, "and I should feel a good bit put out if you thought I was; but passing the parlour door last Sunday, I heard the man at her again! I catched the words, 'We're neither of us growing any younger, Mary Blake,' and then I passed on my way. And coming back a bit later, with my ear open, out of respect for the missis, I heard the man kiss her—I'll swear he did—for you can't mistake the sound if once you've heard it. And she made a noise like a kettle bubbling over. And so of course, I felt that it would be doing less than my duty if I didn't come over and tell you, because your sister's eyes was red as fire at supper table, and 'twas very clear she'd been weeping a bucketful about it. And me and my wife feel 'tis an outrageous thing and something ought to be done against the man."

Well, I went over next morning, and Mary wouldn't see me! For the only time in all our lives, she wouldn't see me. And first I was properly angry with her, and next, of course, I thought how 'twas, and guessed the man had forbidden her to speak to me for fear of my power over her. Him I couldn't see neither, because he was gone to Plymouth. Of course he'd gone for craft, that I shouldn't tackle him. So I left it there, and walked home very much enraged against Bob Battle. Because I felt it was getting to be a proper struggle between him and me for Mary; and that it was about time I set to work against him in earnest.

The climax happened a week later, when the Lord's Day came round again, and we went to church as usual. Then a proper awful shock fell on me and my wife.

For at the appointed time, if the Reverend Batson didn't ax 'em out! "Robert Battle, bachelor, and Mary Blake, spinster, both of this parish," he said; and so I knew the old rascal had gone too far at last and guessed it was time I took him in hand like a man. I remember getting red-hot all over and feeling a rush of righteous anger fill my heart; and an angry man will do anything, so I got up in the eye of all the people —an act very contrary to my nature, I'm sure. The place swam before my eyes and I was only conscious of one thing: my wife tugging at my tail to drag me down. But nought could have shut me up at that tragical moment, and I spoke with a loud and steady voice.

"I deny it and defy it, Reverend Batson," I said, when he asked if anybody knew 'just cause'; and the people fluttered like a flock of geese, and parson made answer:

"Then you will meet me in the vestry after Divine Service, Farmer Blake," he answered, and so went on with his work.

After that I sat down, and my wife whispered: "Now you've done it, you silly gawk!"

But I was too put about to heed her. In fact I couldn't stand no more religion for the moment, and I rose up and went out, and smoked my pipe behind the family vault of the Lords of the Manor, till the people had all got away after service. And then I came forth and went into the vestry. But I wasn't the first, for who should be waiting for me but my sister, Mary, and Bob Battle himself. Bob was looking out of the window at the graves, thoughtful like, and parson was getting out of his robes; but Mary didn't wait for them. She let on to me like a cat-a-mountain, and I never had such a dressing down from mortal man or woman in all my life as I had from her that Sunday morning.

"You meddlesome, know-naught, gert fool!" she said. "How do you dare to lift your beastly voice in the House of God, and defy your Maker, and disgrace your family and come between me and the man I be going to marry? You're an insult to the parish and to the nation," she screamed out, "and 'tis enough to make father and mother turn in their graves."

"I didn't know you was to church," I answered her, "and of course if you're pleased——"

"Pleased!" she cried. "Very like I am pleased! 'Tis a pleasing sort of thing for a woman to wait for marriage till she's in sight of seventy and then hear her banns defied by her own brother! Of course I'm pleased—quite delighted, I'm sure! Who wouldn't be?"

Well, we was three men to one woman, and little by little we calmed her down with a glass of cold water and words of wisdom from his Reverence. Then I apologised to all of them —to Mary first for mistaking her meaning, and to Bob next for being too busy, and to his holiness most of all for brawling under the Sacred Roof. But he was an understanding man and thought nothing of it; and as to Battle, he had meant to come up that very afternoon, along with his betrothed wife, to see us. And it had been Mary's maidenly idea to let us hear tell about it in church first—to break the news and spare her blushes.

Well, I went home with my tail a good bit between my legs, in a manner of speaking; and my sister so far forgave me as to come to tea that day fortnight, though not sooner. And she was cold and terribly standoffish when she did come. We made it up, however, long before the wedding—thanks to Bob himself; for he bore no malice and confessed to me in strict privacy after all was over that it had been a difficult and dangerous business, and that the Chitral Campaign was a fool to it.

"The thing is to strike the right note in these matters," he said. "And it weren't till the third time that I struck it with your sister. Afore that I talked of being her right hand and protector and so on, and I offered to be a prop to her declining years, and all that. And I knew I'd failed almost before the words were spoken. But the third time I just went for her all ends up, as if we was boy and girl, and told her that I loved her, and wanted her for herself, and wouldn't take 'No' for an answer. Why—God forgive me—I even said I'd throw myself in the river if she refused again! But there it was: she yielded, and I kissed her, and she very near fainted with excitement. And I want you to understand this, Rupert Blake: I'm not after her stuff, nor her farm, nor nothing that's worth a penny to any man. Her will must be made again, but everything goes back to you and yours. I only ask to stop along with her till I'm called: for I'm alone in the world and shouldn't like to be thrust out. And if Mary goes first, then I ordain that you let me bide to my dying day in comfort out of respect to her memory. And that's all I ask or want."

I didn't see how the man could say fairer than that, and more did my wife. And it all went very suent I'm sure. They was wedded, and spent eight fairly happy years together, and Bob knew his place till Mary's dying day. He didn't kill himself with work after he'd got her; and he wasn't at church as regular as of old; but he pleasured her very willing most times, and was always kind and considerate and attentive; and if ever they had a word, only them and their Maker knew about it.

She loved him, and she loved the ring he put on her finger, and she loved signing herself " Mary Battle "—never tired of that. And then she died, and he bided on till he was a very old, ancient man, with my son to help him. And then he died too, and was buried along with his wife. He was always self-contained and self-respecting. He took his luck for granted and never made no fuss about it; and such was his character that no man ever envied him his good fortune. In fact, I do believe that everybody quite agreed with his own opinion: that he hadn't got any more than he deserved—if as much.

No. V
WHEN FOX WAS FERRYMAN

No. V

WHEN FOX WAS FERRYMAN

We Dittisham folk live beside Dart river and at what you may call a crossing. For there's a lot of people go back and forth over the water between us and Greenway on t'other bank, and so the ferryman is an important member of the community, and we often date things that happen by such a man who reigned over the ferry at the time, just as we think of what fell out when such a king reigned over the country.

And this curious adventure came to be when Fox was ferryman, and nobody had better cause to remember it than old Jimmy Fox himself, for to him the tale belongs in a manner of speaking, though you may be sure he wasn't the man who used to tell it.

Jimmy Fox not only ran the ferry, but he was master of the 'Passage House' inn, a public that stood just up top of the steps on the Dittisham landing, and as this was the spot where passengers crossed, and there weren't no beer at Greenway, they naturally took their last drink at the 'Passage House' before setting forth, and their first drink there on landing. So it rose to be a prosperous inn enough. Mrs. Fox was the ruling spirit there, because her husband spent most of his daytime working the ferry boat; but Polly Fox—most people called her 'the Vixen' behind her back—had two to help her in the shape of Christie Morrison, a niece of her husband's, and Alice Chick, the barmaid—a good sort of girl enough.

Fox and his wife were a childless couple, and gave out they'd adopted orphan Christie, and claimed a good deal of praise for so doing; but it weren't a very one-sided bargain, after all, for she worked like a pony, and proved more than worth her keep. In fact, there was little in her days but work, and for a young pretty maiden not turned nineteen, there's no doubt the toil and trouble of 'Passage House' and the money-grubbing passion of her uncle and aunt were a depressing state of life.

But she enjoyed the eternal hope proper to youth and looked forward to a home of her own some day, and better times when the right man came along. She got a little fun into her work also, for the river was her delight, and as Jimmy Fox, among his other irons in the fire, rented a salmon net on Dart, Christie now and then had the pleasure of going out along with the fishers, and spending a few hours on the river. But on these occasions she was expected to work like a man and do her part with the nets. That was labour that gave her pleasure, however, and, thanks to the fishery, there came a day when she met a party who interested her more than any other man had done up to that time.

He was a sailor and a calm sort of chap—dark and well-favoured with a lot of fun in him and a lot of character and determination. First mate of a sailing vessel that traded between Dartmouth and Jersey, was Edmund Masters. He had friends at Dittisham, and it was when along with these on the river fishing, that he got acquainted with Christie. Then, as often as his ship, *The Provider*, came to Dartmouth port, he'd find occasion to be up at Dittisham and drop into " Passage House " for a drink and a glimpse of the girl.

As for Jimmy Fox, he thought nothing of it, because a sailor man was of no account in his eyes, and, indeed, he and his wife had very fixed ideas for Christie, which all too soon for her comfort she had now to hear.

After they'd got to bed one night, Mrs. Fox started the subject in her husband's ear.

" 'Tis time," she said, " that William Bassett set on to Christie. She's wife-old now and a good-looking creature, and the men are after her already—that Jersey sailor for one. And it's only making needless trouble for her to go hankering after some worthless youth when you and me and Bassett are all agreed that he must have her."

They'd planned the maiden's future to please themselves, not her ; and such was the view they took of life, that they seemed to think Christie no more than their slave, to be given in marriage where it suited them best.

"There'll be a rumpus," said the ferryman. "But the least said, the soonest mended. William named her to me not long ago, and he brought her a brave dish of plums into the bar only last week. I'll see him to-morrow and tell him to start on her serious and offer himself and say we will it."

But even sooner than he expected did Jimmy see Mr. Bassett, for almost the first passenger as he had for Greenway next day was William. This man owned best part of a square mile of the famous Dittisham plum orchards, and he had a bit of house property nigh St. George's Church also, and was one of our most prosperous people at that time. He was a widower, old enough to be Christie's father; but after five wifeless years he decided to wed again, and having a cheerful conceit of himself and his cash, and reckoning that he had only to drop the handkerchief to any female, decided on Christie Morrison, because her temper was golden and her figure fine, and her character above reproach. As for Bassett, he had a flat face, like a skate, with a slit for a mouth and little pin-point eyes overhung with red hair. He was forty-five and growing bald and his left leg gave at the knee. He was a good sort really, and did kind things for his poorer neighbours. There was a touch of the romantical in him also, and he liked the thought of marrying a pretty girl and making her mistress of his plum orchards and mother of his heir. Because his first had failed him in that matter.

And now, as Fox ferried William over the water on a crisp October morning, he bade him waste no more time, but begin to court Christie like a lover if so be he wanted her.

"We're your side as you know," said Jimmy Fox, "and my wife and I are very wishful to see it happen; but you've got to set on to her, for she's young and a fine sight in the eyes of her own generation. In fact she may fall in love any minute with something better to look at than you."

But William weren't frightened of that.

"She's got a lot of sense, and knows which side her bread is buttered," he said. "She won't trouble about another when she hears, I want her. Because she knows my character, and can count on having a very good time along with me. I'll ax her to tea Sunday, and tell her I'll wed her when she pleases. No need to waste time love-making with a shrewd piece like her. She'll come to me and we'll be married afore Christmas. Then she'll know what it is to wed a romantical man."

"I hope you'll find it as easy as you think for," answered Jimmy, "but you can't take nothing for granted with a maiden girl. However, as you wish it and I wish it, so it's got to be. We've brought her up, and her future lies with us."

"And me," added Bassett, and then the boat touched and he was across.

Christie got her invite to tea that evening and agreed to go. Her aunt had given her an inkling of what was coming; but she hadn't given her aunt an inkling of what had already come, though she might have, and when Polly Fox told her that William wanted her on a very delicate errand, and she must put on her best and look her best, Christie said nothing of the big matter in her own mind. For she very well knew that the Saturday before she went to tea at Mr. Bassett's big red house in the plum orchards, she was promised for a walk to Edmund Master's, and she had a certain belief that before that walk was done Master Teddy would ask her a vital question.

He came, and they went along beside the river, where the wild cherry's leaves fell blood red on the water, and where the hanging woods flamed in afternoon sunshine and made a brave glow. For Dart at autumn time is a fine sight, and the beauty of the scene and the blue of the distant, clear and still beyond all that crimson and gold, tuned Christie to a melting mood. She loved the sailor man very well indeed by now, and knew he loved her; and his calm manner and honest opinions, reposeful sort of nature and unconscious strength won her all the way. For his part he'd never met a girl like her in his travels, and being now twenty-six and wishful to wed, felt that he'd be a very fortunate man to have such a wife as she promised to make. He'd got his eye on a nice little house at St. Helier's, where his relations dwelt, and he'd learned from Christie that she'd be well pleased to dwell there, or anywhere, out of sight and sound of her uncle and aunt Fox. So, when he put the question, she answered it in a way to bring his arms round her and his lips on hers. And though autumn was in the air, spring was in their hearts, no doubt, and they talked the usual hopeful talk, and dreamed the usual cheerful dreams, and knew themselves to be the happiest man and woman walking earth at that particular moment.

Nothing would do, but that Master Ted went off that instant to tell Jimmy Fox the news, and though Christie warned him that her uncle had very different ideas for her, he said, truly enough, that in these cases it was the woman's view of a husband and not her uncle's that ought to count.

But Jimmy very soon showed he wasn't going to take Ted, and had no manner of use for him. In fact, he let go pretty hot, and told Edmund Masters that the likes of him—a seafaring man with a wife in every port, no doubt—wasn't going to have Christie. He blustered and he bullied and he insulted the young man shocking: but the sailor kept his temper very well, and the quieter he was the fiercer old man Jimmy got. And Polly Fox wasn't no better. She spit out her temper on Christie, and wanted to know how a girl, brought up with the fear of God in her eyes, could think twice of a common seafarer.

So seeing they were beyond reason, Masters took up his cap, and left.

"Keep your nerve, my gal," he said to Christie, "and bide my time. Let 'em see we mean what we say; and next voyage I come along, I'll bring my credentials, and if Mr. Fox knows a man with better, then I'll throw up the sponge, but not before."

He took it in that calm and gentlemanlike fashion, but he didn't know his company, or their ideas of proper behaviour; and he didn't know the power her uncle had got over Christie, or the savage nature of the man, that would stick at nothing if crossed.

When he was gone, Fox ordered his niece to her chamber, and when she hesitated, he took her by the scruff of the neck, drove her upstairs to the dormer attic that was hers, pushed her in and locked the door on her.

"And there you shall bide, and there you shall starve till you beg my pardon and your aunt's pardon, and take Mr. Bassett, as we will for you to do," he said.

Stunned and frightened out of her life, the girl very near fainted after such treatment; but the night came and passed, and not a sound of her people did she hear; and in the morning —Sunday—'twas Fox tramped up over the stairs and opened her door and asked if she'd changed her mind. She said "No," of course, and begged him for honour and the love of God to be reasonable; but he only cursed her and locked her in again and went his way.

Later her aunt came, but Christie won no comfort from her tongue, and presently stared out at the shocking truth, that in a Christian country among Christian folks, she was going to be starved to death, because she wouldn't wed William Bassett. On Sunday night Ted would sail again, and she doubted if he'd come to see her till he returned, for his papers were at Jersey along with his mother. Then she thought what lay in her power to do about it, and if it was possible to get at Alice Chick, the barmaid—a very clever creature and very fond of Christie. But there was no chance of that, and she felt sure that Alice had been told she was ill and must not be seen.

But it happened that the other girl knew all about the tragedy, because Mr. Bassett had come in the night before, and Mrs. Fox, who was in the bar, had spoken with him and told what was going forward, and William hadn't liked it none too well. So Alice, though she seemed busy and bustled about as usual, heard the ugly truth, or enough of it to guide her actions.

She thought first of going to William Bassett herself, but she couldn't be sure of him, and so went to her own lover instead. Andrew Beal he was—a fisherman that worked for Fox—and that night Andrew Beal tackled a task somewhat out of the common, for Alice saw him for ten minutes in the road after closing time, and bade him be off to Dartmouth so quick as his legs would carry him with a letter that she'd wrote to Masters. Andrew was to get aboard *The Provider* somehow, and see Ted, and bring his answer in the morning by cock-light. Which things Andrew Beal did do, and before Fox and his wife were stirring,

Alice crept to Christie's door and slipped a letter under it.

And a very clever letter it was.

I hear they've locked you up and mean to starve you if you won't take another man (wrote the sailor). *Well, keep quite calm and save yourself all fear. People who break the rule of law and order and do such devilish deeds as this must be treated to their own high-handed ways, my dear. I'll call for you to-morrow at dusk, Christie, so be ready, and have your things packed, for you'll say good-bye to 'Passage House' a few hours after you get this letter. And if Alice Chick is allowed to see you, tell her I'll not forget her goodness nor yet her man's. We'll have the weather of 'em before nightfall. Cheer O!*

Your loving,

Ted.

Well, that was better than breakfast, no doubt, for the hungry girl, and when her uncle stormed up again, to know if she'd come to her senses and would go over and see Bassett, she said she'd never left her senses, and told him, very bravely, that there was a time coming when his Maker would reckon with him and her aunt also.

He gnashed what teeth he'd got left at her, and told her that he'd break her and make her howl for mercy afore she was many hours older. And then he went down house and dared his wife, who was getting a bit skeared over it, to take the girl a crust.

" 'Tis my will against hers," he said, " and I've got the whip hand. Another day without food will soon bring her to heel; and if it don't, I'll try what a touch of my leather belt will do for the young devil."

Then he went to work, and the few folk he ferried that Sabbath day all said that Jimmy was getting no better than a bear with a sore head, for he hadn't a word to throw at man, or woman, but mumbled in his beard to himself and scowled at the folk as if they were all his natural enemies.

And meantime the hours passed and Christie, though cruel distressed for want of food, did as Ted bade her, and packed her little box with her few treasures, and put on her Sunday clothes, and wondered with all her might however Edmund Masters would be so good as his word.

But she trusted him and doubted not that things would fall out as he said. She knew that *The Provider* sailed for home that night, and guessed her lover meant taking her along with him. Indeed, once out of 'Passage House,' she didn't intend to lose sight of him again. She kept calm and watchful as the sun turned west and the day began to sink. Not a sound had come up to her, but she'd heard her aunt shuffling about the passage once or twice; and once, the old woman, fearful of her silence, had looked in and found her rayed in her Sunday best.

She thought Christie had changed her mind, and was going to William Bassett. So she locked her in again and ran down to tell Jimmy, who was below just going to have his tea.

But a good many hours passed before her husband heard the news after all, for, when his wife got below, he'd just heard the ferry bell calling him from t'other side the river and gone down to his boat and put across.

For when folk came to the little landing-stage at Greenway they rang the ferry bell, lifted up on the high post there, and that brought Fox across to 'em till the hour of dusk. And if they called him after that, they had got to pay double.

Jimmy reckoned it was dusk enough by now to make the fare pay twice over, and he was well used to having arguments on that subject as the evenings began to draw in. But this time he had a surprise—the surprise of his life, in fact—for coming alongside the Greenway steps and telling whoever 'twas to hurry up, a voice from above bade him to moor the boat, and come and lend a hand with a box.

" 'Twill be a shilling more if you've got a box," said Jimmy, and the man up top answered.

" You can charge what you please."

Then Fox made fast and went up the steps, to find the biggest chap he ever set eyes upon waiting for him.

" You ought to pay double fare yourself," he said, " and where's your box ? "

Then the big man calmly gripped him by his neck-cloth as if

he was a kitten and, while he did so, another chap appeared from behind the post that held the ferry bell.

'Twas Edmund Masters, and he explained the situation to Fox in a few words.

" Being an old blackguard above law and order, Jimmy Fox, you give honest men the trouble to teach you manners and explain that you can't starve young women, and treat 'em like dogs and think you're going to have your wicked way with 'em when and how you please. So now your niece will be took away from you for ever, and as she's got no particular wish for you to kiss her 'good-bye,' you can stop here and think over your cowardly sins and cool your heels a bit—till morning, I hope. And this is my best friend, Captain Le Cornu, of *The Provider*, and the strongest man in the Channel Isles. So now you'll know what it feels like to be in mightier hands than your own, you dirty scoundrel. And if you wasn't so old, I'd give you a dozen of the best before we go."

Then he turned to the other.

"Trice him up, skipper."

In half a shake Jimmy Fox found himself bound hand and foot to the ferry bell post. The bell-pull was knotted high out of his reach and a handkerchief tied pretty tight round his mouth.

Two minute sufficed for this job, because no men knew better than those how to handle rope.

" 'Tis a very good bit of Manila hemp," said the captain of *The Provider*.

" And you can use it to hang yourself when you get free again," added Ted.

Half a minute later they were in the ferry boat and away.

Then it was the turn of Jimmy's lady.

The big man stopped in the boat, and Christie's lover, knowing there was no time to lose, bustled into the parlour of the 'Passage House,' and asked Mrs. Fox for the girl.

Whereupon Polly told him to be off, or she'd call her husband to him.

" Give her up, or take the consequences," said Ted, and counting Jimmy would be back every moment, the woman defied him. Luck was on the sailor's side, for the house-place happened to be empty and the bar closed for church hour. So he had it to himself and acted prompt.

"Sorry to touch a woman, though she is a bad old witch that did ought to be drowned," he said, and with that he popped the creature into a big armchair and tied her there.

"Now we all know where we are, Mrs. Fox," he said, "and it won't help you to yowl, because you and your husband are breaking the law and doing a fearful outrage that might send you both to clink for the rest of your evil lives, so you'll do best to keep quiet and thank me for saving you from the wrath to come."

With that he left her, and Alice Chick, who knew all about it and was hiding outside the door, showed him up to Christie's chamber.

The girl was ready for him, and before I can tell it he had her box on his back and was down and away with her at his heels.

A minute later they were in the ferry boat and off to Dartmouth. The tide was just on the turn and helped 'em.

They heard Polly screaming the top of her head off one side the river; while a muffled noise, like a bull-frog croaking, came from the ferry steps at Greenway.

"The owls are making a funny noise to-night sure enough!" said the skipper of *The Provider*.

But Ted was busy. He'd forgot nothing, and now pulled a lot of food out of his pocket for the starving woman.

"Eat and say nought," he ordered, and then he took an oar and helped his friend.

Before dawn the schooner was hull down on her way to the Islands, and folk at Dartmouth stared to see the Dittisham ferry boat adrift in the harbour; but presently there came Jimmy Fox calling on all the law and the prophets for vengeance; and then the nation heard about his troubles and the terrible adventure that had overtook the poor man and his wife. But both were tolerably well known up and down the river, and I didn't hear that anybody went out of the way to show sympathy.

In fact, when the story leaked out, which it did do next time *The Provider* was over, most people agreed with Edmund Masters that he'd done very clever.

Christie was married to Ted at St. Heliers when he came back to her after the next voyage, and Fox and his good lady got wind of it, of course; but 'tis generally allowed they didn't send her no wedding present.

Somebody did, however, for when William Bassett heard how things had fallen out, his romantical character came to his aid, and, such are the vagaries of human nature, that he sent Mrs. Masters a five-pound note.

"Just to show you the sort of man you might have took, my dear," he wrote to her.

No. VI
MOTHER'S MISFORTUNE

No. VI

MOTHER'S MISFORTUNE

I shall always say I did ought to have married Gregory Sweet when my husband dropped, and nobody can accuse me of not doing my bestest to that end. In a womanly way, knowing the man had me in his eye from the funeral onwards, and before for that matter, I endeavoured to make it so easy for him as I could without loss of self-respect; and he can hear me out, and if he don't the neighbours will.

But there it was. Gregory suffered from defects of character, too prone to show themselves in a bachelor man after the half century he turned. He pushed caution to such extremes that you can only call ungentlemanly where a nice woman's concerned, and I never shall know to my dying day what kept him off me. A man of good qualities too, but a proper slave to the habit of caution, and though I'd be the last to undervalue the virtue which never was wanted more than now, yet, when the coast lies clear and the sun's shining and the goal in sight, and that goal me, 'twas a depressing thing for the man to hold back without any sane reason for so doing.

Being, as you may say, the centre of the story, for Milly Parable and my son, Rupert, though they bulk large in the tale, be less than me, it's difficult to set it out. And the affair itself growed into such a proper tangle at the finish that my pen may fail afore the end; but I'll stick so near as memory serves me to the facts, and, though others may not shine too bright afore I finish, the tale won't cast no discredit upon me in any fairminded ear.

I married at twenty and had four children and they was grown up, all but Albert, before I lost John Stocks, my first husband. Albert, top flower of the basket, he died as a bright child of ten year old. His brain was too big for his head and expanded and killed him. And that left Jane, my first, married to Ford, the baker, and John, called after his father, and known to me as 'Mother's Joy,' and Rupert, who got to be called 'Mother's Misfortune,' because he was a shifty and tolerable wicked boy with lawless manners and no thought for any living creature but self. John was good as gold, but a thought simple. He married and had five childer in four years and never knew where to turn for a penny. But the good will and big heart of the man was always there, and if he could have helped his parents and come by money honest, he'd have certainly done it. A glutton for work and in church twice every Sunday; but his work was hedge-tacking and odd jobs, and he never done either in a way to get any lasting fame. I wouldn't say I was proud of him, and yet I knew he went straight and done his duty to the best of his poor powers. His wife was such another—the salt of the earth in a manner of speaking, if rightly understood, but no knack of making her mark in the world—in fact a very godly, unnoticeable, unlucky fashion of woman. I knew they'd be rewarded hereafter, where brains be dust in the balance, but meantime I'd sometimes turn to mark Rupert flourishing like the green bay tree and making money and putting it away and biding single and keeping his secrets close as the grave.

I never saw none of his earnings and more didn't his father. He was under-keeper to Tudor Manor and very well thought on; but a miser of speech, as well as cash, and none knew what was in his heart. He lived at the north lodge of the big place and woke a lot of curiosity, as secrecy will; but at eight-and-twenty years of age he was granted to be a man very skilled in his business, and the head-keeper, Mr. Vallance, thought a lot of him, and the two men under him went in fear. So also did the poachers, for he was terrible skilled in their habits, and only his bringing up and a patient father and mother had turned the balance and made him the protector of game instead of a robber himself. So there it was: my eldest had a heart of gold and no intellects, as often happens, while Rupert hadn't no heart at all, but the Lord willed him wits above ordinary. He'd come to supper of a Sunday and eat enormous; though never did we get anything in return but emptiness and silence. He'd listen to his father telling, and my John, being a hopeful man, never failed to hint that a few shillings would help us over a difficult week and so on ; but Rupert only listened. My John, you see, was one of they unfortunates stricken with the rheumatism that turns you into a living stone, so his usefulness was pretty undergone afore he reached sixty and but for my little bit, saved in service, and an occasional food-offering from my daughter's husband, it would have gone hard with us. This my eldest son well understood and often the tears would come into his eyes because he couldn't do nothing ; but no tear ever came into Rupert's eyes. Once I saw him stuff his father's pipe out of his own tobacco pouch and only once ; and we thought upon that amazing thing for a month after and wondered how it happened.

Well, that's how it stood when the Almighty released my husband and in a manner of speaking me also. He had been comforted by good friends during his long illness and not only our eldest son, John, would often make time to sit by him and have a tell, but there was the Vicar also and his wife—peaceful and cheerful people, that my poor sufferer was always glad to see. And besides them Mr. Sweet often came in and passed the news, though owing to his high gift of caution he'd seldom tell you anything that wasn't well known a month before. And Arthur Parable was not seldom at the bedside, for he was among our oldest friends and tolerable cheerful along with John, because the sight of a sick person had a way to cheer him and make him so bright as a bee. He'd be very interested to hear about my husband's pangs and said it was wonderful what the human frame could endure without going under. But a nice, thoughtful man who had seen pecks of trouble himself and could spare a sigh for others. He'd often bring my husband a pinch of tobacco, or an old illustrated newspaper ; and he liked to turn over the past, when his wife was alive and he'd many times been within a touch of taking his own life.

Arthur was a handsome fellow, and might well have wed again, but no desire in that direction overtook him, and when Dowager Lady Martin at Tudor Manor took sick and had two nurses, his daughter Minnie, gived over her work, which was lady's maid to the old lady, and come home to look after her father. I'd say to Mr. Parable sometimes that, at his age and with his personable appearance, he might try again in hope; but "No," he said. "I've had my little lot and there's Minnie. My girl would never neighbour with a step-mother and I don't want no more sour looks and high words in my house."

"Girl" he called her, but in truth Minnie Parable was five-and-thirty and far ways from being girlish in mind or body. Old for her age and one of they flat, dreary-minded females with a voice like the wind in a winter hedge, eyes without no more light in 'em than a rabbit's, and a moping, down-daunted manner that made the women shrug their shoulders and the men fly. Not a word against her, and the fact she was lady's maid for ten full years to the Dowager can be told to prove her virtues; but then again, the Dowager was a melancholy-minded old woman, along of family misfortunes, and no doubt Minnie's gift for looking at the dark side suited that ancient piece, who always did likewise.

But there it was. With her melancholy nose, thin shoulders and sand-coloured hair, Minnie woke up no interest in the men, and there was only one person surprised to find it so, and that was herself.

She told me once, in her poor, corncrake voice, that she'd never had an affair in her life, though she'd saved money. "I'd always thought to have a home of my own some day," she told me, "for it ain't as though I was one of them women that shun the male and plan to go through life without a partner; but they hold off, Mrs. Stocks, and the younger girls get married."

"Plenty of time," I said—to pleasure her—though knowing only too well there would never be the time for Minnie. "You wait," I said. "All things come to them who wait."

Little did I guess I was speaking a true word, but I went on:

"Them as marry for the eye often find they're mistook, and with your homely looks, my dear, you've always got the certainty no man will snatch at you like he would at a pretty flower. When he comes, your husband will look beneath the surface and there he'll find what's better than pink cheeks and a glad eye. So you wait," I said, "for a chap who's past the silly stage and wants a comfortable home and a good cook and helpmate who'll look at both sides of sixpence before she spends it."

'Twas well meant, but like a lot of other well-intending remarks, fell a good bit short to the hearer. In fact the woman's reply threw a bit of light on character and showed me a side of Minnie's mind I had not bargained for. She flickered up as I spoke and stared out of her faded eyes, and for a passing moment there came a glint in 'em, like the sun on a dead fish.

"I didn't know I was so plain as all that!" she snapped out. "There's uglier than me in the village, unless I can't see straight, and whether or no, when I marry, it'll be for love, let me tell you, Mary Stocks, and not to count my husband's sixpences!"

"May he have more than you can count, my dear, when he do come," I said, for the soft answer that turns away wrath has mostly been my motto. And then I left her, champing on the bit, so to say; and I wondered where the poor soul had seen a less fanciable maiden than herself in our village, or any other. But 'tis the mercy of Providence to hide reality from us where 'tis like to hurt most, and no doubt if our neighbours knew the naked truth of their queer appearances and uncomfortable natures, there would come a rush of them felo-de-sees and a lot of unhappiness that ignorance escapes.

Well, my poor John went, but before he'd done so it was plain to mark that our old and valued friend, Gregory Sweet, had me upon his mind. Never a word he said while there was a spark of life in John and never a word he said afterwards either for a full year, and I liked him the better for it; but though cautious, he was not a concealer, and never attempted to hide his regard and hope where I was concerned. A woman knows without words, being gifted by nature to understand signs and signals, whether of danger, or the reverse; and so I knew Gregory was very much addicted to me and only waiting the appointed time to offer. For a long while I thought he would put the proposal in a letter, and then, remembering his caution and his terror of the written word, I guessed he'd never so far commit himself as to set it down. But I was ready and willing, for Greg had a tidy little greengrocer's business and they counted him a snug man. A bachelor of sixty-two he was—clean as a new pin of a Sunday and very well thought upon. A bearded man, with a wrinkled brow and eyes that looked shifty to a stranger; but 'twas only his undying caution made them so. As straight as any other greengrocer, and straighter than some. And I was tolerable poor, but not lacking in gifts to shine, given the chance; and I knew Gregory inside out, you may say, and felt that in the shop and the home, he'd be a happier man for my company.

So, when the year was out and he still kept hanging on, though never a day passed but he looked in, or brought a bunch of pretty fresh green stuff, I felt the man's hand must be strengthened.

"I'll save him from himself in this matter," I thought. "He's got a way of thinking time and eternity be the same thing, and he's looked all round the bargain for more'n a year, so 'tis up to me to help him in the way he very clearly wants to go." And I set about him and made it easy for him to see he wouldn't get "No" for an answer when he brought himself to the brink. I made it so clear as a woman could that I cared for Sweet, and I aired my views and dropped a good few delicate-minded hints, such as that he didn't look to be getting any younger and more didn't I; and when the Rev. Champernowne preached a very fine performance on the words, "Now is the accepted time," I rubbed it in fearlessly when Mr. Sweet next came for a smoke and talk after his supper.

"Time don't stand still with the youngest," I said, "and for my part it seems to go quicker with the middle-aged than anybody; and many a man and woman too," I said, "have lived to look back and see what a lot they missed, through too much caution and doubt. 'Nothing venture, nothing have,' is a very true word," I said, "and when a man have only got to open his mouth to win his heart's desire, he's a good bit of a fool, Greg, to keep it shut."

I couldn't say no more than that, and he nodded and answered me that he didn't know but what I might be right.

"There's not your equal for sense in the parish," he told me, and being worked up a bit that evening, I very near gave him an impatient answer; but that ain't my way: I just held in and told him that I was glad he thought so, and I believed he weren't the only one. Then he took a curious look at me and said " Good evening," and went on his way.

And, strange to tell, that last word of mine gave me an idea. Looking back I can see what tremendous things was hid in that chance speech, for it decided my life in a manner of speaking. Of course when I told Greg he weren't the only one, I used a figure of speech and no more, because there weren't none else and never had been ; but now, as I unrayed for bed, I asked myself how it would be if there was another after me, and though very well knowing that no such thing could possibly happen, I let the thought run, pictured myself with another string to my old bow, and wondered what Mr. Sweet would do then.

I certainly paid the man the compliment of feeling sure, when he heard that, he'd throw caution to the winds and go for me ; and since there wasn't in sober truth another as had looked upon me with any serious resolves, I had to set about the matter. The Lord helps those who help themselves, but not if they be up to anything underhand or devious, as a rule, and though I might have invented a tale to hoodwink Gregory Sweet, that must have got back on my conscience, besides being a dangerous thing. Deceived, the poor man had to be—for his own good, but my story must be made to hold water and ring true, else, with his doubting and probing nature, I well knew he'd ferret out the facts and very like leave me a loser.

But one man there was, who could well be trusted to play his part in this difficult matter, and he knew the circumstances and had already asked me time and again when Gregory was going to take the plunge. So I went to Arthur Parable and explained the situation and hoped, as an old friend and a well-wisher and a man far above suspicion, he'd lend a hand.

" It's like this, Arthur," I said. " I can trust you with my secrets, you being a man never known to talk and also a great friend of poor John's." And then I explained how it was with Mr. Sweet and how he only wanted just a clever push from outside to propose and be done with it.

Arthur heard me in silence, then he spoke. "You don't want me to tell the man to offer for you?" he asked, and I replied:

"No Arthur—far from it; but I want you to fall in with a little plot. There's nothing quickens a man like Gregory so fast as finding he isn't the only pebble on the beach; and if he was to hear my praises on your lips, or find us two taking a walk by the river, or drop in and see you drinking your dish of tea along with me once and again, I'm tolerable sure that he'd find the words. It won't throw no shadow on you," I said, "if you was to pretend a little interest in me; but when Gregory found out you was doing so, and heard the name of Mary Stocks in your mouth, and guessed you find your mind occupied with me off and on, then 'twould be the match to the powder in my opinion; and I should never forget your great goodness and bless your name."

He took a good long time before he answered, and I was feared of my life he would refuse to have any hand in the affair. He cast his eyes over me that searching that I felt I might have gone too far; but then he grinned, which was an expression of pleasure very rare indeed with Arthur, and his brow lifted, and he went so far as to wink one of his pale grey eyes, the one with a drooping lid.

"For John's sake," I said.

"As to John," he answered, "I never heard him say he was particular anxious for you to take another, and many husbands feel rather strong on that subject, as you can see when you hear their wills after they be gone; but as poor John hadn't nothing to leave, he couldn't make no conditions to hamper your freedom of action, and for my part I see no reason why you shouldn't marry Gregory Sweet if you want to."

"I do," I said. "He's a man you could trust, and you put safety first at my time of life."

Well, Arthur dallied a bit and didn't throw himself into it exactly; but none the less, before I left him he promised to do his part and make Mr. Sweet jealous if he could without casting any reflections upon himself.

For I found that Arthur had his share of caution also, and

before we parted he made me sign a paper acknowledging the cabal in secret against Greg.

"You shall have it back the day he offers for you," promised Arthur Parable, "and I only require it so that if any hard things was said of me, or I was accused of toying with your finer feelings, or anything like that, I can show by chapter and verse under your signature that the man's a liar. And meantime I'll sound your praises if I see Sweet and say you'd teach him the meaning of true happiness, and so on. And I'll come to tea Sunday."

Well, I thanked the man from my heart and since one good turn called for another I asked after him and his girl and hoped Minnie was being a kindly daughter to him and so on. But he didn't speak very fatherly of her.

"She's a melancholy cat in a house," he said, "and women will be melancholy in her stage of life. She's terrible wishful to leave me and find a husband—so set on it as yourself—but of course with no chance whatsoever; for no self-respecting man would ever look at a creature like her. As a rule, with her pattern, they have got sense enough to give up hope and take what Nature sends 'em in a patient spirit. But not Minnie. Hope won't die and, in a word, she's a plaguey piece and she's got a sharp tongue too, and when I'm too old to hold my own she'll give me hell."

"Why don't she go into one of them institutions?" I asked. "There's plenty of places where good work is being done by ugly, large-hearted women, looking after natural childer, or nursing rich folk, and so on. Then she'd be helping the world along and forget herself and lay up treasure where moth and rust don't corrupt."

"You ax her," answered Arthur. "You give her a hint. I'd pay good money to man or woman who could tempt her away from looking after me. And if she thought I was minded to take another wife, I'd get the ugly edge of her tongue up home to my vitals, so us must watch out."

"Don't you let her in the secret, however," I prayed the man, "because if she knew she'd spoil all."

"Fear nothing," he answered; "I can take her measure."

But unfortunately for all concerned, Arthur over-praised himself in that matter, and before a fortnight was told, while we developed our little affair very clever, and I smiled on Arthur in the street afore neighbours, and now and again he invited himself to tea—if Minnie didn't dash in and put the lid on! What I felt I can't write down in any case now, things happening as they did after; but at the time, I'd have wrung the woman's neck for a ha'porth of peas. But she thought she knew the circumstances, and being filled with hateful rage that her father was thinking on another, she struck in the only quarter that mattered and, before I knowed it, I was a lone woman and hope dead.

A good bit happened first, however, and Arthur played up very clever indeed. He'd come along and pass the time of day and I'd look in his cottage to give an opinion on some trifle; and when he came to a tea on which I'd spent a tidy lot of thought, he enjoyed it so much and welcomed the strength of it and the quality of the cake so hearty that once or twice us caught ourselves up.

"Dammy!" said Arthur, "we'm going it, Mary. Us had better draw in a thought, or our little games will end in earnest."

"Not on my side," I said, and that vexed him I believe, for a man's a man. However, I reminded him of his first, and that always daunted his spirit, so he soon went off with his tail between his legs.

But all the same, I couldn't help contrasting Arthur with Gregory, and though Greg might be called the more important and prosperous man, yet there was always a barrier he wouldn't pass, while Arthur, though brooding by nature, could get about himself now and again, and in them rare moments, you felt there was a nice, affectionate side to him that only wanted encouraging.

It was three days after that tea and his praises of my hand with a plum cake, that I found myself left.

It came like a bolt from the blue sky, as they say, and I was messing about in my little garden full of an offer I'd got to let my cottage, or sell it, and wondering if I should tell Gregory, when the man himself came in the gate and slammed it home after him. And I see when I looked in his determined eyes that the time had come. His jaws were working, too, under his beard, and I reckoned he'd got wind of Arthur and was there to say the word at last. And I was right enough about Arthur, but cruel wrong about the word.

"I'll ax you to step in the house," he said. "I've heard something."

"I hope it's interesting news," I answered. "Come in by all means, Gregory. Always welcome. Will you drink a glass of fresh milk?"

For milk was his favourite beverage.

"No," he answered. "I don't take no milk under this roof no more."

So then I began to see there was something biting the man, though for my life I couldn't guess what.

However, he soon told me.

He sat down, took off his hat, wiped his brow, blew his nose and then spoke.

"I've just been having a tell with Minnie Parable—old Parable's daughter," he said.

"Have you?" I said. "Would you call him old?"

"Be damned to his age," he answered. "That's neither here nor there. But this I'd wish you to understand. I've respected you for a good few years now."

"Why not?" I asked, rather short, for I didn't like his manner.

"No reason at all till half an hour agone," he replied. "But now I hear that, while you well knew my feelings and my hopes and might have trusted a man like me to speak when he saw his way, instead of following my lead and remembering yourself and calling to mind the sort of woman such as I had the right to expect, and waiting with patience and dignity for the accepted hour, you be throwing all thought of me to the winds and rolling your eyes on the men and axing them to tea, and conducting yourself in a manner very unbecoming indeed for the woman I'd long hoped to marry."

I felt myself go red to the bosom; but I done a very clever thing, for though a thousand words leapt to my tongue, I didn't speak one of 'em; but kept my mouth close shut and looked at him. Nought will vex an angry man more than to be faced with blank silence after he's let off steam and worked up to a fine pitch; and now Greg expected me to answer back; and it put him out of his stride a lot when I didn't.

I dare say we was both dumb for three minutes; then he got up off his chair and prepared to go.

"And—and," he began again "— and I want you to understand here and now—here and now—that it's off. You've played with my affections and made me a laughing stock—so Minnie Parable tells me—and I hope you'll live to repent it—yes, I do. And I'll say good evening."

"Good evening, Mr. Sweet," I said, "and may God forgive you, because I never won't. You've put the foul-mouthed lies of that forgotten creature before a faithful, wholesome woman and listened to libellious falsehoods spoke against me behind my back, and talked stuff I might have you up for. And 'tis you are disgraced, not me; and when you find a straighter, cleaner-minded and more honourable creature than what I am, and one as would make you a finer partner, or had more admiration and respect for your character and opinions than what I had until ten minutes ago, then I shall be pleased to wish her luck."

"It's all off, all the same," he said, and began to shamble down the path; but he'd lost his fire.

"Yes," I said, following him to the gate. "It's off all right, and angels from heaven wouldn't bring it on again. I never had it in my mind for an instant moment to take any man but you, and if I haven't been patient and long-suffering, waiting till your insulting caution was at an end, then God never made a patient woman. But it's off, as you truly remark, and I'm very well content to remain the relic of John Stocks, who valued me and who died blessing my name."

He went out with his head down and his nose very near touching his stomach; and after he'd gone I got in the house so limp as a dead rat. I'd bluffed it all right to Gregory; but when my flame cooled, I found the tears on my face and let 'em run for an hour. Then I calmed down and licked my bruises, so to speak, and felt a terrible wish for to hear a friendly fellow creature and get a bit of sympathy out of someone. For I'm a very sociable kind of woman; so I put on my bonnet and was just going round to see Mrs. Vincent and ask after the new baby and then tell my tale, her being a dear friend to me and her family also, when another man came to my door and there stood my son Rupert—him known as 'Mother's Misfortune,' to distinguish him from my dear eldest one.

I wasn't in no mood for Rupert, and I told him so, but I marked he was mildly excited, and that being a most unusual state for him, I stopped five minutes and axed him what he'd come for.

"You'll laugh," he said sitting down and lighting his pipe.

"I ain't in a very laughing temper," I answered, "and if I laugh at anything you say, it will be the first time in your life I ever have done."

"Dry up," he said, "and listen. I've just come for a bit of a tell with Minnie Parable."

Then I forgot myself.

"To hell with Minnie Parable!" I cried out. "I don't want to hear nothing about that misbegot vixen."

For once Rupert was astonished, but he weren't so astonished as me a minute later.

"I'm sorry you take that view," he replied; "because she'll be your daughter-in-law in six weeks. I be going to marry her."

I never can stand more'n one shock a day, and now I felt myself getting out of hand terrible fast. But I drawed in a deep breath of air and fell on my chair.

"There's a good deal more in that woman than meets the eye," went on Rupert. "Her face would frighten a hedge-pig, no doubt, and her shape be mournful; but I ain't one to marry for decorations. She's a woman, and she can cook and she knows the value of money, and also knows my opinions on that subject. I didn't find her a bad sort by no means. She's got sense and she ain't a gadder, and would rather work than play, same as me."

"But her temper, Rupert, her famous temper," I murmured to the man, and her woeful, craakin voice."

H

"Nobody won't hear no more about her famous temper," he said, "not after she's married me. If I don't cast her temper out of her in a week, then I ain't the man I count myself; and as for her voice, that won't trouble me neither. I'm a peace-lover, and her voice will damned soon be stilled when I'm home to hear it."

It didn't sound promising to my ear, and if it had been any other she but Minnie Parable, I might have felt sorry for the woman.

"D'you mean she's took you?" I asked, still fluttering to the roots.

"She will," he answered. "I was waitin' till I happened to fall in with her, and having done so, I said I wanted a wife, because it was time I had one, and I told her that I saw the makings of a useful woman in her and invited her to turn it over. She was a good bit surprised and couldn't believe her luck for a bit. In fact, if I'd pressed her, or kissed her, or anything like that, she'd have said 'Yes' instanter. But I bade her to keep shut till to-morrow morning, and then be at the north lodge at five-thirty with her answer. And she'll be there."

Rupert had never talked so much in his life afore, and I could see he was tired. In fact he rose up after that last speech and went off without another word. And I knew that Minnie would be up to time also, for she weren't going to say "No" to the first and last as was ever like to offer for her.

And I turned over the mystery and very soon felt in my bones there must be something hidden. Rupert might have had a dozen girls, for there's lots of meek women like his overbearing, brutal sort and would have been very well content to take him, well knowing he spelled safety if no more; but for him, a saver and dealer in the main chance to marry at all, let alone an object like Minnie, meant far more than I could fathom out. He'd said himself there was more to her than met the eyes, and no doubt there was; but her promise was hidden from me, and I puzzled half that night and three parts of the next day, though all in vain.

There was my own sad case also, and, of course, a very painful duty lay in front of me. But I ain't one to let misery fester and so, twenty-four hours after my shocking adventure with Gregory, I went right over to Arthur Parable and told him all.

He was a good bit amused, in fact I never heard him laugh so hearty, and I got a thought hot about it ; but he hadn't nothing much to say except I was well rid of Mr. Sweet. "A man like that," said Arthur, " was never meant to wed. Caution such as his in the home would mighty soon have drove you daft. And there's the makings of a tyrant in Gregory, by your own showing, for the man who resents freedom to his woman before marriage, may very like lock her up afterwards."

"I weren't his woman," I said, "and I didn't take it lying down, neither. He got the truth, and he didn't like it."

"I'd have give a finger off my hand to have heard you," declared Arthur, and then he laughed again ; and then he grew serious and offered hope.

"Mark me," he said. "He ain't done with you. This is no more than a fit of silly temper and I dare say, though you think you're defeated, you'll find you've conquered before a week's sped."

"I don't want to conquer," I answered. "I wouldn't take the man now if he was twice what he is. Along with you I've found that there's better than Greg. I've got over the shock and I won't take him now, even if he wants me. There's a tyrant hid behind the man, as you say."

Arthur considered.

"I wouldn't swear but what you might be right," he declared.

And then I let drop a hint or two, though well within manners.

"If there was more like you," I told Arthur, "I might be tempted, but since I've heard you, I very well know Mr. Sweet at his best never held a candle to you."

"Once bit twice shy," said Parable, and strange to say, from that moment I took a violent fancy to the man. However, he'd grasped my meaning, as his answer showed, and next time I met him, he was happier than I'd ever known him to be. Joy blazed in his face and he walked like a young man.

"My, Arthur!" I said, "who's left you a fortune?"

"Better than that," he answered. "Your Rupert have

offered for Minnie and wants to be married in six weeks. It sounds like a fairy story; but there's no doubt seemingly; and don't you put him off her, or I'll never speak to you again, Mary."

"It would take more than me to put Rupert off anything he wanted," I replied. "And, to tell truth, this is no surprise to me. He's very well pleased with his bargain, and I do hope you see your way to give Minnie a pinch of cash, for that will lighten Arthur's heart amazing and keep him faithful till they be wed."

"So I thought," replied Arthur. "In fact I've gone so far as to name one hundred pounds if they're man and wife afore Michaelmas."

"Then fear no more," I said. "It will happen."

The same night affairs rushed on to their amazing conclusion and Rupert staggered me once more. For the first time in his life he willed to pleasure me, and it showed the secret power of the man, that again he talked as if a deed was already done afore the difficulties had been faced.

Minnie had told him all about my adventures, indeed they was common knowledge now, and many had heard how Mr. Sweet had fallen off. Some came to say they was sorry, and some thought it a pretty good escape, and some of his friends would never know me no more. But Rupert didn't waste no time on Gregory; he was in a wonderful amiable mood and I could see Arthur's hundred pounds had touched him in his tenderest spot. And then, in his blunt way, he went to the centre of the situation and asked me if I'd like to marry Arthur.

"Because," he said, "if you would, you shall!"

"You'll puzzle me to my dying day," I answered. "And how be it in your power to give me Arthur Parable, supposing I was to want him? It's a delicate subject," I said, "and he will never take another, having all he wanted with his first."

"Don't jaw," my son answered me. "For once I can do you a turn; but if you're going to bleat about it, I shall not. Do you want Arthur Parable, or don't you?"

An indecent man was Rupert, and always above any of them nice shades in conversation that manners point to and proper feeling expects. However, that sort don't think the worse of you for sinking to their level, and I well understood that he meant what he said and would be off if I didn't answer straight.

"Between mother and son, I may speak," I answered Rupert, "and if you want to know, though what business it is of yours I can't say, I should be willing to take Mr. Parable if the idea got in his mind."

"Right then," answered Rupert. "It damn soon will get in his mind."

And he was gone.

I heard the end of the tale next day, when Arthur himself looked in.

He was a bit comical tempered at first, but he thawed out after a drop and asked me to marry him, and I asked whether it was from the heart, or there lay anything behind. And then he told me that Rupert had been to see him and told him that I wanted him cruel and that he must take me; and that if he didn't, he wouldn't wed Minnie! "Your son's a man," said Arthur, "as I won't neighbour with, Mary, and you mustn't expect I shall; but there's a hateful, cold-blooded power about your Rupert. And there's mysteries hid in him. And he's one too many for me, or any other decent and orderly spirit. Of course, if I've got to choose between having my darter on my hands for ever and another wife, only a lunatic would hesitate, and since it had to be, I'd a lot rather it was you than any other I can call to mind. And truth's truth, and I hope you'll allow for the queerness, and take a man who's very addicted to you and can be trusted to serve you as you deserve."

With that I told him he must court me without any regard to Rupert, and explained the whole plot was Rupert's, and not mine.

"There's something devious about it," I said, "or it wouldn't be Rupert. You exercise your manhood, Arthur," I said, "and make up your own mind, and don't let my son make it up for you. 'Tis past bearing," I said, "and I won't stand for it. Who be he to drive us?"

"You swear afore your God it wasn't your own idea,"

ordered Arthur, and he cheered up when I put my hand on the Book in my parlour and swore most solemn I'd never thought of no such thing.

"In that case," he said, "I feel a good bit hopefuller, and when you ax if Rupert looked ahead with his eye to the main chance, of course he did. If you come to me, mine's yours when I go to ground, or else Minnie's, so Rupert knows the future's safe either way."

"There's my son John," I said, "but this I tell you, Arthur, I'll come to you on one condition only, that you leave all to Minnie after I'm gone. For it shall never be said that I stood between her and her own. Her, or her childer, must be the gainers."

He laughed at the thought of childer, with Minnie and my Rupert for their parents; and from that time he warmed up and showed his true nature, and we was tokened three days later, so as I was able to tell Mr. Sweet about it, when he'd thought over his mistake and crept on to the warpath again.

And the marriages took place in due course, and me and Arthur was properly happy; and when old Dowager Lady Martin went home, we found the mystery solved.

You see, Rupert had been told off one shooting day to look after a young lawyer and give him some sport, because his Lordship wanted to please the young man's father, who was his own man of business. This chap took to Rupert, by reason of his queer nature, and when they was eating their sandwiches, he must needs talk and chaff my son. He told Rupert about a will as he'd drawed back along for the Dowager, and how an old butler at Tudor Manor was down for five hundred, and the cook for two hundred, and a lady's maid, as served her before she took to her bed and had two nurses, was down for five hundred. But the lawyer named no names and didn't know that Rupert knew who that lady's maid was. And in any case the rash youth never ought to have opened his mouth, of course, on such a secret subject.

But twenty-four hours later, my 'Mother's Misfortune' was tokened to Minnie Parable, and when the Dowager died, of course the money came Rupert's way.

MOTHER'S MISFORTUNE

Strange to relate, it was a tolerable happy marriage as such things go. They bore with one another pretty fair, and though you couldn't say it was a homely pattern of home, and struck shivers into most folk as saw it, it suited them. She never put no poison in Rupert's tea, and he never cut her throat nor nothing like that. One child they had and no more; and he'll get his grandfather's little lot when I don't want it, and John'll get mine.

Rupert's child weren't one for a Christmas card exactly; but they set a lot of store by him. Minnie saw through it, of course, when the Dowager died; but she'd got Rupert which was what mattered to her, and she knew the money was bound to goody all right in her husband's hands; which it did do.

No. VII
STEADFAST SAMUEL

No. VII

STEADFAST SAMUEL

SAMUEL BORLASE was one of them rare childer who see his calling fixed in his little mind from cradlehood. We all know that small boys have big ideas and that they fasten on the business of grown-up people and decide, each according to his fancy, how he be going to help the world's work come he grows up. This child hopes to be a chimney-sweep, and this longs to be a railway-porter; scores trust to follow the sea and dozens wish for to be a soldier, or a 'bus-conductor, a gardener, or a road-cleaner, as the ambition takes 'em. My own grandson much desired to clean the roads, because, as he pointed out, the men ordained for that job do little but play about and smoke and spit and watch the traffic and pass the time of day with one another. He also learned that they got three pounds a week of public money for their fun, and half-holidays of a Saturday, so to his youthful mind it seemed a likely calling.

But most often the ambitions of the human boys be like to change if their parents get much luck in the world, so when you see a steadfast creature, like Samuel Borlase, answer the call in his heart almost so soon as he can walk and talk, you feel the rare event worth setting down.

When he was four year old (at any rate, so his mother will take her oath upon) Sam said he'd be a policeman, and at twenty-four year old a policeman he became. What's more, chance ordained that he should follow his high calling in the village where he was born, and though the general opinion is that a lad, who goes into the civil forces, be like to perform better away from his surroundings, where he was just a common object of the country-side with none of the dignities of the law attaching to him, yet in this case it fell out otherwise and Borlase left home to become a policeman and in due course returned, the finished article.

Naturally with such a history behind him and the ambition of a lifetime to fall back upon, the authorities found no difficulty with Samuel, because he had a policeman's mind and a policeman's bearing and outlook upon life from his youth up. He thought like a policeman about the mysteries of existence; he regarded his neighbours with a policeman's inquiring eyes, because a policeman has a particular glance, as you'll find if you have much to do with 'em; and he moved like a policeman with the might and majesty of law and order ever before his eyes.

He confessed in later time that he pushed his great theories of perfection rather hard in his earlier years; and he came back to his native village of Thorpe-Michael full of high intentions to lift the place higher than where it already stood. He had an unyielding habit of tidiness and hated to see children playing in a road; and he hated worse to see a motor-car come faster round a corner than it did ought; or any sign of unsteady steps in a man or woman, who'd stopped too long at the 'Queen Anne' public-house, or anything like that. He weren't what you might call an amusing man and he hadn't yet reached the stage to make allowances and keep his weather eye shut when the occasion demanded it; but these high branches of understanding was likely to develop in time, and Inspector Chowne, who ruled over him when these things fell out, always held of Samuel Borlase that the material was there and the man hadn't took up his calling without promising gifts to justify it.

"I'd sooner see him fussy than careless," said Chowne, "because life cures a chap of being fussy, if he's got a brain and a sensible outlook; but the careless and slack sort go from bad to worse, and I ain't here to keep my constables in order: they be here to strengthen my hands and keep the rest of the people in order."

He didn't judge as Samuel would ever rise to the top of the tree, any more than what he'd done himself; for Chowne was one who had long lost illusions as to a leading place. He'd made a woeful mess of the only murder case that ever happened to him, and he well knew that anything like great gifts were denied him. But he saw in Samuel such another as himself and judged that Borlase was born to do his duty in the place to which he had been called, and would run his course and take his pension without any of the fierce light of fame.

Of course, Samuel had his likes and dislikes, and he knew which of the community might be counted to uphold him and which might prove a thorn in his side. In fact he was acquaint with most everybody, and as happens in every village, where there's game preserves and such-like, the doubtful characters were there ; and Thorpe-Michael chancing to lie up a creek near the port of Dartmouth, there was river-rats also—said to do a little in a mild way at smuggling from the Channel Islands—a business long sunk from its old fame. Yet the grandsons of vanished 'free-trade' grandfathers were thought to carry on a bit when chance offered.

It was a subject about which there were two opinions, and Billy Forde and others vowed most certain that the law was far too strong to allow of any free-trading nowadays ; but, just because Billy and his friends were so sure, the policeman mind of Sam Borlase suspected 'em. He judged it suited Billy's convenience to declare that no such things happened, the more so because Mr. Forde's own father was well known to have broke a preventive officer's arm in his youth and done time for the same.

But a man by the name of Chawner Green it was that caused Samuel the greatest mistrust. He had nought to do with the creek, but lived in his own cottage, a mile out of Thorpe-Michael ; and the keepers at the big place by name of Trusham, hard by, declared that Mr. Green was a fearsome poacher and hated the sight of the little man, though never had they catched him red-handed, nor been able to fetch up legal proofs against him.

There was a bit of a complication with Chawner Green, because Inspector Chowne happened to be related to him by marriage. In fact, Chawner had married the Inspector's sister five-and-twenty years before, and though Mrs. Green was long since dead, the Inspector never quarrelled with his brother-in-law and regarded him as a man who had got a worse name in the parish than he deserved. So there it was : the keepers at Trusham always felt that Chowne stood against 'em in their valiant endeavours to catch out Chawner ; while the officer took his stand on the letter of the law and said that he held the balance of justice as became him, but weren't going to believe no tales nor set the law in motion against Mr. Green until the proofs stood before him.

It chanced that the under-keeper at Trusham was but three year older than Samuel Borlase himself and a lifelong friend, so Samuel got influenced and came to view Chawner Green very unfavourable. He found himself in rather a delicate position then, but his simple rule was to do what he thought his duty. To look at, Samuel was a big, hard man, rather on the lean side, with a blue chin and a blue eye, which don't often go together. His brow was a bit low and his brain didn't move far out of his appointed task; but a country policeman has a lot of time on his hands, and upon his long country beats, while his eyes surveyed the scene, Sam's intellects would turn over affairs and, no doubt, arrive at conclusions about 'em. And his conclusion about Chawner Green was that he must be a devious bird, else he wouldn't be so idle. For Samuel held that a chap of five-and-fifty, and hard as a nut, which Chawner Green was known to be, did ought to do honest work—an occupation never connected in the public mind with Mr. Green.

There'd been a wedding a bit back along and Chawner's daughter had married a respectable shopkeeper at a neighbouring town; and Samuel Borlase reflected rather gloomily that the small shopkeeper was a fish and poultry merchant—also a seller of game. To his policeman's mind there was a lot more in that than met the eye; and no doubt the born policeman do see a lot more in everything than what us everyday people may remark. Then, on a lonely beat, one autumn day to the north side of Trusham, there came, like a bolt from the blue, the great event of Sammy's life, not only from a professional standpoint, but also an affair that led to far higher things in the shape of a female.

There was a bit of rough, open land there that gave from the covert edge, with scattered brake-fern and a stream in the midst and a lot of blackthorn scrub round about. A noted place for a woodcock, also a snipe, and a spot from which trespassers were warned very careful. So Samuel took a look over to see that all was quiet, and there, in the midst, he marked a big girl struggling with a sloe-bush! But, quick though he was, she'd seen him first, and before he could call out and order her back to the road and take her name, she cried out to him:

"Will 'e lend me a hand, Mister Policeman, if you please? I be catched in thicky sloan tree."

So Borlase went to her aid and he found a basket half full of amazing sloes and a maiden the like of which he never had found afore. A tall piece with flaxen hair and a face so lovely as a picture. Her eyes were bluer than Samuel's and twice so large, and she had a nose a bit tip-tilted and a wonderful mouth, red as a rose and drawn down to the corners in a very fascinating manner. She was sturdy and well rounded, and looked to be a tidy strong girl, and her voice struck the policeman as about the most beautiful sound as he'd heard out of human lips. He saw in half a shake as she weren't in no trouble really, but had just challenged to take the wind out of his sails; and when she'd got free of the thorns, she thanked him with such a lot of gratitude for rescuing of her that 'twas all he could do to keep his face. A lovely thing sure enough; and such is the power of beauty that Samuel felt a caution might be sufficient. He was out to fright her, however, and he was terrible interested also, because he'd never seen the maid before and felt a good bit thunderstruck by such a wonder. She disarmed his curiosity without much trouble, and the truth decided him to do no more; because he found she had a way to her that made him powerless as a goose-chick.

"Didn't you see the board?" he asked; and she assured him that she had not.

"I'm a stranger in these parts as yet," she said, "and I was by here yesterday and marked these wonderful sloan, so I came to-day with a basket, because my father's very fond of sloe gin, you understand, and I'm going to make him some, if you'll be so kind as to let me keep the berries. I much hope you'll do so, please young man, and I give you my word solemn and faithful never to come here no more."

Their blue eyes met and 'twas Samuel's that looked down first.

"Who might your father be?" he asked.

"Mr. Chawner Green," she answered. "'Tis this way with us, you see. My sister, that kept house for him, have just married, and so now I be come to take care of father."

"He can take care of himself by all accounts," answered Samuel, but in quite an amiable tone of voice, because the girl's magic was already working upon him.

"Can he?" she said. "I never heard of no man that can take care of himself. Can you? Anyway, my father can't. He's as helpless as most other men be without a woman to mind 'em. And I love to be here. I was in service, but this is a lot better than service, and Thorpe-Michael's a dear little place, don't you think?"

Samuel didn't say what he thought of Thorpe-Michael. He'd got a powerful feeling in him that he wanted to know her name, and he asked her to tell him.

"You ain't going to put it down in your policeman's book, are you?" she said. "Because I sinned in ignorance and it would be very ill-convenient if I got in trouble with the police afore I'd been here a fortnight."

"You'll never get in trouble with the police," explained Samuel. "In the first place, Inspector Chowne is related to your father."

"He's my uncle," she answered, "and a dear man."

"And he's a tower of strength," continued Samuel, "and, as for getting in trouble with me, that I can promise you you never will do if you behave."

She looked up at him under her eyelids and felt a flutter at her heart-strings, for if ever there was a case of love at first sight it happened when Chawner Green's younger daughter was catched in the sloan bushes by Sam Borlase. If he liked her voice, she liked his, and if he admired her nice shoulders, she was equally pleased with his great broad ones. Just the old craft of nature once more, as happens at every time in the year and turns all seasons into spring.

"I'm called Cicely," she said—"'Sis' for shortness. And what be you called?"

"My name's Samuel Borlase," he answered, and she nodded.

"I'll remember," she said.

In five minutes they were walking side by side to her home, which lay along the policeman's beat; and he carried her basket and talked about local affairs.

He was a bit shaken, however, to know she belonged to Chawner, and wished with all his heart that she had not.

Mr. Green was in his garden when they came along and he struck a tragical attitude and poked fun at 'em, for no man loved a joke better than what he did.

"Already!" he cried. "Have she fallen into evil already, Borlase? Be the sins of the fathers visited on the childer so soon?"

But the girl hastened to explain.

"He's been merciful, dad," she explained. "Mr. Borlase catched me stealing sloe berries for your sloe gin; but I didn't know I was stealing, you see, for I thought they were free, so he's forgiven me and I ban't to hear no more of it this time."

"Then he can come in and have a drop of the last brew," declared Chawner; "but just look round afore he enters and see as no fur nor feathers be about in the house-place to fret him."

Samuel, however, with all his virtues, weren't much a man for a joke, and at another time this speech would have earned a rebuke from him in the name of law and order. But afore Cicely, and in sound of her voice, he felt amazed to find law and order sink into the background for a minute, though for a minute only, of course.

He explained he was on duty and mustn't have no refreshment just then; but such is the power of passion that he loitered a full sixty seconds after he'd set down Cicely's basket.

"You come in and taste my sloe gin another day, then," said Green, who knew Samuel was in the other camp with the gamekeepers and liked the thought of pulling his leg; but the surprise was Chawner's then, for instead of a short answer, Samuel thanked him as mild as milk, vowed that to his way of thinking sloe gin couldn't be beat and said he'd certainly accept the invitation and come for a drop. Nor did he leave it doubtful when he would come. He acted very crafty indeed and invited Chawner to name the time and hour; on hearing which the girl showed so much interest as he did himself and fixed the time and hour for him.

"Fetch in to tea o' Sunday, Mr. Borlase," she said. "I

make father put on his black ' Sundays ' of an afternoon, and I'll see he's to home."

Then Sam went his way, and when he was gone Cicely praised him for a very understanding chap.

"The sloan in them thickets be a joy," she said, "and if you'll buy the gin, I'll get the fruit. And I dare say he'll catch me there again come presently. He's a handsome fellow, whatever else he may be."

So it began that way, and then the majesty of love got hold upon 'em and enlarged both their minds as it be wont to do. For there's nothing further from the truth than the saying that love makes a man, or a woman, a fool.

Anyway, Samuel come to tea, and he ate a big one and drank two glasses of the sloe gin after; and when he went away, he knew he loved Cicely Green better than anything in the world, and she knew she loved him. But while the man went home and confessed his secret to his mother, a good bit to her astonishment, the girl hid her heart from her father and only showed it in her eyes when she was all alone. The signs amazed her, for she had never loved before, and when she found as she couldn't trespass for no more sloes after all, it broke in upon her that she must already be terrible addicted to Samuel. Because to obey any such order from an ordinary policeman would have been difficult to her nature.

Of course, Chawner very soon found it out and was a good bit amused and a thought vexed also, since he counted on a year at least of Cicely's company, though well knowing such a lovely young woman weren't going to devote herself to his middle-aged convenience for ever. He inquired concerning Samuel Borlase, and Inspector Chowne gave it as his opinion that the material was there, but explained that Sam stood all untried as yet and his value still doubtful.

And meantime Cicely took tea along with Samuel's mother and his old aunt, who lived with them, and told her father they were dear old people and a very nice and interesting pair indeed; because if you're in love, the belongings of the charmer always seem quite all right at first and worthy of all praise.

In fact, Sam and Cicely lived for each other, as the saying is, afore six weeks were spent, and on Christmas Day, being off duty at the time, the policeman took an afternoon walk with Cicely Green and asked her to marry him.

"You know me," he said, "and very like a common constable lies far beneath your views, as well he may; but there it is: I love you, to the soles of my feet, and if, by a miracle of wonder, you was to think I could win you, I'd slave to do so for evermore, my dinky dear."

"'Tis no odds you're a policeman," she said. "You've got to be something. And you very well know I love you, and life's properly empty when you ain't with me. There's nought else in the world that matters to me but only you."

With that the man swallowed her in his great arms and took his first kiss off her. In fact, the world went very well for 'em, till they stood afore Chawner, who demanded time. Indeed, he appeared to be a good bit vexed about it.

"Dash my wig!" he said, "who be you, you hulking bobby, to come upsetting my family arrangements and knocking my well-laid plans on the head in this fashion? Sis came here to look after me, didn't she, not to look after you. And 'tis all moonshine in my opinion, and I doubt if you know your own minds, for that's a thing this generation of youth never is known to do. And, be it as it will, time must pass—oceans of time—afore I can figure all this out and say whether 'tis to be, or whether it ain't."

They expected something like that, and Cicely had a plan.

"If Sam was to come and live along with you, father," she said, "then I shouldn't leave you at all and we would go on nice and comfortable together."

"For you, yes," said Chawner, winking his eye. "But what about me? I don't intend to neighbour so close as all that with a policeman, I do assure you, my fine dear. And so us'll watch and wait, and see if Samuel Borlase have got that fine quality of patience so needful to his calling—also what sort of hold he can show me on the savings bank, and so on."

Then he turned to the young man.

"I know nought against you, Samuel," he said, "but I know nothing for you neither. So it will be a very clever action if we just go on as we're going and see what life looks like a good year hence."

More than that Chawner wouldn't say; but he recognised they should walk out together and unfold their feelings, and he promised that in a year's time he'd decide whether Samuel was up to the mark for his girl.

He was a good bit of a puzzle to Borlase, but the younger, in justice, couldn't quarrel with the verdict, and he only hoped that Cicely wouldn't change her mind in such a parlous long time; for a year to the eye of love be a century.

Well, as elders in such a pass will do, Chawner took careful stock of Sam, and the more he gleaned of the young man's opinions the better he liked him. Old Green was tolerable shrewd, and along with a passion for natural history and its wonders, he didn't leave human nature out of account. He was going on with his own life very clever, unknown to all but one person, and among his varied interests was a boy-like love of practical joking. But among his occupations the story of Samuel Borlase came first for a bit, and he both talked and listened to the young fellow and was a good bit amused on the quiet to find Samuel didn't hold by no means such a high opinion of him as he began to feel for the policeman.

Of course, Cicely was always there to help his judgment; but though the natural instinct of the parent is to misdoubt a child's opinions—generally with tolerable good reason—it happened in this case that love lit the girl's mind to good purpose. She'd laugh with her father sometimes, that Sam hadn't no dazzling sense of fun himself, and it entertained her a lot to see Sam plodding in his mind after her nimble-witted father and trying in vain to see a joke. But what delighted her most was Sam's own dark forebodings about Mr. Green's manner of life, and his high-minded hopes that some day, come he was Chawner's son-in-law, he would save the elder man's soul alive. That always delighted Cicely above everything, and she'd pull a long face and sigh and share Samuel's fine ambitions, and hope how, between them in the future, they'd make her father a better member of society than the Trusham gamekeepers thought he was.

Not that Borlase could honestly say the marks of infamy came out in Mr. Green's view of life. He showed a wonderful knowledge of wild birds and beasts and plants even, and abounded in rich tales of poaching adventures, though he never told 'em as being in his own personal experience. He declared no quarrel with the law himself, but steadfastly upheld it on principle. At the same time a joke was a joke, and if a joke turned on breaking the game laws, or hoodwinking them appointed to uphold right and justice, Chawner would tell the joke and derive a good deal of satisfaction from Sam's attitude thereto.

So time passed and near a year was spent, but Chawner dallied to say the word and let 'em wed; and the crash came on a night in October, when the policeman suddenly found himself called to night duty by Inspector Chowne. 'Twas a beat along the Trusham covers, and a constable had gone ill, and the gamekeepers were yowling about the poachers as usual, instead of catching 'em. So Samuel went his way and looked sharp out for any untoward sign of his fellow-man, or any unlawful sound from the dark woods, where Trusham pheasants harboured of a night. He was full of his own thoughts too, for he wanted cruel to be married, and so did Cicely, and the puzzle was to get Mr. Green to consent without a rumpus.

Nought but a pair of owls hollering to each other did Samuel hear for a good bit. The moon was so bright as day, for the hunter's moon it happed to be at full, and all was silence and peace, with silver light on the falling leaves and great darkness in spruce and evergreen undergrowth. 'Twas at a gate that Sam suddenly heard a suspicious sound and stood stock-still. Footsteps he thought he heard 'tother side of a low broken hedge, where birches grew and the gate opened into a rutted cart-track through the woods. The sound was made by no wild creature, pattering four-foot, but the quick tramp of a man, and when Sam stood still the sound ceased, and when he went forward he reckoned it began again. There was certainly an evil-doer on the covert side of the hedge, and Borlase practised guile and pretended as he'd heard nothing and tramped slowly forward on his way. But he kept his eyes over his shoulder and, after he'd gone fifty yards, stepped into the water-table, as ran on the south side of the beat, and crept back under the darkness of the hedge so wily as a hunting weasel. Back he came as cautious as need be, and for a big and heavy chap he was very clever, and the only noise he made was his breathing. He got abreast of the gate, still hid in night-black shadows, and then he heard the muffled footfall again and a moment later a man sneaked out of the gate with a gun in one hand and a pheasant in the other. Sam licked his hands and drew his truncheon, and then the moon shone on the face before him and the light of battle died out of his eyes. For there was Chawner Green, with a fur cap made of a weasel skin drawed down over his head and the moonshine leaving no doubt as to his identity.

Chawner stood a moment and peeped down the road to see if the policeman was gone on his way. Then out strode Samuel and the elder man used a crooked word and stared upon him and dropped his pheasant in the road. He turned as to fly but 'twas too late, for Sam's leg-of-mutton hand was on his neckerchief and Mr. Green found hisself brought to book at last.

And then Samuel saw a side of Chawner's character as cast him down a lot, for the man put up a mighty fight—not with fists, because he was a bit undersized and the policeman could have put him in his pocket if need was; but with his tongue. He pleaded most forcibly for freedom, and when he found his captor was dead to any sporting appeal, he grew personal and young Borlase soon found that he was up against it.

At first Chawner roared with laughter.

"By the holy smoke," he said, "I'm in luck, Sam! I thought 'twas Billy King had catched me, and then I'd have been in a tight place, for Billy's no friend of mine; but you be a different pair of shoes, thank the Lord! Take your hand off, there's a bright lad, and let me pick up my bird."

"I'm cruel sorry for this—cruel sorry," began Samuel in great dismay. "I'd rather have any misfortune fall to my lot than have took you, Mr. Green."

"Then your simplest course will be to forget you have done so," answered the older man. "You go your way and I'll go mine. Your job's on the road, so you stop on it, Sammy, and if they busy chaps pop along, you can say you've heard nought moving but the owlets."

"Duty's duty," replied Sam. "You must come along with me, I guess. Give me your air-gun, please, and pick up thicky bird."

Green thought a moment, then he handed over the gun and picked up the pheasant and began on Borlase most forcible. He pleaded their future relationship, the disgrace, the slur on his character and the shame to his girl; and Samuel listened very patient and granted 'twas a melancholy and most misfortunate affair; but he didn't see no way out for either of 'em.

"Duty's duty," he kept saying in his big voice, like a bell tolling.

And then Chawner changed his note and grew a bit vicious.

"So be it, Borlase," he said. "If you're that sort of fool, I'll go along with you this instant moment to the police-station; but mark this: so sure as a key's turned on me this night, by yonder hunter's moon I swear as you shan't marry Cicely. That's so sure as I stand here, your captive. If there's a conviction against me, you'll whistle for that woman, and God's my judge I'm telling truth."

Well, Samuel weren't so put about at that as the other apparently expected to find him. He well knew the size of Cicely's love for him, and he'd heard her praise his straightness a thousand times. 'Twas true enough she set great store on her father; but love's love, and Sam was quite smart enough to know that love for a parent goes down the wind afore love for a lover. He looked forward, therefore, and weren't shook of his purpose by no threats.

"That's as may be," he said, "and you've no right, nor yet reason, to speak for her. She loves me as never a woman loved a man, and if she saw me put my love afore my duty, I'll tell you what she'd say—she'd say she'd been mistook in me."

"And don't she love me, you pudding-faced fool!" cried Chawner. "Don't she set her father higher than a man she hasn't known a year? Be fair to yourself, Borlase, or else you'll lose the hope of your life. My honour's her honour and my reputation is her reputation. She thinks the world of me and she's a terrible proud woman; and you can take it from me so sure as death that she'll hold my side against you and cast you off if you do this fatal thing."

Samuel chewed over that a minute; but he decided as he didn't believe a word of it.

"We haven't kept company in vain for ten months and four days, Chawner Green," he said. "I mean me and your girl. She's the soul of upright dealing, and if you was a better man, you'd know it so well as I do."

"She may be," said the other, "but she'll honour her father's name afore she'll see him in your hands. She'll think the same as I do about this night's work, and dare you to lay a finger on me if ever you want to look in her face again."

They argued over that a bit and Chawner cussed and swore, because he said the keepers would be on to 'em in half a minute and all lost.

And then he got another idea and challenged Samuel for the last time.

"List to this," he said. "Cicely will be sitting up, though it have gone midnight. She knows I'm out on my occasions—lawful or otherwise—and she'll be there with a bit of hot supper against my return. We pass the door. And if you're still mad enough to hold out against me, you can hear her tell about it with your own ears and see if you are more to her than what I am. She'll hate your shadow when she hears tell of this."

And Samuel, though his mind was in a pretty state by now, agreed to it. Chawner's confidence shook him a bit, for he wasn't a vain man; and yet he saw pretty clear that Cicely would be called to decide betwixt father and lover in any case, and felt the sooner the ordeal was over the better for all concerned. They went their way and never a word more would Borlase answer, though Green kept at him like a running brook to change his mind and act like a sensible man and not let a piece of folly spoil his own life. But he bided dumb until they reached the home of the Greens; and there stood Cicely at the gate with the moon throwing its light upon her and making her lint-white locks like snow.

"Powers in Heaven!" cried Cicely. "What be this, father?"

And her parent made haste to tell her, while Sam stood mute. But when she heard all, the maiden made it exceeding clear how she felt on the subject and turned upon Borlase very short and sharp.

"Let's have enough of this nonsense, Sam," she said. "You know me and I know you. You be more to me than ever I thought a living man could be, and I love the ground under your feet, and I be your life also, unless you're a liar. So that's that. But a father's a father, and because my father is more to me, after you, than all the world together, I'll ask you please to drop this tragedy-acting and go about your business and let him come in the house. Give me that gun and get to your work, and kiss me afore you go."

She stretched out her hand for the gun, but he wouldn't part with it. He stared upon her and the sweat stood in beads all over his big face.

"This be a night of doom seemingly, and I little thought you'd ever beg for anything I could give as would be denied, Sis," he said; "but you be called to see this with my eyes. I've had the cruel misfortune to catch Mr. Green doing evil, and well he knowed he was; and duty's duty, so he must come along with me. And if you know me, as well as you do know me, you know there's nought else possible for me now."

She lifted her voice for her father, however, and strove to show him what a pitiful small thing it was.

"What stuff are you made of, my dear man?" cried Cicely. "Be a wretched bird that nobody owns, and may have flown to Trusham from the other side of the country, going to make you outrage my father and disgrace his family? I could be cross if I didn't reckon you was in a waking dream."

She ran on, but he stopped her, for he knew his number was up by now and didn't see no use in piling up no more agony for any of 'em.

"Listen!" he shouted out, so as the woods over against 'em echoed with the roar of his big voice. "Listen to me, the pair of you, and be done. I can't hear no more, because there's higher things on earth than love of woman. I'm paid—I'm paid the nation's money, you understand, to do my duty. I'm paid my wages by the State, and I've made an oath afore God Almighty to do what I've undertaken to do to the best of my human power. And I've catched a man doing evil, and I've got to take him to justice if all the angels in heaven prayed me to let him free."

"If the angels in heaven be more to 'e than her you've called an angel on earth, Samuel," answered back Cicely, "then be it so. I understand now the worth of all you've said—and swore also; but your oath to the police stands higher than your oaths to me seemingly, so there's no call to waste no more of your time, nor yet mine. Only know this: if my father sleeps in clink to-night, I'll never wed you, nor look at you again, so help me, God! And now what about it?"

"Think twice," he said, walking very close to her and looking in her beautiful eyes. "Think twice, my dear heart."

But she shook her head and he only see tears there full of moonshine.

"No need to think twice," she answered. "You know me, Samuel."

He heaved a hugeous sigh then and looked at the waiting man. Chawner was swinging his pheasant by the legs and regarding 'em standing up together. But he said nought.

Then Samuel turned and beckoned Mr. Green with a policeman's nod that can't be denied. And Chawner followed after him like a dog, while Cicely went in the house and slammed home the door behind her.

Not a word did either man utter on their tramp to the station; but there they got at last, and the lights was burning and Inspector Chowne, whose night duty it happed to be, was sitting nodding at his desk. And when Sam stood before him and in a very disordered tone of voice brought the sad news of how the Inspector's brother-in-law had been took red-handed coming out of Trusham, a strange and startling thing followed. For, to the boy's amazement, Inspector Chowne leapt from his seat with delight, and first he shook Chawner's hand so hearty as need be and then he shook Sam's fist likewise; and Chawner, the fox that he was, showed a lot of emotion and his voice failed him and he shook Samuel by the hand also! In fact, 'twas all so contrary

STEADFAST SAMUEL 139

to law and order, and reason also, that Samuel stared upon the elder men and prayed the scene was a nightmare and that he'd wake up in his bed any minute.

And then the Inspector spoke.

"Fear nothing, Borlase," he said. "You're saved alive, and you can take a drink out of my whisky bottle in the cupboard if you've got a mind to it. 'Tis this way, my bold hero. My brother-in-law, Mr. Green here, have a sense of fun as be hidden from the common likes of you and me. He's a great naturalist, and he haunts the woods for beetles and toadstools and the like; and I may tell you on his account that he's a person of independent means, and would no more kill a pheasant, nor yet a guinea-pig, that belonged to another man, than he'd fly over the moon. But when he heard the Trusham keepers thought he was a poacher, such was his ove of a lark that he let 'em go on thinking so, and he's built up a doubtful character much to my sorrow, though there ain't no foundation in fact for it. But he laughs to see the scowling faces, though after to-night he'll mend his ways in that respect I shouldn't wonder."

Samuel stared and looked at the gun in his hand and the pheasant in Chawner's. It comed over him now that Inspector was going back on him and meant to take Green's side.

"What about these?" he said.

"I'll come to them," continued Chowne. "Now you fell in love with my niece and, as becomes a father, Mr. Green have got to size you up. And he took a tolerable stern way so to do; but there again his sense of fun mastered him. He told Sis you was still untried and a doubtful problem, though nought against you, and she said, being terrible trustful of you, that nought would come between you and your duty. And so this here man thought out a plan; and if the devil could have hit on a craftier, or yet a harsher, I'd be surprised. But mark this, Samuel: he laid it afore Cicely afore he done it. And such was her amazing woman's faith, she agreed to it, because her love for you rose above all doubt. 'Twas a plant, my boy; and if you'd let Mr. Green go his way, you'd have lost your future wife; but because you've done your duty, you've got her; and may she always have the rare belief in you she has to-night."

Still Sam found it hard to believe he was waking. But he done a sensible thing and went to Inspector's private tap and poured himself four fingers.

"Here's luck," he said; and Chawner Green always told afterwards that it was the first and last joke his son-in-law ever made.

'Twas he who spoke next.

"Now look at this pheasant," ordered Chawner; and the young man handled the bird and found it stiff and cold.

"How long should you judge it had been dead?" inquired Mr. Green. "Anyway, I'll tell you. Sis bought that creature at her sister's husband's fish and poultry shop two days agone. You'll certainly make a policeman to talk about, Sam; but I'm fearing you'll never rise to be a detective."

They went out together five minutes later, Sam to his beat and Green to his home. And the elder was in a very human frame of mind, but Samuel hadn't quite took it all in yet.

Then they came to the elder's house, and there was the girl at the gate waiting for 'em as before.

"When she went in and banged the door, you thought she'd gone to weep," said Chawner; "but for two pins, Samuel, I'd have told you she was dancing a fandango on the kitchen floor. 'Tis a very fine thing for a woman to know her faith is so truly founded, and she's got the faith in you would move mountains; and so have I; and you can wed when you've a mind to it."

So Chawner left 'em in each other's arms for five minutes, and then Samuel went on his way.

A very happy marriage, and a week after they joined up, Chawner married a new-made widow, which he had long ordained to do in secret; but she wouldn't take him till a year and a day was passed.

And Samuel would often tell about his wife's faith in after-time and doubt if the young men he saw growing up around him would have rose to such fine heights as what he done.

But then Cicely would laugh at him and tell him that his own son was just so steadfast as ever he was, and plenty other women's sons also.

No. VIII
THE HOUND'S POOL

No. VIII

THE HOUND'S POOL

By day the place was inviting enough and a child wouldn't have feared to be there. Dean Burn came down from its cradle far away in the hills and threaded Dean Woods with ripple and flash and song. The beck lifted its voice in stickles and shouted over the mossy apron of many a little waterfall; and then under the dark of the woods it would go calm, nestle in a backwater here and there, then run on again. And of all fine spots on a sunny day the Hound's Pool was finest, for here Dean Burn had scooped a hole among the roots of forest trees and lay snug from the scythe of the east wind, so that the first white violet was always to be found upon the bank and the earliest primrose also. In winter time, when the boughs above were naked, the sun would glint upon the water; and sometimes all would be so still that you could hear a vole swimming; and then again, after a Dartmoor freshet, the stream would come down in spate, cherry-red, and roll big waters for such a little river. And then Hound's Pool would be like to rise over its banks and drown the woodman's path that ran beside it and throw up sedges and dead grasses upon the lowermost boughs of the overhanging thicket to show where it could reach sometimes.

'Twas haunted, and old folk—John Meadows among 'em— stoutly maintained that nothing short of Doomsday would lay the spectrum, because they knew the ancient tale of Weaver Knowles, and believed in it also; but the legend had gone out of fashion, as old stories will, and it came as a new and strange thing to the rising generation. 'Tis any odds the young men and maidens would never have believed in it; but by chance it happed to be a young man who revived the story, and as he'd seen with his own eyes, he couldn't doubt. William Parsloe he was, under-keeper at Dean, and he told what he'd seen to John Meadows, the head-keeper; but it weren't till he heard old John on the subject that he knew as he'd beheld something out of another world than his own.

The two men met where a right of way ran through the preserves—a sore trial to the keepers and the owners also, but sacred under the law—and Harry Wade, the returned native, as had just come back to his birthplace, was walking along with Parsloe at the time.

The keepers were a good bit fretted and on their mettle just then, because there was a lot of poaching afoot and pheasants going, and a dead bird or two picked up, as had escaped the malefactors, but died after and been found. So when Parsloe stopped Mr. Meadows and said as he'd got something to report, the old man hoped he might have a line to help against the enemy. One or two law-abiding men, Wade among 'em, had been aiding the keepers by night, and the police had also lent a hand; but as yet nobody was laid by the heels, nor even suspected. So it looked like stranger men from down Plymouth way; and the subject was getting on John Meadows' nerves, because his master, a great sportsman who poured out a lot of money on his pheasants, didn't like it and was grumbling a good bit.

Then William Parsloe told his tale:

"I was along the Woodman's Path last night working up to the covers," he said, "and beside Hound's Pool I fell in with a hugeous great dog. 'Twas a moony night and I couldn't be mistook. 'Twas no common dog I knowed, but black as sin and near so large as a calf. He didn't make no noise, but come like a blot of ink down to the pool and put his nose down to drink, and in another moment I'd have shot the creature, but he scented me, and then he saw me, as I made to lift my gun, and was off like a streak of lightning."

John Meadows stared and then he showed a good bit of satisfaction.

"Ah!" he said. "I'm glad as it is one of the younger people seed it, and not me, or some other old man; because now 'twill be believed. Hound's Pool, you say?"

Parsloe nodded and Harry Wade asked a question. He

was a tall, handsome chap tanned by the foreign sun where he'd lived and worked too.

"What of it, master?" he said.

"This of it," answered Meadows. "Bill Parsloe have seen the Hound and no less. And the Hound ain't no mortal dog at all, but he was once a mortal man and the tale be old history now, yet none the less true for that. My father, as worked here before me, saw him thrice, and his highest good came to him after; and Benny Price, a woodman, saw him once ten year ago, and good likewise came to him, for Mrs. Price ran away with a baker's apprentice at Buckfastleigh and was never heard of again. And since you've seen the Hound, Parsloe, I hope good will come to you."

Neither of t'other men had heard the tale and Harry Wade was very interested, because he minded that, when a nipper, his mother had told him something about it. And Parsloe, who was pretty well educated and a very sharp man, felt inclined to doubt he hadn't seen a baggering poacher's mongrel; but old John wouldn't tell 'em then. He was a stickler for his job and never wasted no time gossiping in working hours.

"'Tis too long to unfold now," he said, "because Bill and me have got to be about our duty; but if you'll drop in o' Sunday and drink a dish of tea, Wade, you can hear the truth of the Hound; and you can look in on your way to work, Bill, and hear likewise if you've a mind to it."

They promised to come and upon the appointed hour both turned up at the gamekeeper's cottage on Thurlow Down, where the woods end and the right of way gives to the high road. And there was John and his wife, Milly, and their daughter, Millicent, for she was called after her mother and always went by her full name to distinguish her. Meadows had married late in life and Milly was forty when he took her, and they never had but one child. A very lovely, shy, woodland sort of creature was Millicent Meadows, and though a good few had courted her, William Parsloe among 'em, none had won her, or tempted her far from her mother's apron-strings as yet. Dark and brown-eyed and lively she was, with a power of dreaming, and she neighboured kindlier among wild things than tame, and belonged to the woods you might say. She was a nervous maiden, however, and owing to her gift of make-believe, would people the forest with strange shadows bred of her own thoughts and fancies. So she better liked the sunshine than the moonlight and didn't travel abroad much after dark unless her father, or some other male, was along with her.

Another joined the tea-party—a very ancient man, once a woodman, and a crony of John's; and the keeper explained to the younger chaps why he'd asked Silas Belchamber to come to tea and meet 'em.

"Mr. Belchamber's the oldest servant on the property and a storehouse of fine tales, and when I told him the Hound had been seen, he was very wishful to see the man as had done so," explained Mr. Meadows. "You may say the smell of a saw-pit clings to Silas yet, for he moved and breathed in the dust of pine and larch for more'n half a century."

"And now I be waiting for the grey woodman to throw me myself," said Mr. Belchamber. "But I raised up as well as threw down, didn't I, John?"

"Thousands o' dozens of saplings with those hands you planted, and saw lift up to be trees," answered Meadows, "and scores of dozens of timber you've felled; and now, if you've took your tea, Silas, I'd have you tell these chaps the story of Weaver Knowles, because you'll do it better than what I can."

The old man sparked up a bit.

"For my part, knowing all I know, I never feared the Hound's Pool," he said, "though a wisht place in the dimpsey and after dark as we know. But when a lad I drew many a sizeable trout out of it—afore your time, John, when it weren't poaching to fish there as it be now. Not that I ever see the Hound; but I've known them that have, and if I don't grasp the truth of the tale, who should, for my grandfather acksually knowed the son of old Weaver Knowles, and he heard it from the man's own lips, and I heard it from grandfather when he was eighty-nine year old and I was ten."

"Then we shall have gospel truth for certain," said Harry Wade, with his eyes on Millicent Meadows.

"Oh, yes," answered Silas, "because my grandfather could

call home the taking of Canada and many such like far-off things, so that shows you the sort of memory he'd gotten. But nowadays the learning of the past be flouted a good bit and what our fathers have told us don't carry no weight at all. Holy spells and ghostesses and——"

"You get on to Hound Pool, Silas," said John Meadows, "because Parsloe will have to go to his work in ten minutes."

"The solemn truth be easily told," declared Mr. Belchamber. "Back along in dim history there was a weaver by name of Knowles who lived to Dean Combe. Him and his son did very well together and he was a widower with no care but for his work. Old Weaver, he stuck to his yarn and was a silent and lonely fashion of man by all accounts. Work was his god, and 'twas said he sat at his loom eighteen hours out of every twenty-four. Then, coming home one evening, the man's son heard the loom was still and went in and found old Knowles fallen forward on the top of his work, dead. So they buried him at Buckfastleigh.

"Then young Knowles, coming home to his empty house after the funeral, suddenly heard the music of the loom and thought his ears had played him false. But the loom hummed on and he crept up over to see who was weaving. In a pretty good rage he was, no doubt, to think of such a thing; but then his blood turned from hot to cold very quick, I warn 'e, for there was his father sitting on the old seat and working weft through warp as suent and clever as if he was alive!

"Well, young Knowles he glared upon his dead parent and felt the hair rising on his niddick and the sweat running down his face; but he kept his nerve pretty clever and crept away and ran for all his might to the village and went to see Parson. They believed more in those days than what they do now, and Parson, whatever he may have thought, knew young Knowles for a truth-teller and obeyed his petition to come at once. But the good man stopped in the churchyard and gathered up a handful of sacred ground; and then he went along to the dead weaver's house.

"Sure enough the loom was a-working busy as ever; but it couldn't drown Parson's voice, for he preached from one of they old three-decker pulpits, like a ship o' war, and his noise, when the holy man was in full blast, would rise over a thunderstorm.

"'Knowles! Knowles!' he cried out; 'Come down this instant. This is no place for you!'

"And then, hollow as the wind in a winter hedge, the ghost made answer.

"'I will obey so soon as I have worked out my quill, your reverence,' replied the spirit of Weaver Knowles, and Parson didn't raise no objection to that, but bade the dead man's son kneel down; and he done so; and the priest also knelt and lifted his voice in prayer for five minutes.

"Then the loom stopped and old Knowles came forth and glided downstairs; and not a step creaked under him, for young Knowles specially noted that wonder when he told my grandfather the adventure.

"At sight of Old Weaver, Parson took his churchyard dust and boldly threw it in the face of the vision, and afore you could cross your heart the shadow had turned into a gert black dog—so dark as night. The poor beast whimpered and yowled something cruel, but Parson was short and stern with it, well knowing you can't have half measures with spirits, no more than you can with living men if you will to conquer 'em. So he takes a high line with the weaver, as one to be obeyed.

"'Follow me, Knowles,' he said to the creature. 'Follow me in the name of the Father, Son, and Ghost'; which the forlorn dog did do willy-nilly; and he led it down the Burn, to Hound's Pool, and there bade it halt. Then the man of God took a nutshell—just a filbert with a hole in it bored by a squirrel—and he gave it boldly into the dog's mouth.

"'Henceforth,' he said, 'you shall labour here to empty the pool, using nought but this nutshell to do so; and when you have done your work, but no sooner, then you shall go back whence you came.'

"And the Hound will be on the job till the end of the world afore he gets peace, no doubt, and them with ears to hear, may oft listen to a sound in the water like the rattling of a loom to this day; but 'tis no more than that poor devil-dog of a Knowles at his endless task."

Millicent poured the old man another cup of tea and Parsloe went to work and Wade applauded the tale-teller.

"A very fine yarn, uncle," he said, "and I'm glad to know the rights of it; and if the Hound brings luck, I hope I'll see him."

"More would see him if faith was there," answered old Belchamber. "But where do you find faith in these days? For all I can see the childer taught in school don't believe in nothing on earth but themselves. In fact, you may say a bald head be a figure of scorn to 'em, same as it was in the prophet's time."

"Youth will run to youth, like water to the sea," said Harry Wade. "But a very fine tale, master, and I hope I may be the next to meet thicky ghost Hound I'm sure."

"You've had your luck, Mr. Wade, by all accounts," laughed Millicent, but the returned native was doubtful. They chatted and he told 'em some of his adventures and how, at the last gasp, prospecting along with two other men, they had found a bit of gold at last.

"Not any too much for three, however," said Harry; "but enough for a simple customer like me. They say lucky in life unlucky in love; but I much hope I haven't been too lucky in life to spoil my chance of a home-grown partner."

Mr. Belchamber departed then, because he was rather tired after his tale, but Harry stopped on, because Mrs. Meadow had took a liking to his talk and found he'd got a very civil way with old women. He'd listen to her and, as she loved to chatter, though she'd got nothing whatever to say, as so often happens with the great talkers, his attention pleased her and she asked him if he'd bide to supper. And Millicent liked him also, being drawn to the man by his account of great hardships and perils borne with bravery; for though Harry wasn't the hero of his own tales no more than his mates had been, yet he had gone through an amazing lot and done some bold and clever things. And the girl, being one of the timid sort, liked to hear of the courage of a man, as they will. Wade was an open speaker, and had no secrets from 'em. He confessed that he'd got a clear four hundred pounds a year out of his battle with life.

"Not much for what I endured," he said, "yet a lot more than many poor chaps, who went through worse. And now I'm in a mind to settle down and find a bit of work and stick to Dean Prior for evermore."

Mrs. Meadows laughed at her daughter when Harry was gone, for she had quick senses and was a good bit amused to see her shy girl open out and show interest in the man; but to chaff Millicent was always the way to shut her up, and she wouldn't let her mother poke fun at her.

"Now I'll never see him again," vowed Millicent, "and all along of you, mother, for I'd blush to the roots of my hair if he spoke to me any more while I knew your cruel sharp eye was on me."

However, see him again she did, because Wade had asked 'em all to come and drink tea long with him and witness the curiosities he'd fetched home from Australia; and though the girl made a hard try to escape the ordeal, her father bade her go along with him. Mrs. Meadows didn't go when the day came, because she weren't feeling very well; and out of her ailments sprang a surprising matter that shook 'em all to the roots.

Harry Wade lived in a little house all alone and did for himself very clever as old campaigners know how to do. He'd planned a very nice meal for 'em and laid out his treasures and was very sorry when John and his daughter explained the absence of Mrs. Meadows. And sorrier still he declared himself to be when they cut their visit a bit short, because for the need to get home pretty quick to the suffering woman.

He was engaged for the most part with Millicent's father that visit, though he pressed food of his own cooking upon her and tried to make her chatter a bit. But he got little out of her, for she weren't a talker at best, and she couldn't forget her mother had laughed at her for being so interested in the man, and so she was shyer than usual.

But though she said nought, she liked to hear her father praise Harry as they went home along, for John thought well upon him.

"He's a man who have got a regular mind despite his

dangerous past," said the old chap. "You might think such a venturesome way of life would make him reckless and lawless; but far from it. His experience have made him see the high value of law and order."

"He's brave as a lion seemingly," ventured Millicent, and her father allowed it was so.

"An undaunted man," he admitted, "and his gifts will run to waste now, because, unless you're in the police, or else a gamekeeper, there's little call for courage."

Mrs. Meadows was a lot worse when they came home and they got her to bed and put a hot brick in flannel to her feet; but she'd had the like attacks before and John weren't feared for her till the dead of night; and then she went off her head and he touched her and found she was living fire. So he had to call up his girl and explain that, for all he could tell, death might be knocking at the door.

Such things we say, little knowing we be prophets; but in truth a fearful peril threatened the Meadows folk that night, though 'twas Millicent and not her mother was like to be in highest danger.

"'Tis doctor," said John, "and I can't leave her, for she may die in my arms, so you must go; and best to run as never you run before. Go straight through Dean Wood and don't draw breath till you've got to the man."

She was up and rayed in less than no time and away quick-footed through the forest; and so swift had been her actions that she hoped to cheat her own fear of the darkness and get through Dean Woods afore she had time to quail. But you can't hoodwink Nature that way, and not long afore the trees had swallowed her up Millicent felt nameless dread pulling at her heart and all her senses tingling with terror. She kept her mind on her mother, however, and sped on with her face set before her, though a thousand instincts cried to her to look behind for the nameless things that might be following after.

'Twas a frosty night with a winter moon high in the sky, and Millicent, who knew the Woodman's Path blindfold, much wished it had been darker, for the moonlight was strong enough to show queer faces in every tree-bole and turn the shadows from the trees into monsters upon her path at every yard. She prayed as she went along.

"My duty—my duty," she said. "God help me to do my duty and save mother!"

Then she knew she was coming close to the Hound's Pool and hesitated for fear, and wondered if she might track into the woods and escape the ordeal. But that wasn't possible without a lot of time wasted, and so she lifted up another petition to her Maker and went on. She'd travelled a mile by now and there was another mile to go. And then she came alongside the Pool and held her hands to her breast and kept her eyes away from the water, where it spread death-still with the moon looking up very peaceful out of it. But a moment later and poor Millicent got the fearfullest shock of her life, for right ahead, suddenly without a sound of warning, stark and huge with the moonlight on his great open mouth, appeared the Hound. From nowhere he'd come, but there he stood within ten yards of her, barring the way. And she heard him growl and saw him come forward to meet her.

One scream she gave, though not so loud as a screech owl, and then she tottered, swayed, and lost her senses. If she'd fallen to the left no harm had overtook her; but to the right she fell and dropped unconscious, face forward into Dean Burn.

The waters ran shallow there, above the Pool, yet, shallow or deep, she dropped with her head under the river and knew it not.

Many a day passed afore the mystery of her escape from death got to Millicent's ears; but for the moment all she could mind was that presently her senses returned to her and she found herself with her back against a tree and her face and bosom wet with water. Slowly her wits worked and she looked around, but found herself a hundred yards away from the Pool. Then she called home what had befallen her and rose to her feet; and presently her blood flowed again and she felt she was safe and the peril over-got. 'Twas clear the Hound had done her no hurt and she felt only puzzled to know why for she was so wet and why, when she went fainty beside the Pool, she'd come to again a hundred yards away from it. But that great mystery she put by for another time and thanked God for saving her and cleared the woods and sped to doctor with her bad news.

And he rose up and let her in and, hearing the case was grave, soon prepared to start. And while he dressed, Millicent made shift to dry herself by the heat of a dying fire. Then he put his horse in the trap and very quick they drove away up to the gamekeeper's house. But no word of her amazing adventure did the woman let drop in doctor's ear; and the strange thing was that peace had come upon her now and fear was departed from her heart.

Milly Meadows had got the influenza very bad and, guessing what he'd find, the physician had brought his cautcheries along with him, so he ministered a soothing drug and directed her treatment and spoke hopeful words about it. He was up again next day and found all going very orderly, and foretold that, if the mischief could be kept out of Milly's lungs, she'd recover in due course. So the mind of her husband and her daughter grew at peace when Milly's body cooled down; and then the girl told her father of what had befell her by Hound's Pool, and he was terrible interested and full of wonder.

In fact, naught would do but they went there together the morning after, and there—in the chill light of a January day, Millicent pointed out where she stood when the vision come to her and presently the very tree under which she had returned to life.

But John, being skilled in all woodland craft, took a pretty close look round and soon smelled out signs and wonders hid from common sight. He'd been much pleased with the tale at first, for though sorrowful that his girl had suffered so much, he hadn't got enough mind himself to measure the agony she'd been through; and, whether or no, since the Hound brought good luck, he counted on some bright outcome for Millicent presently, if it was only that her mother should be saved alive. But when he got to his woodcraft, John Meadows weren't so pleased by any means, because he found another story told. Where the girl had fainted and dropped in the water on seeing the Hound was clear to mark; but more than that John discovered, for all round about was the slot of a big dog with a great pad and claws; and, as if that weren't enough, the keeper found something else also.

He stared then and stood back and scratched the hair on his nape.

"Beggar my shoes!" said John. "This weren't no devil-dog, but a living creature! The Hound be a spirit and don't leave no mark where he runs; but the dog that made these tracks weighs a hundred and fifty pound if he weighs an ounce; and look you here. What be this?"

Well, Millicent looked and there weren't no shadow of doubt as to what her father had found, for pressed in the mire and gravel at river edge was the prints of a tidy large boot.

William Parsloe came along at the moment; but he knew nought, though he put two and two together very clever.

"'Tis like this," he said; "you ran into the poachers, Millicent, though what the blackguards was up to with a hugeous dog I couldn't tell you. And now I'll lay my life that what I saw back along was the same creature and he whipped away and warned his masters."

"But me?" asked the girl. "Why for if I fainted and fell into the river, didn't I drown there for you or father to find next day?"

"Yes," added John. "How came that to be, Bill?"

"I see it so clear as need be," explained Parsloe, who had a quick mind. "You fell in the water and the dog gave tongue. The blackguards came along and, not wishful to add murder to their crimes, haled you out. Then they carried you away from the water, loosened your neckerchief and finding you alive, left you to recover."

"Dear God!" said Millicent, shivering all down her spine, "d'you mean to tell me an unknown poaching man carried me in his arms a hundred yards, William?"

"I mean that," answered Parsloe, "and if we had the chap's boot, we should know who 'twas."

So they parted, and John he went home very angry indeed at such triumphant malefactors, and though Millicent tried her bestest to be angry also, such is the weakness of human nature that she couldn't work up no great flood of rage. And when she was alone in her bed that night, for it was her father's turn to watch over her mother, she felt that unknown sinner's arms around her again and his wicked hands at her neckerchief, and couldn't help wondering what it would have been like if she'd come to and found herself in that awful position.

Then Milly Meadows recovered and John, along with William Parsloe, Harry Wade, and a few more stout men, plotted a plot for the poachers and combed the plantations on a secret night in a way as they'd never done afore; but they failed and had Dean Woods all to themselves, though the very next night there was another slaughter and a lot of birds lost.

And a bit after the pheasant season finished, John Meadows heard that the master reckoned 'twas time his head-keeper made a dignified retirement and let a younger man—William Parsloe in fact—take his place.

But while John felt sorry for himself in this matter, yet was far too sane and common-sensible to resent it, another wondrous thing fell out, and Harry Wade got in a rare sort of fix that promised more fret and strain than all his other adventures put together. For, along of one thing and another, though the true details never reached but two ears, he was up against a new and tremendous experience and from being a heart-whole man with no great admiration on the women, he felt a wakening and a stir and knew 'twas love.

For Millicent Meadows he went through the usual torments, and his case weren't bettered by William Parsloe neither, because when he confessed to the man, who had got to be his friend, that Millicent was a piece very much out of the common, Bill told him that he weren't the first by many as had thought the same.

"But she's not for men," said Parsloe. "All sorts have offered, and good 'uns, including myself I may tell you in confidence; but the man ain't born to win Millicent Meadows."

However, Wade, he set to it, and after a lot of patient skirmishing he began to see faint signs of hope. He held in, however, so powerful as his nature would let him until the signs heartened the man for a dash at last, and 'twas by Hound's

Pool on a May day with the bluebells beside the water, and the cherry blossom tasselling over their heads—that he told the girl she was the light of his spring and the breath of his life.

And she just put her hand in his'n and looked up in his face and took him without any fuss whatever.

Not for a week, however, till he felt safe in his promised state, did Harry ever open out his dark secrets to her; but then, for her ears only, out it came.

"You mind that fatal night?" he asked; and they were beside the Pool again, for she loved it now, because 'twas there he begged her to marry him.

"Ess fay and I do, but I don't hate the Pool no more—not after you told me you loved me there," said Millicent.

"'Twas I that saved you," he confessed. "At a loose end and for a bit of a lark—just sport, you understand, not wickedness—I done a bit of poaching and picked off a good few birds, I fear."

She looked at him round-eyed.

"You wretch!" she cried; but his arms were close about her, and she was powerless.

"Oh, yes. And my great dog it was as I kept hid on a chain by day. And when he frightened you into the water that night, I was behind him and had you out again and in my arms in half a second. And then I carried you away from the river, and when I held you in my arms I knew you'd be my wife or nobody would."

"Thank the watching Lord 'twas you!" she gasped.

"I waited till I see you come to and knew you'd be all right then; but I followed you, to see what you was up to, and didn't go home till I saw you drive away with the doctor. My dog was my joy till that night—a great mongrel I picked up when I was to Plymouth and kept close of a day. Clever as Satan at finding fallen birds in the dark, though unfortunately he didn't find 'em all. But after the happenings I took him back to Plymouth again on the quiet, and he won't frighten nobody no more."

Then 'twas her turn and she dressed him down properly and gave him all the law and the prophets, and made him promise on his oath that he'd never do no more crimes, or kill fur or feather that didn't belong by rights to him.

And he swore and kept his oath most steadfast.

" I've catched the finest creature as ever harboured in Dean Woods," he said, " and her word be my law for evermore."

But nobody else heard the truth that Wade was the unknown sinner, for Millicent felt as her father would have been cruel vexed about it.

They was wed in the summer and Wade found open-air work to his taste not a mile from their home. But often, good lovers still, they'll go to Hound's Pool for memory's sake and sit and hear Weaver Knowles working unseen about his task.

No. IX
THE PRICE OF MILLY BASSETT

No. IX

THE PRICE OF MILLY BASSETT

MEMORY, as we old folk know, be the plaything of time, and when trouble comes and we wilt and reckon life's ended, the years roll unresting on, and the storm passes, and the dark breaks to grey again, and, may be, even the sun's self peeps forth once more. For our little wits ain't built to hold grief for ever, else the world would be a lunatic asylum and not the tolerable sane and patient place we mostly find it.

It was like that with my friend, Jonas Bird. When his wife died, and left him and three young childer, his light went out, and though no more than thirty-five years of age, he felt 'twas the end of the world. He comforted his cruel sufferings with the thought of a wonnerful tombstone to Sarah Bird, and there's no doubt that tombstones, though they can't make or mar the dead, have, time and again, softened the lot of the living. And you may say that poor Sarah's mark in the churchyard was the subject that first began to calm Jonas. But it did a lot more than that.

He was a sandy-headed man with old-fashioned whiskers, a long face like a horse, blue eyes and a wondering expression. In fact, life did astonish him a good bit, and being a simple soul, most things that happened were apt to puzzle him. A carpenter by trade, he did very well in that walk of life and had saved money. But he had long lived for one thing only, and that was Sarah, and when she dropped sudden and left him with two little boys and a girl babe, he was more puzzled than ever and went in a proper miz-maze of perplexity that such things could be.

Everybody liked Jonas, for he was a kindly and well-intending creature, and his wife had been such another, and a good few women rushed to the rescue when the blow fell. And his master, a childless man and very fond of Bird, offered to adopt one of his boys and take the lad off his hands. But Jonas clung to all three, because, as he truly said, they each had a good bit of their mother in 'em and he couldn't spare a pinch of Sarah. And his wife's first and dearest woman friend it was who came to the rescue at this season and stopped along with Jonas, for the children's sake and the dead woman's.

Milly Bassett, she was called, and she ministered to the orphaned children and talked sense to the widow man; and though an old maid here and there didn't think it a seemly thing for Milly to take up her life under Bird's roof, the understanding and intelligent sort thought no evil. For of such a creature as Milly Bassett no evil could be thought.

She was the finest-minded woman ever came out of Thorpe-Michael in my opinion, and she only had one idol and that was duty, and when Sarah, on her death-bed, prayed Milly to watch over Jonas and the family till the poor man recovered from his sorrows and wed again, then Milly promised to do so. And her promises were sacred in her eyes. And if any was mean enough to think ill of her for so doing, she'd have said such folk didn't know her and their opinions were no matter.

A flaxen woman—grey-eyed and generous built—was Milly. She lived with an old mother who was a laundress, and the old mother took it very ill when her daughter went to mind the dead woman's little ones; but, as Milly herself said, there was only one man who needed to be considered before she went to her holy task, and that was William White.

You see, Miss Bassett had long been tokened to William, and if he'd objected, it must have put her in a very awkward position with the promise to a dead woman pulling one way and her duty to a live lover pulling the other. But it happened that William White was a very good friend to Jonas, like everybody else, and he didn't see no good reason why for his sweetheart shouldn't lend a hand at such a sorrowful time.

Moreover, there was a bit of money in it, and Milly's William happened to be a man whose opinions and principles had never been known to stand between him and a shilling. So when Jonas insisted on paying Milly Bassett ten bob a week over and above her keep—all clear profit—William raised no objection whatever. He weren't a jealous man—quite the contrary— and his engagement to marry Milly weren't an affair of yesterday. In fact, at this time, they'd been contracted a good two years, and though the man felt quite willing to wed when ever Milly was minded to, she'd got her ideas and she'd made it clear from the very start that not until her intended could show her four pound a week would she take the step.

And William White, though a good horseman and a champion with the plough and well thought upon by Farmer Northway, could not yet rise to that figure, though he went in hope that it might happen. He'd tried round about on the farms to better his wages, for he was amazing fond of money, but up to the present nobody seemed to think William was worth more than three pound ten, or three pound with a cottage.

So Milly waited. She loved William in a temperate sort of way, though there was points in his character she didn't much hold with; but she'd given her word to wed him in fullness of time, and she was the sort never to part from her word for no man. They kept company calm and contented, with no emotions much to either side, though now-and-a-gain William would venture to say he thought she might bate her terms and take him for ten shillings less. But this she weren't prepared to do; and so it stood when Mrs. Bird died and Milly, who had worshipped the dead woman, came to take her place till time had worked on Jonas and he was able to look round for another. For that his Sarah had always wished he should do, well knowing the poor man couldn't carry on without a spouse.

Jonas was terrible obliged to Milly for coming, and to William for letting her do so, and he was the soul of goodness in the whole matter and made William free of his house and saved him the price of many a meal. In fact William rather exceeded reason in that matter and dropped in at supper-time too often for decency; but it was his sweetheart and not Jonas who opened his eyes to his manners and told him there was reason in all things.

They weren't none too mad in love, as Jonas found out in course of time. In fact Milly was temperate in all things and had never known to lose her nerve or temper; while as for William White, he'd got her promise and knew she was the faithful-unto-death sort and would wait till he could raise what she considered the proper income for a married woman to begin upon.

The widower soon found out the fashion of sense that belonged to Milly for, while still in his great grief, he began to talk of spending fifty pounds of capital on Sarah's grave, and she heard him and advised against.

"As to that," she said, "I knew your dear wife better'n anybody on earth but yourself, Jonas, and this I will say: if she thought you'd heaved up fifty pounds' worth of marble stone on her, she wouldn't lie quiet for an instant moment. You know that modesty was Sarah's passion, and she'd rather have a pink daisy on her pit and a blackbird pulling a worm out of the green grass than all the monuments in the stone-cutter's window."

He listened and she ran on:

"Her virtues be in our hearts, and it won't better it to print 'em in the churchyard; and if I was you and wanted to make heaven a brighter place for Sarah than it already is, I'd lift up a modest affair and put a bit of money away to goody for your little ones."

"I dare say that's a very clever thought," admitted Jonas.

"Yes, it is, then," went on Milly. "She didn't help you to be a saver for vain things like grave-stones that don't bring in no interest to nobody. And if it was the measurement of your sorrow, I'd say nothing, but 'tis well known remorse be at the foundation of half the fine monuments widow men put up to their partners, and you don't need to tell nobody in Thorpe-Michael what you thought of Sarah and how she was the light of your house, for we well know it."

"I won't do nothing skimpy, however," said Jonas.

"I'm sure you won't," she answered, "but in the matter of monuments 'tis a very good rule to wait till the grave be ready to carry 'em; and by that time the bereaved party have generally settled down to take a sensible view of the situation."

He nodded, and from that evening he began to see what a fine headpiece Milly had got to her. In fact she was a very entertaining woman and as time went on and his childer grew to love her, Jonas was a lot puzzled at the thoughts that began to move in his brain. He turned to work, which is a very present help in trouble, and he did overtime and laboured something tremendous at his bench. In fact, if he'd belonged to a Trades Union, Jonas would have heard of it to his discredit, for there's nothing the unions dread more than a man who loves work and does all he knows for the pride of it plus the extra money. But Jonas was on his own and independent to all but his conscience—and his master didn't see no sin in paying him what he was worth.

He'd always been a saver, and his wife had helped him in that respect, but now his money was no more than dust in the corners of his mind, for there weren't no eye to brighten when he told of a bit more put by and no tongue to applaud and tell him what a model sort of man he was. He found, however, as he came to know Milly Bassett better, that though his good fortune and prosperity was nothing to her, yet she could praise him for it. So, little by little, he gave her a peep into his affairs and found she was one of them rare people who can feel quite a bit of honest interest in their neighbour's good luck, with no after-clap of sourness, because their own ain't so bright.

'Twas natural the woman should contrast her horseman with Jonas and wish he'd got the same orderly sort of mind; but she had the wit to see that it takes all sorts to make a world, and while William liked money a lot better than earning it, Jonas liked the earning and didn't set no lustful store on the stuff itself.

Still money's a power, and there's no doubt 'twas the hidden power of his purse which presently tempted the carpenter to a most unheard of piece of work. Never a man less likely to do anything out of the common you might have thought, yet life worked on him and time and chance prompted until that everyday sort of chap was finally lifted up to an amazing deed.

Round about a year after his wife died, the thought came to him and gradually growed till it mastered him and led to a wonderful stroke. And it showed, if that wanted showing, that you never know what gifts be hid in anybody, or what the simplest man will rise to in the way of craft, given the soil to ripe his wits and the prompting to lift him up.

Jonas found himself more and more interested in the love affair of William and Milly, and having studied the situation in all its bearings and measured the characters of the man and woman and taken the subject also to the Throne of Grace, for he was a prayerful creature, he finally considered that it now lay in his power to make the first move, since that had to come from him. And the second move would have to be made by William White; and it all depended upon William whether there remained an opening left for Jonas, or whether the affair was closed. For he was a most honourable chap in all things and never one to best a neighbour even if opportunity offered.

Some men, for example, might have tried to tempt Milly Bassett away from William and hold out the attractions to be got with such a husband as Jonas; but no such thought ever darkened the carpenter's mind. He'd certainly got to a pitch when he dearly wanted Milly, for with his soul at rest and memory growing fainter, she seemed to reflect all the beauties of his late partner, along with several of her own; but Jonas well knew that she was tokened to William and would never leave him for another, but wait till time cured all. To tempt Milly was out of the question; yet he couldn't see no particular reason why he shouldn't tempt William, or at any rate inquire into William's attitude on the subject. And knowing the horseman exceeding well by now and perceiving that, strictly speaking, William couldn't be considered in the least worthy of such a wife as Milly, Jonas went his way and done his dashing deed.

On a day in early spring White was ploughing and Jonas Bird, who'd gone to Four Ways Farm to measure up for a new pigs' house, took care to come home along past the field where White was at work. And he knew that at noon William's horses would have their nose-bags and the ploughman would be sitting in the hedge eating his dinner. And there he was, in a famous lew hedge facing the sun, where the childer find the first white violets of the year.

So Jonas pitched beside the man and said they was well met.

"I've been wanting to meet you all alone this longful time," said Jonas; "and I'm very wishful to ask you a question, Bill. You mustn't think me impertinent nor nothing like that. You and me be very good friends and long may we remain so; but I've took careful note of your character, and you know me just so well, so you'll understand, please, I be asking in a very gentlemanly spirit and not for no vulgar curiosity nor nothing like that."

"My!" said William, "what a lot of talk, Jo! Spit it out. I'll answer any question you like to ask if I can so do."

"'Tis just this, then, and you go on with your meal," answered Jonas. "What's the thing you set highest in all the world?"

"Money," said William, and Jonas nodded.

"So I thought," he replied, "and if it had been any other thing, I'd have left it at that; but as I've got your own word, I may take it that money comes first."

"First and last and always," answered William. "And hell knows I don't get my share."

"Money comes first and Milly Bassett second—that would be a fair way to put it?" asked Jonas.

Well, White thought a minute before he replied. "When you say 'Milly,'" he began, "you touch a delicate subject, and I ain't none too sure if I didn't ought to tell you to shut your mouth. But still, I don't deny but that's about the size of it. Me and Milly have been tokened very near three years, and perfect love, Jo, on them terms may cast out fear and a lot else, but it don't get you no forwarder—quite the contrary. Love don't keep for ever, more than a leg of mutton will, and sometimes it comes across me it may go a bit stale, if not actually bad. I fear nought myself, of course, because Milly's a woman of her word and knows no changing; but that cuts both ways and, while she's so firm as a rock about my wages and in a manner of speaking puts money before love, then I sometimes wonder who could blame me for doing the same. We'm very good friends, and she'll be a damned fine wife, no doubt—when I get her; but, meantime, things run a little on the cool side and I can't pretend I feel so furious set in that quarter as I did three year agone. She ain't the only pebble on the beach, to say it kindly, though a most amazing wonder and well worth waiting for in reason. But there's others—not a few very comely creatures as would reckon me along with three ten a week quite good enough. I can't hide that from myself."

Well, this was meat and drink to Jonas, but he hid his heart for the present, though his great excitement made his voice run up till it broke and he had to begin again—a thing that happened to him sometimes.

"That being so," he said, "that being so, Bill, how would you feel if anybody was to say : ' Here's good money for changing your future career, if you ain't too addicted to Milly Bassett to take it ? ' "

" Money for her ? " asked William.

" Money enough to turn your affections into another quarter and let her go free."

"God's truth, Jo ! You've gone and loved her ! " shouted William.

"No," answered the carpenter. "By this hand I have not, Bill. I'm not one to love any created woman as be tokened to another man and well you know it. To do so would be a wicked thing. But this I may tell you open and honest : if Milly were a free woman, then I should love her instanter."

"Dammy, Jo ! You want to buy her ! " said William.

But Jonas shook his head.

" I reverence the woman far, far too much to want any such thing," he said. " You can't buy and sell females in a Christian land ; but this I'll say, if you can honestly feel that a good dollop of money would recompense you for losing Milly, things being as they are, then I'm your man. Of course if you feel money's dross before the thought of her, then I shall well understand and we won't touch the subject no more. And, in any case, never a breath must get to her ears else she'd leave my house like a whirlwind, and quite right to do so. But if you feel that you could make shift with another fine woman and might tear yourself away from Milly Bassett for a bit in the bank—*if* you feel that, William, and only so, then we can go on talking."

William White laughed and ate a bit of pie that hung on his

fork. Then he drank from his cider runlet. "What a world!" he said.

Jonas didn't answer and let his great thought sink into the man.

Presently William put a nice point. "Needless to ask if you've whispered any of this to her?"

"God's my judge, Bill."

"Well, there's one thing I'd put afore you, Jo. Suppose we can agree to a price, what happens if, when your turn comes to offer, she turns you down and we're both left?"

"A natural question, Bill, and I'd thought of it, for there's no vanity in me and it might very likely happen. And my understanding of that position is this: If she says 'No' to me, after you've given her her liberty, then I've made a bad investment and my feeling would be to cut a loss; but if on the other hand she says 'Yes,' then I'd go a bit higher."

"A sum down when I've chucked her, and a bit over if you get her."

"When you say a sum down, Bill, you'd better consider of it," explained Jonas. "A sum down there will certainly be; but if you saw your way to take the money by instalments, then you'd benefit considerable in the upshot, because, by instalments, I could pay a good bit more than I could in a lump."

"I see that," admitted the horseman. "Well, on the general questions, Jo, I may say that I'll do business. That far I'm prepared to go; but when it comes to figures, I'd very much like to hear your ideas. This is a bit out of my experience; but I warn you, you've got to pay money."

"I know that," answered Jonas. "I know that very well indeed. I can't pay half nor yet a quarter of what she'd be worth to me, for the reason a king's ransom wouldn't do it; but money I will pay. I'll pay you a hundred a year for four years, William."

"And interest while 'tis running?" asked the horseman.

"Yes," answered Jonas, "interest while 'tis running."

"That's if you don't get her?"

"No, Bill; that's if I do get her."

White considered. 'Twas very big money, of course, but he tried for a bit more.

"You must remember that when I throw her over I'm a disgraced man, Jo."

"I wouldn't say that. 'Twill be a shadow on your name for a minute, but such things fall out every day and be very quickly forgot. Milly's the only one that matters and I don't think you're the best partner in the world for her, else I'd never have touched the subject. But if you use your cleverness and put it to her that 'tis undignified for you both to go on waiting for ever, she'll very likely see it."

"She might, or again she mightn't."

"She would," declared Jonas. "I ain't watched you and her for a year for nothing. This ain't going to be the shattering wrench for her you might think, William."

White knew that very well, but dwelt on his own downfall, and loss. "Make it five hundred—win or lose," he said at last, "and I'll oblige you."

And Jonas Bird agreed instantly, for at the bottom of his heart he weren't feeling it no wildgoose chase for him; because, though a simple man in some ways, he didn't lack caution, and he'd unfolded his feelings pretty oft to Milly, speaking, of course, in general terms; and he well knew that she felt high respect for his character and opinions and good position.

Then William spoke.

"If you'd like it in writing, you can have it," he said, "but for my part I trust you, and I doubt not you trust me, and I'm inclined to think the less that be put down on paper about it, the better. 'Tis a deed of darkness, in a manner of speaking, and written documents have often brought disasters with 'em afterwards, so us had best to trust each other and sign nought."

Jonas agreed to this most emphatic and then they parted.

But it weren't twenty-four hours later before the carpenter felt the deed was afoot, for he soon saw that Milly had got a weight on her mind. She said nought, however, till a week was past and then told Jonas, confidential, that she savoured something in the air.

"There's some people can smell rain," she said, "and others, if they go in a churchyard, know to a foot when they be walking over their own future graves; and though I'm not one to meet trouble half-way, it's borne in on me that I be going to face changes afore long."

"In what direction?" asked Jonas, cunning as a serpent.

"God send you don't mean that William be going to get his rise and take you away?"

"I do not," she said. "Quite the contrary. I mean that William be going to change his mind about me."

"And would you call that meeting trouble exactly, or contrariwise?" asked Bird.

"Well," she answered. "Between you and me, I may say that I shall doubtless get over it; but I'm a good bit hurt, because it had got to be an understood thing and I little like changes. But there it is: the man's getting restless and be pruning his wings for flight if I know him."

"'Tis beyond belief that any living man should want to fly from you," declared Jonas. "I wouldn't come between lovers for a bag of gold; but in a case like this, feeling for you as I always have done since you kept your promise to Sarah with such amazing perfection—feeling that, if you say the word, I'll talk to William White as no man yet have talked to him."

"Do nothing," she said. "Let nature take its course with William; and if it takes him away from me, so be it. I can very well endure to part from the man and, so like as not, when I'm satisfied that things are so, I shall tell him I understand, and give him his freedom."

"Such largeness of mind I never heard tell about in a woman," answered Jonas.

And six weeks later William and Milly were cut loose, without any fuss on her part but to the undying amazement of Thorpe-Michael. And then Jonas paid his first instalment at dead of night and got a receipt for the same.

'Twas after that the carpenter's anxieties began. He'd hoped that Milly would be a lot cast down by this reverse and that he'd fill the gap and comfort her and support her through the sad affair; but she didn't want no support. In fact she talked most sensible about being jilted and confessed that it might be all for the best in the long run. "Nought happens save by the will of Heaven," she said, "and I can look at it with a good conscience which be a tower of strength, and I can even go so far as to tell myself that Daisy Newte may make a better wife for Bill than me ; for that's where his eyes are turning."

"Daisy Newte! Good God—the blindness of the bachelor male!" swore Jonas.

And from that day forward he was at her—respectful, but unsleeping.

His fear was that, now she stood free of a man, her nice feeling would take her from under his roof and of course there was plenty of women who pointed this out to Milly Bassett ; but in her fine way she despised the mind that thinks evil for choice and said 'twas a pity that good thoughts was not put into the human heart instead of bad ones.

She said : "If my character can't rise above Thorpe-Michael, 'tis pity. And the man, or woman, who could whisper a bad thought against Jonas Bird be beneath my notice and his'n."

And then he offered for her and she took him ; and then, after that, of course, she left his home till the wedding.

And the carpenter's childer yowled their heads off when she went, and couldn't very easy be made to understand that Milly was only away for a few weeks and would soon be back to bide with 'em. William tried hard to get a bit more cash out of Jonas when he heard the glad news ; but, though feeling kindly to heaven above and earth beneath after his wonnerful triumph, Milly's future husband felt that with his new calls and doing up his home and buying poultry for his wife—birds being a thing she doted on—that William must be content. He paid another fifty down and made it clear that no more must be counted on for six months. And the horseman said no more at that time, being a good bit occupied with Daisy Newte by then. For she was walking with him and very near won. And afore Christmas, he'd got her.

All went well and everybody wished Jonas joy and Milly luck. 'Twas thought a very reasonable match, for Bird stood high in the public esteem and the folk had long since felt that Milly might do much better than William. But they admired her honesty and the way she'd stuck to him and felt she'd been richly rewarded. In fact Jonas and Milly were a devoted pair and not a cloud darkened their wedded life for a good few years.

Then came the fatal affair of the bargain, and though pretty easy about the instalments till he'd got three children of his own, from that time forth there's no doubt William began to fret Jonas cruel. Because, you see, the crafty toad had bargained for interest running, and Jonas, not understanding these things and guessing such matters was always five per centum and no more, had agreed to pay it. But this is where William got the better of him, for White went to a friend of his at Dartmouth and between them they figured up a very clever scheme which caused Jonas a lot of inconvenience.

They explained to him the wonderful ways of compound interest, and though he couldn't see 'em, he had to feel 'em, and he found, as time passed, that far from paying off William's five hundred, do what he might the money still piled up against him. There was complications, too, for of course he had no other secret than this from his wife, and Milly read him like a book, and after they was wed four years, Jo reached a pitch when he couldn't conceal his anguish. For presently, puzzling over the figures for the hundredth time, he came to the fearful conclusion that he'd already paid William over five hundred pounds, and yet, if White was to be trusted, there was three figures of money still owing to him by compound interest.

He had it out with William the next time he got him alone; but the horseman declared himself as a good bit surprised that a little thing like cash should fret such a happy and prosperous creature as Jonas Bird.

"Good powers!" he said, "haven't you found out that Milly was worth all the money in the Bank of England? And then to grouse because you bain't out of debt for her! Hell!" said William White, "you needn't think I wouldn't be off the bargain to-morrow and gladly pay you all the money twice over for Milly back again!"

Because, you see, his Daisy, though a nice girl up to a point, was very human in some things and had failed, both as a wife and a mother, owing to her fatal fondness for liquid refreshment. 'Twas a family weakness which had been kept out of William's knowledge while he was courting; but marriage and the cares of childer and so on, had woke a thirst in Daisy that made her difficult. So William weren't in a mood to lighten up for Jonas. and he said that figures can't lie and the loan must run its appointed course if it took ten years to do so. He'd got the whip-hand, no doubt, because it weren't a subject for any other ear, though Jonas, in his despair, did once think of going to parson with it. But the thought of laying bare the past and seeing parson's scorn was more than he could face, and he hid it up.

At last, however, he felt the tax past bearing, for it was making an old man of him; and then he braced himself and called on his Maker to see him through and done the wisest thing that ever he had done. In a word, he told Milly. He told her when they'd gone to bed one Christmas night and unbosomed his troubled mind. He'd paid William another fifty only the week night before and, as he presently confessed to Milly,' twas the last straw that broke his back and sent him to throw himself on her mercy.

He bade her list, then told the tale from the beginning, told it honest without straining truth in any particular. And Milly listened and said not a word till he was done.

"So there it is," finished Jonas—" a choice of evils for me 'twixt stripping up the past afore your eyes and letting William bleed me to my dying day seemingly. And knowing you, I reckoned the wisest thing was to come to you with the naked tale and hide naught. William says figures can't lie, and he may or may not be right, but I've got it fixed in my mind that he's making 'em lie; and, be it as it will, he's had enough, and I'm properly sick of putting big money in his pocket instead of yours, where all that is mine belongs by right."

Milly kept silent a bit, but he knew by her calm breathing that she weren't going to throw the house out of windows over it, or make a scene. In fact, she'd never been known to make a scene in all her life and weren't likely to begin now.

She spoke at last.

"There's some women would be a good bit put about to hear these things, Jo," she said, and he granted the truth of it.

"I can't call home one but yourself as wouldn't," he said,

"but you are the top flower in the basket of women at Thorpe-Michael, and have got intellects and the wit to see 'twas nothing but my great passion for you as led me into this mess. And though business is business and no man can ever say I drew back in a bargain, yet I've got a good bit enraged with William lately, and I feel 'tis more'n time this here compounded interest come to an end."

"How much have he had?" asked Milly, and Jonas gave her the figures, which was branded in letters of fire on his mind, so to say.

"Five hundred and seventy-eight," he said, "and still he's got the front to swear I owe him near two more hundred."

"I've puzzled sometimes where your money was going," she told him, "but, knowing you, I well understood 'twas safe."

"Thank God you came to the task with your usual high courage and sense," he answered. "And thank God, also, that you think none the worse of me. And don't you imagine I grudge the money itself. On the low level of cash you was worth the Mint of England ten times over; but the question afore me is, looking at my deal with William as a money bargain between man and man, whether he ain't going a bit over and beyond doing me in the eye."

"I reckon he is," said Milly. "Five hundred and seventy-eight's enough, Jo, and I'm proud, in a manner of speaking, you could rise it. I'm very fortunate in having you for a husband, because the man wasn't born to suit me better; and I should never have neighboured with William so fine as what I have done with you. But you was fortunate, too, in finding a chap as would take cash for what you was so willing to buy."

"I was," he granted. "Providence never done any member of my family such a turn as it done me when it sent you to my roof; but, outside that, touching William Bird, I be growing to feel—— However, if you say 'Go on paying, William,' I'll do so very well content; but if, on the other hand, you reckon that the man's Jewing me and did ought to be spoke to, then I'll be still better content."

"He shall be spoke to," she answered, "and I'll speak to him. We are very good friends and I'm sorry for him, because he's drawn a blank; and I've noticed, now and again, he's looked at me as if he was a good bit vexed we ever parted. And no doubt he's had queer thoughts and weighed his money against me and wondered whether it has served him better than what I should."

"Damn queer thoughts, I'll lay my life," said Jonas. "And I'm sorry for him, also as a Christian man, because he's quite clever enough to know what he's lost, and the bitterness no doubt runs into my compound interest."

"Go to sleep now," she said, "and fret no more. You can leave the rest to me."

So he blessed her for the wonder she was, and, with the load lifted from his heart, soon slept like a child.

Milly Bird took an early chance to see William, and what passed between them would have been very exciting to know and perchance an interesting side-glance on human nature; but none ever heard it save their Maker; and not Jonas himself, though he was cruel inquisitive, ever larned no details.

"'Tis no matter," said Milly to her husband. "We had a tell about it, and William's all right and won't want no more money. He's a very clever chap and ain't wishful for nobody to hear tell of his doings in the past, least of all poor Daisy. So that's that. And there shan't be no ill blood and there shan't be no more cash, and all friends notwithstanding."

Which fell out just as the remarkable woman ordained it should.

No. X
THE AMBER HEART

No. X

THE AMBER HEART

THE Lord chooses queer tools to do His purpose and we know that the stone the builders rejected was took by Him to be head of the corner; but in the case of the amber heart, it might be too much to say that the way that particular object worked for good was His almighty idea, for the reason, there was something a bit devious about the whole matter, and you'd be inclined to think a woman's craft rather than the Everlasting Will was at the bottom of the business.

And amber ain't a stone, anyhow, for while some people say 'tis sea-gulls' tears petrified by sea water, and others, equally clever, tell me it comes out of a whale, yet in either case you couldn't call it a mineral substance; and let that be as it will, what sea-gulls have got to cry about is a subject hidden from human understanding, though doubtless they've got their troubles like all mortal flesh.

Well, there was four of 'em—two maidens and two young men —and James White, the farmer at Hartland and Mary Jane White his sister, were two, and Cora Dene, who lived along with her old widow aunt, Mrs. Sarah Dene, was the third of the bunch, and Nicholas Caunter, who worked as cowman at Hartland Farm, came fourth.

And at the beginning of the curious tale James White was tokened to Mrs. Dene's niece, while his cowman had got engaged to Mary Jane. Folk said none of 'em was particular well suited, but the thing had fallen out as such matters will, and there weren't no base of real love behind the engagements, except in the case of White's sister.

There's no doubt James White loved Cora Dene for her cooking, as well he might, because she was a wonder in that art. She was also a very pretty woman, with a headpiece well furnished within as well as beautiful without, and when she first took James, Cora honestly believed she loved him and liked the thought of reigning at Hartland. But more than the love of the couple had gone to the match, because Mrs. Dene, Cora's aunt, was very wishful for it to happen on the girl's account and meant to make other arrangements for her own comfort.

She liked Cora very well, you understand, and knew she'd miss her cooking, if not her pretty face and her commonsense; but she had a great feeling for a man round her house, which was lonely, and on the moor-edge by the river, half a mile from Little Silver village, and her ambition was to engage a married couple who could tend home and garden, poultry and pigs; because Mrs. Dene, though fairly well to do, was an energetic creature and liked to be busy and add to her income in a small way.

So when she learned through his sister that James White wanted Cora, she done her best to help on the match and found the girl not unwilling. In fact, Cora accepted Jimmy before she knew quite enough about him to do so; and then, after she got to understand his nature and found he was merciless about money and cruel close, and grudged a sovereign for a bit of fun, her heart sank. Because she didn't know that love can't stem a ruling passion, and ain't very often the ruling passion itself in a male, and she found, as many other maidens have afore her, that a man's love affairs don't stand between him and life, or change his character and bent of mind.

So when she discovered that James was a miser, Cora began to see other things, because, once there's a spot for doubt to work, the tarnish soon spreads. James would not buy her a ring, but put five pounds in the bank for her, which didn't interest Cora much; and that's how it stood with them; while as to the other pair, the friction was a bit different.

You see, Nicholas Caunter, the cowman, only got interested in his master's sister when he found she was terrible interested in him. He was very good looking and a simple, charming sort of a man unconscious of his fine appearance; and there's no doubt that Mary Jane fell in love with him a week after he came to Hartland. And, when he found that out, being heartwhole at the time and poor as a mouse, he couldn't but see that to wed

Mary Jane would be a pretty useful step ; because she had her own money and was a nice enough woman, though not very good-looking.

However, she was healthy and hearty and there was a lot of her, so Nick told himself it all looked very promising and proper and he started making love to her, and foxed himself presently that it was the genuine article and there weren't nobody for him on earth but Mary Jane.

Then, a week after he'd offered for her and she'd wasted no time saying " Yes," but was in his arms almost afore the words had got out of his mouth, the young woman brought Nicholas acquainted with Cora Dene, because she said it was well he should know her brother's future bride.

So there they was—Cora betrothed to James White and Mary Jane White fixed up with Nicholas Caunter, though he'd only been at Hartland a month. And then the trouble began. First, Cora slowly discovered that James was close as a shut knife ; and if she'd been clever enough to read a man's mouth and eyes, she'd have seen his character stamped upon 'em. But that was the first secret disturbance ; and then Nicholas, he got a painful jar and found out there was only one girl on earth for him and that was Cora.

He'd never been properly in love till then, and if poor Mary Jane was a shadow before he met t'other girl, she sank to be less than nothing at all so soon as Nicky had seen James White's sweetheart the second time.

In a fortnight, from being an easy-going creature, very fond of cows, and with just an ordinary eye to the main chance, Nicholas Caunter found himself alive and tingling to the soles of his feet with a passsionate desire for Cora. Everything else in life sank out of sight, and he cussed Providence good and hard for playing him such a cruel trick, not seeing it was his own desire for the line of least resistance that had landed him plighted to Mary Jane.

So you see James and his sister both well content, and reckoning in a dim way at the back of their minds that each was going to be boss in the married state, because the money and position was with them. And James had reached the point when he saw himself married in another six months, after he'd done the autumn work on his farm and could afford three days' holiday. He reckoned such a lapse would be largely waste of time, for money-making was his god; but a honeymoon appeared to be counted upon by Cora, and he'd yielded reluctantly in that particular. Then Mary Jane, she hoped to be wedded along with her brother, and counted on a very fine holiday with Nicholas after, and even thought of going so far as London for it.

So that's how they stood; and meantime, though Nicholas managed still to hide his misery from Mary Jane, because they'd only been tokened a fortnight, his heart, in truth, was long since gone to Cora. As for her, she stood in perplexity because she liked her close lover less and less and saw his smallness of vision and lust for the pence with growing hatred and clearness; while, worse still, she couldn't but see that 'twas all bunkum about Nicholas caring a straw for Mary Jane.

And far deeper than that she saw, because not only did the maiden discover that Caunter was thinking a million times more about her than the other girl; but to her undying amazement she found that Nicholas was working on her heart very fierce indeed and that, though he played the game to the best of his powers and respected her engagement and stood up for James White and said he was a good man, though mean as an east wind and so on, yet she very well knew what had happened to the pair of 'em, and being a brave woman and much the cleverest of the four, she faced the situation in secret and put it to herself in plain English.

Meantime, Cora's aunt was casting about for her own comfort, after the girl should wed with White, and planning her arrangements without a thought that clouds were in the sky.

And then came the amber heart into the affair, and to Cora's immense astonishment James gave her a gift.

Him and his sister had talked on the subject of presents and she'd told him that 'twas rather a surprise to her that Nicholas hadn't produced no tokening ring as yet, and James had supported Nicholas in that matter, and said money was money, and his cowman hadn't got much at best and far too little anyway to waste ten shillings in sentiment.

"Let him keep his money for the wedding-ring," said James. "That you must have, though even that's a silly waste in my opinion."

But Mary Jane weren't with him there, and was casting about to give Nicholas a present herself and so lift him to give her one back; when James White, down to Ashburton after a very successful sale, happed to look in a window and see the amber heart.

'Twas just a honey-coloured thing carved to the familiar pattern and a bit bigger than your thumbnail, and with a thin little silver chain hung to it. And fired to a rash deed, he thought on Cora and went in the shop and asked the price.

A hopeful jeweller said he could have it for ten bob, so James took a chair and cheapened it. He sat there haggling for half an hour; and finally he got the trinket for six shillings and six pence, and returned to his hoss and rode home, thinking small beer of himself for a silly piece of work.

He was a secretive sort of man and didn't whisper his purchase to nobody; but the next Sunday, when Cora came to Hartland to tea and for a walk on the moor and a bit of love-making after, James fetched out the prize when they were alone. It had grown to be high summer time just then, and James was amazed to see the crop of whortleberries lying ripe for the picking. They made him forget all about Cora and the amber heart for a bit.

"If us have the childer out here, there's pounds and pounds of the fruit to be picked and they run a shilling a pint at market," he said. "Pay 'em twopence a pint for picking, and there's a five pound note for me afore the summer's over."

Then he was pleased to see his honey bees hard at work in the heather.

"I respect a bee more than most any creature," James told Cora, "because the insect rises above holidays and works seven days a week all its life till it drops."

Then he minded the amber heart, and said he doubted not 'twas going to be an heirloom in the White family, to be handed down from mother to daughter for generations. And he warned her to take a lot of care of it, and look cruel sharp that no misfortune ever befell the trash.

Cora thanked him very gratefully and put it on, and he said it looked very fine and became her well; but he bade her only to wear it on great occasions, and watch over it very close and jealous.

"There's money there," said James, and she wondered how much, but knew exceedingly well he hadn't put no great strain on a fat purse when he bought it.

He ordered her to keep the thing a secret for the present, and she promised to do so; and then came on the next queer scene of the play, for meeting with Nicholas down in Little Silver a week later, the man unfolded his feelings a bit and give Cora a glimpse of his heart. But such were her own feelings by then that what he hinted at didn't surprise her. In fact, he told her what a hundred things had told her already. He dwelt on Mary Jane first, however, and said he was a lot put about in that quarter and shamed of himself and wishful to give her a bit of a gift for the sake of peace.

"Such things must be done gradual and decent," he said. "'Tis clear as light I can't marry her now, because I moved like a blind man and made a shocking mistake; but I've only been tokened to the woman a month, though it seems like eternity, and afore I cut loose, I must carry on a bit longer and let the shock come gradual."

"I know very well how it is with you, Nick," she answered. "Such things will happen and 'tis very ill-convenient; but, I'm tolerable understanding, the more so because I'm finding myself in much the same sort of a mess as you."

They skated on thin ice, of course, and Nicholas found silence the safest when along with Cora; but they opened out bit by bit, and they both knew very well by now that they was meant for each other and no other parties whatsoever.

Then began the craft of Cora, and such was the amazing cleverness of the woman, doubtless quickened by love, that she worked single-handed, and whereas a lesser female might have taken Nicholas into her confidence, she did not, but struck a far-reaching stroke for them both, all unknown by him. She hoped it might happen as she'd planned for it to do, and reckoned no great harm would result if it failed; but her arts and her knowledge of Caunter's habit of mind carried her through and advanced the tricky and parlous affair a pretty good stage.

Cora knew two or three things now and she fitted 'em together. She knew the holiday people was apt to picnic round about on famous spots beside the river, and she knew sometimes they would leave odds and ends behind 'em worth the picking up.

She also knew that Nicholas Caunter would smoke his pipe by the river of an evening, when he could escape from his sweetheart, and she knew that poor Mary Jane was worrying a bit about a token of affection from Nicholas, which he weren't in any great hurry to produce. For, since the crash, the cowman soon felt less and less disposed to carry on his pretence, or do aught to encourage the false hopes of Mary Jane.

So, fortified by all these facts, Cora watched out for Nicholas one evening, saw him coming, and dropped her amber heart in the way where it would lie under his nose as he came along.

Her only fear was that he'd miss it, and she hid, so close as a hare in its form, to watch how it might go. But since Nicky's eyes were on the ground and the sunset light glittered very brave upon the toy, miss it he did not.

She saw him pick it up with a good bit of interest and then his eyes roamed about; but there was nought in sight of him but the river and some fragments of paper and a burned-out fire, where holiday folk had took their tea. So away he went with the amber heart in his trouser pocket, and after he was gone Cora came forth well pleased with the adventure; because she knew all was tolerable safe now, and reckoned the next stage would happen next day as she had foretold to herself. Which it did do.

She met Nicky after work hours and he was full of his find and very wishful for Cora to take it. But that weren't her purpose by no means.

"No, Nick," she said. "This fix we be in wants a power of careful thought and management, and we've got to go slow. You ain't a very downy man and can't see much beyond the point of your beautiful nose; but I can, and I'll ask you to go on as you are going for a bit and leave the future to me."

"I'd trust you with my life," he said, and then she told him what he was to do.

"You give this thing to Mary Jane," directed the devious woman. "You needn't be telling you picked it up and that 'tis no more than a come-by-chance, because then she'd set no store upon it. But just say 'tis a gift for her, and she'll be pleased and axe no questions."

Of course Nicholas couldn't see the point; but Cora just told him to trust her and do what she said.

"You leave the future to me," she told him. "I know a lot more about this than what you do, and if there's one thing above all else it is for you to trust me. You'll do a mighty sight more than you think you're doing when you give that rubbish to Mary Jane."

Well, he felt with a woman like Cora Dene, his strong suit was to obey and not argue, for he understood now, by a sure instinct, that such a creature was a tower of strength if she loved a man, and had best be let alone to work out her plans in her own way. And he presented the amber heart to Mary Jane and endured her joy and her kisses, though his heart sank under 'em and he puzzled all night to know how such a stroke was going to work for good. And if he'd known the proper tempest that had to rage afore there was peace, doubtless his pluck would have quailed under it.

And the very next morning, so proud as punch, Mary Jane came to breakfast with her amber heart flashing under her chin, and when James sat down to his meal, the first thing he catched sight of was his gift to Cora on his sister's bosom.

His eyeballs jingled no doubt and he put down his knife and fork and stared as if he'd seen a spectrum instead of the homely shape of Mary Jane behind the teapot.

"What—what in thunder be that hanging round your neck?" he asked.

"A little momentum from Nick," she answered lightly. "He gave it to me yesterday and was wishful for me to let him see me wear it."

"Caunter gave you that?" he said. "Let me look at it."

Well, she was a bit surprised, of course, to see James tighten up and set his jaws as he was wont to do before ugly news; but she put it down to astonishment and no more and handed the heart and the chain to James. She knew nought about his gift to Cora, and so when he dropped it, after squinting close at it, and said : " My God in heaven, 'tis the same ! " then Mary Jane felt proper amazement.

" The same what ? " she asked.

" The same treasure that I gave Cora for a heirloom," he answered, his jaws like a rat-trap.

" You gave Cora ! " gasped Mary Jane. " What stuff are you telling ? "

And then the woman in her conquered, because she knew the value of things as well as another.

" And a treasure it ain't any way," went on Mary Jane, " because a few shillings would buy it. But Nicholas is poor and 'tis the thought behind that I value."

" Damn the thought behind ! " thundered out James. " It weren't his to give, you silly owl. This was my gift to Cora Dene, and not a month ago, neither."

" Nonsense ! " she answered. " There might be fifty like it."

But he knew better, because he'd marked the thing very close when he bought it, and there was a stain in the amber which had knocked off two bob.

He said no more but ate his poached eggs and cleaned up the plate after with a piece of bread, according to his habit. Then he drank his tea, and ten minutes later he was off on his pony to old Mrs. Dene's house to have a tell with his sweetheart. And nobody ever went to the woman of his choice in such a foaming passion as Jimmy White that fine morning.

There was another outlet for Cora's remorseless and far-reaching activities at this time besides James, for the woman had an uncanny power of looking far ahead and, while she'd planned the affair of the amber heart outside her home, she was also working very hard within it. Her purpose there was to please her aunt as never she'd pleased her until that time ; and for two reasons.

Cora well knew that there was going to come a fearful strain on Mrs. Dene's goodwill, and was anxious to plan her own life after the crash had fallen, because she little doubted Mrs. Dene would cast her out. Indeed, she reckoned on it. But over and beyond that was the time to come, and Cora had so behaved of late that she meant the old woman should feel the gap when she was gone. Because a sudden upheaval and parting will oft be the only adventure to bring a thing home to anybody, and it isn't until the even, pleasant everyday life comes to an end and a thousand hateful problems call to be solved, that some people know their luck and realise their good time was in the present, though they were always waiting for the good time to come in the future.

And Cora had been giving her aunt a very fine time indeed, which is easy if anybody makes a god of their food and you happen to be a peerless cook. She was a heaven-born hand at food, was Cora, and Mrs. Dene, loving her food next to her hope of salvation, revelled in her niece's kitchen art. In fact, Cora went from strength to strength in that particular ; and a thousand other things she'd done during the last month to endear herself to her aunt.

Her craft was to plant in old Sarah Dene's mind the picture of a helpmate very much out of the common ; and she done so, and on the night before James White came along, Cora's aunt had gone so far as to admit it would be a dark day for her when the girl was wed and had took her many gifts to Hartland.

So that's how it stood when Jimmy lighted off his pony, and two minutes later he was holding the amber heart under his sweetheart's astonished eyes.

"Good morning, James," she said. "You'm early."

"What's this?" he asked, wasting no words in politeness.

She was a play-actor to the roots of her being, Cora was, and she started and stared.

"Not another, my dear man, surely?" she asked.

"No," he answered. "Not another. But what I'd like to know is, where be yours?"

"In your hand, thank God," she answered, and put out her fingers to take it ; but he wasn't giving it back to her no more.

He commanded her to tell him how it come about that his gift to her—a sacred heirloom evermore—come to be on his sister's neck that morning, and she marvelled at a tale so strange and wondered what the world was coming to.

"I'll tell you the truth," she said—suspicious words in

Jimmy's ear, because, to market or elsewhere, he'd often noted that when a fellow creature begins a tale like that, truth be often the one thing lacking. But Cora's story sounded as if there weren't much wrong, and perhaps another sort of man might have believed her.

"I broke my word and I own it," she told him. "I was so proud of the necklace that I couldn't but wear it, James, for I wanted the holiday people to see it round my neck, and the other girls to see it too. And, coming home from gathering whortles for a pie for my aunt—which she dearly loves—I found to my undying grief as I'd dropped the precious trophy somewhere. And back along I went and hunted till dusk and dewfall, and drowned myself with tears; and for two whole days I couldn't gather pluck to tell you the fearful news. I've lost pounds of solid flesh fretting and be so weak as a goose-chick about it; but I was coming to confess my sins to-day. And now you rise up, like the sun over a cloud, and turn my sorrow into joy, I'm sure."

"You needn't think so," he said, "because there's a lot more in this than meets the eye, and I doubt you're lying."

She stared at that.

"I should hope all's well that ends well, James," she answered him, "and no call for no such insult as that. What was lost be found, such as it is, and I'm very wishful to know where Mary Jane picked it up."

"She didn't pick it up at all," he answered. "'Twas Nicholas Caunter—his gift to her."

"What a world!" exclaimed Cora. "So Nicholas found it! Or, since you think I'm lying, perhaps you'll say 'twas me gave it to him, because your sister thought 'twas more than time she had a present off him?"

"How he came by it I've yet to find out," answered the man, "and if that's true and you thought to hoodwink Mary Jane and me also by a trick like that, then you're a bad lot and not worth your keep to any man. But all that matters to me be this: you disobeyed me on your own showing and risked a valuable jewel, messing about on the moor for vanity, or some worse reason. And them that be careless of a lover's wishes before marriage won't care a cuss for 'em after. In a word, I've done with you. This is the last of a lot of pin-pricks you've given me lately, and I've caught ideas and opinions from you during the past month that made me ask myself some difficult questions. It's off, you understand."

'Twas true she'd been saying things to shake up James pretty frequent; but this was better than her highest hopes, of course. She hid her joy, however, and put her apron up to her eyes and shook her slim shoulders a bit; then, as he was going, she told him a thing that astonished him.

"Whether or no," said Cora, " the amber heart, trash though it is, be mine, not yours, James, and I'll thank you to return it to the lawful owner. Since you be going to say ' good-bye,' we'll part friends, but thicky necklace is mine, whatever your godless intentions."

He glared at her, stuffed the toy in his pocket and went back to his pony without a word. But she followed him down the pathway and smiled at him as he mounted, and even dared to rub the pony's nose, for she'd often been suffered to ride the creature herself.

"If you won't give me the amber heart, Jimmy, I'll have you up for breach," she said. And then he let fall a few crooked words and drove his heels into the beast and galloped off in a proper fury of rage, cussing the whole sex to hell and Cora Dene in particular.

With that she went in and told her aunt the tale; but now she was all shame and grief, and after she'd given the details and said how James White had cast her off, she vowed that her last day on earth had dawned.

"I'd call on the hills to cover me if they would do so," sobbed Cora. "But as they will not, I'll call on the river, and I'll go and drown myself to-night, for I can't face Little Silver no more after this downfall."

And Mrs. Dene, who had always thought a lot of James White and been proud of the match, weren't particular helpful, nor yet comforting. In fact, she was very disappointed about it and lost her temper with Cora. So the bedraggled maiden went out of her sight and looked as never she'd looked before. And on the evening of that day, under cover of darkness, she met Nick Caunter and heard his news.

" 'Tis in a nutshell and all very shameful, but very convenient," said Nicholas. "White faced me about the amber heart after dinner, and axed me where I'd bought it, and, took unawares, I said at Moreton. Then he told me I was a liar and could clear out of Hartland at the end of my month. And then I owned up that I'd found the blessed thing on the moor and thought it would sound better in Mary Jane's ear if I said I'd bought it. Then he flattened me out by telling me 'twas his gift to you, and the whole trick had been planned by us both, as an insult to him and his sister. Then I looked at Mary Jane and found, to my great thankfulness, she was in a mood to believe James; and then I went out of their sight that instant moment, before she had time to relent. I packed my bag and I cleared, and I ain't going back again, neither."

She was very pleased indeed, Cora was.

"You couldn't have done no better," she said. "You couldn't have carried on cleverer than that if I'd advised you. 'Tis a very sad affair for everybody, I'm sure, but better be troubled for a week than for a lifetime. Now you go to Moreton and put up the banns and leave the rest to me, if you please."

"What a day!" he said. "If I didn't know you, I should reckon you was going mad along of so much plotting. How can I put up the banns—me out of work and not a job in sight? And where will you stand with Mrs. Dene when she hears that White have thrown you over?"

"Don't waste your time axing questions," she answered. "I want your address in Moreton and that's all there is to it for a fortnight till after we be wed. You've got enough money to carry on, because you can draw out your twenty-five pounds from the Post Office Savings Bank; and I can draw out my fifteen, and that's forty. And don't you look for no work, unless it's jobbing work, but leave the future in my keeping till we meet again."

With that they praised the Lord for all His mercies and the man went on his way, to tramp to Moreton and Cora returned home. But the river ran at the bottom of her aunt's garden and she popped down and dipped in it, clothes and all, before she returned to Mrs. Dene.

The old woman was sitting up in a bit of a stew, because the hour grew late and she minded what her niece had threatened. In fact, she was half-inclined to go down to the police-station when the girl came in, soaking from head to heel, and told her story.

"I flinged myself in, as I ordained to do," she said, "and by the wisdom of God a man was passing and heard the splash and saved me. 'Twas Nicholas Caunter, the cowman at Hartland, who fought for my life, and he made me promise faithful I wouldn't go in no more. So I've got to live after all, Aunt Sarah."

"In that case, you'd best to unray and get out of them clothes and go to bed," said the old woman, hiding her relief, "else you'll very likely die in earnest—and no great loss if you did."

So Cora went to her chamber after a busy day; but she was one of them terrible clear-minded women who work when they work and sleep when they sleep, and she never had a better night's rest.

Two days later came news of where Nicholas was stopping; and there also arrived for Cora a little box left by a farm-hand from Hartland. There wasn't no letter with it, but Cora found herself disappointed in a way, because she rather liked the thought of fetching James White up for breach if it could be done; and the fact that he had so far shunned the prospect of the law as to send her back the trinket showed that he was fearful too. Because James White had a proper dread of lawyers.

And then came the last fine act but one of her make-believe, and when Mrs. Dene had swallowed the pill and begun to see that, but for the shame, she'd be a lot better with Cora than without, and set to work to make her niece bide along with her and live it down, the girl vowed that such a thought was beyond belief and she couldn't face Little Silver as a forlorn woman passed over and disgraced.

"I'll go to Moreton," she said, "and find honest work; and as the world's crying out for cooks, with a hand like mine, no doubt I'll struggle in somewhere and make new friends; but to stop here all forlorn without a man's courage and strength to defend me, be asking too much. And I never shall forget your goodness and loving-kindness, Aunt Sarah; and the Lord won't forget 'em either. I'll always pray for you in my prayers, and I'll always pray for that poor chap, Nicholas Caunter, as saved me alive, because when it got to Mr. White's ears as he'd done so and kept me from a watery death, him and his sister turned against poor Nicholas and threw him over, and he's a wanderer on the face of the earth this minute, though such a clever, big-hearted soul as him be sure to find a warm welcome somewhere, I hope."

Well, Mrs. Dene, who was broke down by now and terrible wishful for Cora to stay, pleaded with her in vain to do so; but the girl went on cooking to a marvel, and excelling in surprises, and being a proper angel in the house for a fortnight; and then crying oceans of tears, she packed her belongings, and Farmer Maitland, the widower, carried her off to Moreton in his market cart on market day.

'Tis said he offered her marriage before they were halfway up Merripit Hill and out of sight of her native village; but he was unsuccessful, and afore noon Cora found herself in the arms of Nicholas Caunter. Two days after, the day being Sunday, him and her were married and off to Ashburton for a bit of a honeymoon. And then, when their united money was down to ten pounds, Cora struck her last stroke.

She waited and watched the *Moreton Trumpet*, the paper her aunt took up, and then come the expected advertisement telling how Mrs. Sarah Dene of Little Silver was wishful to employ a man and his wife; and on the day after it appeared, off she went along with Nicholas in a hired trap and drove into the village so bold as need be.

Then Cora left her husband at the 'Three Travellers' and walked down to Mrs. Dene, and found her aunt sitting helpless afore a score of letters from married folk all very wishful to join her.

Cora told her news and how she'd found and married Nicholas; and then she brought peace and order and hope into her aunt's heart, according to her custom; and the sight of her awakened a great hope in Mrs. Dene, though it sank again when she grasped that Cora was no more a free creature, but given over to the keeping of a man.

And then, of course, the old woman said exactly what her niece knew she would say. Cora had looked through the applications and didn't feel too hopeful about any of 'em.

"The first thing is the cooking," she declared. "A bad cook's going to shorten your life, Aunt Sarah, and my mind always sinks when I think of it. You're thinner than when I saw you last, for that matter, and I'm going to make one of my mutton pies for you this day before I say 'good-bye.'"

And then—a world of anxiety in her eyes—Mrs. Dene wondered if 'twas in the power of possibility that Nicholas Caunter would see his way to come to her if all she'd got was left to Cora in the hereafter, under her will.

And the young woman stared with amazement, and declared no such thought as that had ever crossed her mind.

"Wonders never cease with me," she said, "but Nicky's all for foreign parts, I'm afraid, and a State-aided passage to Canada. I've begged him to think twice, I may tell you, because the sea between you and me is a very cruel thought; but since you want a man and his wife, which was always your ambition, and since I should certainly lengthen your days if I was to bide along with you, and be happier far than I should be anywhere else on earth, I'll strive with my husband about it and try my bestest to change his plans."

So she went for Nicholas and he came along. Of course, he couldn't play-act like his wife; but she'd schooled him pretty well, and he came out with flying colours and sacrificed his hopes of Canada so that Cora and her aunt shouldn't be parted.

It worked very well indeed, and the old woman had five more happy years afore a tremendous Christmas dinner finished her.

And then Cora came by the house and three hundred a year.

You'd think, in your worldly wisdom, that such a woman as her might have been rather doubtful as a wife, and was like to trade on her fatal cleverness when up against the changes and chances of married life; but no such thing was ever reported against Cora Caunter. She loved Nick and ran straight in double harness, and brought the man four very fine childer. And the eldest girl wears the amber heart to chapel on Sundays; because, as Cora told Nicholas, 'tis no use having a heirloom if you don't let the peope see it.

As for James White, one dose of romantics was enough for him and he never went courting no more; but Mary Jane found a very good husband and left Hartland along with him after marriage. She quarrelled with James about the wedding-breakfast because she wanted for him to pay, but he would not.

No. XI
THE WISE WOMAN OF WALNA

No. XI

THE WISE WOMAN OF WALNA

I

WHEN farmer Badge died, his widow kept on at Walna, and some people thought the world of her, same as I always did, but some was a bit frightened, because of her great gifts. Charity Badge certainly did know a terrible lot more than every-day folk, which was natural in the daughter of a white witch ; but she weren't no witch herself—neither black nor white—and, as she often said to me: " 'Tis only my way of putting two and two together that makes the difference between me and the other women round about these parts."

Walna was a poor little bit of a place up the Wallabrook Valley, and when Charity died it all went to pieces, for there was none to take it again. Tramps slept there till the roof fell in, and then the hawks and owls took it over ; but fifty years agone she flourished and did pretty well there, one way and another, though 'twas more by the people that visited her for her wisdom than anything she made out of the tumble-down farm. More'n a cow or two she never had no cattle, and the last sheep to Walna went to pay for farmer Badge's coffin.

I was a maiden then and worked for Mrs. Badge, so I comed to see a lot about her and marked her manner of life. Half the things she did was thought to be miracles by the Postbridge people, yet if you saw the workings of 'em from inside, you found that, after all, they was only built on common sense. Still, I'll grant you that common sense itself is a miracle. 'Tis only one in a million ever shows it ; and that one's pretty near sure to be a woman.

Charity was a thin, brown creature—birdlike in her ways, with quick movements, quick hands, and quick eyes. She never had no childer, and never wanted none. In fact, she was pretty well alone in the world after her husband died. There was a lot of Badges, of course, and still are ; but she never had no use for them, nor them for her.

And now I'll tell the story of Sarah White and Mary Tuckett and Peter Hacker, the master of Bellaford.

Sarah was a lone creature up fifty year old, and she come along to Mrs. Badge one fine day with a proper peck of troubles. She crept down the path to Walna from Merripit Hill, like a snail with a backache, and weren't in no case at all for merriment ; yet the first thing she heard as she come in was laughter ; and the first thing she seed was pretty Mary Tuckett sitting on Mrs. Badge's kitchen table, swinging her legs, and eating bits of raw rhubarb out of a pie as my mistress was trying to make.

Mary was a beauty, and a bit too fond of No. 1, like most of that sort.

" 'Tis too bad," she said to the new-comer, " ban't it too bad, Mrs. White ? Here's Charity, well known for the cleverest woman 'pon Dartymoor, won't tell me my fortune or look in her crystal for me, though I be offering her a two-shilling piece to do so."

" You go along," said Charity. " Don't you waste no more of my time, and let your fortune take care of itself. It don't want a wise woman to tell the fortune of such a lazy, good-for-nought as you."

Then Mary went off laughing, and poor Mrs. White began her woes.

" I could have told that woman something as would have changed her laughter to tears," she began. " But time enough for that. Can you list to me for an hour, Charity ? I'm in cruel trouble, look where I will, and if there's any way out, I'll be very glad to pay good money to know it."

" Let me put the paste 'pon this here pie, then I'll hear what you've got to grumble at," answers the wise woman ; and five minutes later she sat down and folded her hands and shut her eyes and heard what Sarah had got to tell.

" When my husband was alive, he worked for Peter Hacker's father at Bellaford, and lived in a little cottage on a newtake field a mile from Bellaford Farm. Old Hacker often said to my husband that when he'd paid rent for fifty year for the cottage, he'd let him have it for his own. 'Twas common knowledge that he intended to do it. But now, with my husband dead in his grave—and he died just six months after he'd paid his fiftieth year of rent, poor soul!—Peter Hacker have told me that the cottage ban't to be mine at all, and that 'tis all rubbish, and not a contract. I tell him that the ghost of my poor Thomas will turn his hair grey for such wickedness; but you know Peter Hacker. Hard as the nether millstone, and cruel as winter— with women. Very different, though, if a brave man beards him. Now he's dunning me for two years' rent, and even when I told him all that hangs on my keeping the cottage, he won't change or hold to the solemn promise his father made my husband. In fact, he'll turn me out at midsummer."

"And what do hang on your keeping the house?" asked Charity.

Mrs. White sniffed and cooled her tearful eyes with her handkercher.

"Johnny French hangs on it," she said. "We'm keeping it close till next autumn, but he wants for to marry me, and we'm both lonely souls, and we've both lost a good partner; and so it falls out very suent and convenient like that we should wed. But now he hears tell as I ban't to have the cottage, he's off it. He won't hear of marrying if there's no cottage. So the fag end of my life's like to be ruined one way or another."

"Let's see," says Charity, in her slow, quiet way. "Firstly, Peter Hacker's dunning you for two years' rent and will turn you out if you don't pay it; and secondly, he refuses to be bound by what his father promised your Thomas long years afore you married; and thirdly, you'm tokened to old Johnny French; but he won't take you if you're not to have the cottage free gratis and for ever."

"That's how 'tis; and, as if all this misfortune wasn't enough I've just heard of the death of my only brother, Nathan Coaker, in Ireland."

"That terrible handsome man, as had all the girls by the ears in Postbridge afore he went off?"

"Yes—only thirty-five—killed steeple-chasing. He was a huntsman, you know, and a great breaker of hosses. And now one's broke him. Dead and buried, and nought for me but his watch and chain and a bill from his undertaker. It happened in Ireland three weeks ago; and I've only heard tell to-day; and I thought if Mary Tuckett knowed, 'twould soon have turned her laughter into tears, for she was cruel fond of him, and wept an ocean when he went. In fact, they was tokened on the quiet unknown to her father, and Nathan hoped to marry her some day and little knew she'd forgot all about her solemn promise."

"I'm very sorry for you. I'll think about this. It don't look hopeful, for Peter Hacker's very hard all through where women are concerned. There's no milk of human kindness in him, and he don't like me. He thinks—poor fool—that I overlooked his prize bullock, that died three days afore 'twas to start to the cattle show."

"He might be tenderer, for he's only human, after all," said Mrs. White. "He's courting that very girl that was here a minute agone. In fact, they be plighted, I believe. It do make me bitter when I think upon it, for my poor Nathan's sake. She had sworn to marry my brother, remember, for Nathan told me so, and, no doubt, he counted upon it to the end of his days. But out of sight out of mind with her sort. Peter's riches have made her forget Nathan's beautiful face. And now he's in his grave."

"Stop!" says Charity. "You'm running on too fast. Let me think a minute. There's a lot here wants sifting. Let's come to business, my dear, and stick to the point. You want your cottage and you want Johnny French. What will you give me if I get your cottage for 'e out of Peter?"

Mrs. White was known to have saved a little bit, or, rather, her late husband had for her. He was a lot older than her, and had thought the world of her.

"I'll give 'e a five-pound note," she said at last.

"And what if I get Johnny French up to the scratch also?"

"If you do one, you'll do t'other," said Sarah. "He depends on the cottage, and won't take me without it, but be very willing to have both together. Still, I'll meet you gladly if there's anything you can do, and the day I'm wed I'll give you another five-pound note, Charity. And well you'll have earned it, I'm sure."

"So much for that then. And now, what like was your brother? Let's talk of him," said Mrs. Badge. "I'm awful sorry for you—'tis a great loss and a great shock. Horsemanship do often end that way."

Sarah was a thought surprised that t'other should shift the conversation so sudden; but she felt pretty full of her dead brother and was very well content to talk about him.

"A flaxen, curly man, with a terrible straight back, and a fighting nose and blue eyes. He hunted the North Dartmoor Hounds and every girl in these parts—good-looking and otherwise—was daft about him. They ran after him like sheep. There was a terrible dashing style to him, and he knowed the way to get round a female so well as you do the way to get round a corner. They worshipped him. Just a thought bowed in the legs along of living on hosses. A wonder on hossback, and very clever over any country. Great at steeple-chasing also, but too heavy for the flat—else he'd been a jockey and nothing else. And he would have married Mary Tuckett years ago if her father had let him. But old Tuckett hated Nathan worse than sin and dared Mary to speak with him or lift her eyes to him if they met. So away he went to Ireland; but not before that girl promised to wait for ever, if need be."

They talked a bit longer; then Mrs. Badge said a deep thing.

"Look here: don't tell nobody that your brother be dead for the minute. Keep it close, and if you must tell about it, come up here and tell me. I'll listen. But not a word to anybody else until I give the word."

"Mayn't I tell Johnny French?"

"Not even him," declared Mrs. Badge. "Not a single soul. I've got a reason for what I say. And now be off, Sarah, and let me think a bit."

With that Mrs. White started; but she hadn't reached the tumble-down gate of Walna—in fact, 'twas the head of an old iron bedstead stuck there and not a gate at all—when Charity called after her.

"Go brisk and catch up that girl Mary Tuckett," she said. "Tell her, on second thoughts—for her good and not for mine—that I'll do what she wants. Go clever and brisk, and you'll over-get her afore she's home again."

So Mrs. White trotted off, and very soon found Mary looking over a hedge and helping a young man to waste his time, according to her usual custom when there was a coat about.

But Sarah gave her message, and fifteen minutes later Mary was back along with Mrs. Badge.

II

"I've changed my mind about 'e, Mary," said the wise woman. "I'm terrible unwilling to tell young people concerning the future as a rule—for why? Because the future of most people be cruel miserable, and it knocks the heart out of the young to hear of what's coming; but you'm a sensible girl, and don't want to go through life blind. And another thing is this: 'tis half the battle to be fore-warned; and a brave man or woman can often beat the cards themselves, and alter their own fate—if they only know it in time."

After all this rigmarole Charity Badge bade Mary take a seat at the table. Then she drawed the blind, and lighted a lamp; and then she fetched out a pack of cards and her seeing-crystal. 'Twas all done awful solemn, and Mary Tuckett without a doubt felt terrible skeered even afore t'other began. Then Mrs. Badge poured a drop of ink into her crystal—some said 'twas only the broken bottom of an old drinking glass; but I don't know nothing about that. Next she dealt out the cards, and fastened on the Jack o' hearts and the Jack o' oaks,* and made great play with 'em. And, after that, she sat and gazed upon the crystal with all her might, and didn't take her eyes off of it for full five minutes.

"Now list to me, Mary Tuckett," she says, "and try to put a bold face on what be coming, for there's trouble brewing for 'e—how much only you yourself can tell."

With that she read out the fortune.

---

* Oaks—Clubs.

"There's a dark, rich man after you, Mary. He's fierce as a tiger, and the folk don't like him, but he's good at bottom, and he'll make you a proper husband. But there's another chap who have more right to you according to the cards, and I see him in the crystal very plain. He's flaxen curled with a straight back and a fighting nose, and blue eyes. Very great at horsemanship seemingly, and he'll have you for a wife, so sure as death, unless something happens to prevent it. He's on the way to you this minute. He's the Jack o' hearts; and t'other man's Jack o' oaks. Now hold your breath a bit while I look in the crystal and see what happens.

"Good powers!" cried the girl, creaming with terror down her spine. "'Tis Nathan Coaker as you be seeing! I thought he'd forgot me a year agone!"

"Hush! Don't be talking. No, he ain't forgot you by the looks of it. Quite the contrary."

Mary went white as curds, and sat with her hands forced over her heart to hear what the wise woman would see next.

"Them men will meet!" she said, presently. "There! They crash together and fight like dragons! There'll be murder done, but which beats t'other I can't tell yet. The picture's all ruffled with waves. That means the future's to be hid—even from me. But one thing is only too clear; there'll be a gashly upstore and blood spilled when Jack o' oaks meets Jack o' hearts; and the end of it so far as you be concerned is that you'll have no husband at all, I'm afeared—poor girl."

So that was the end of the fortune-telling, and Mary wept buckets, and Mrs. Badge reminded her of the florin but wouldn't take it.

"No," she said, "money like that be nought in such a fix as you find yourself. The thing is to help you if I can. I don't want to know no names. 'Tis better I should not; but 'tis clear there's a fair, poor man coming here to marry you; and there's a dark, rich man also wants to do so. Now maybe I can help. Which of 'em is it you want to take? Don't tell me no names. Just say dark or pale."

"The d-d-d-dark one," sobs out Mary. "I thought 'twas all off with the pale one years ago, and I wouldn't marry him for anything n-n-n-now—specially if he's so poor as when he went."

"And what'll you do for me if I can save you from him? I don't say I can, for 'tis a pretty stiff job; but I might do so if I took a cruel lot of trouble."

"I'll give you everything I've got, Charity—everything!" cries the girl.

"I'm afraid that ban't enough, my dear. Will you give me ten pound the day you'm married to the dark one? That's a fair offer; and if I don't succeed, I'll ax for nothing."

The girl jumped at that, and said she thankfully would do so; and Mrs. Badge bade her keep her mouth close shut—knowing she would not—and let her go. Poor Mary went off expecting to meet Nathan Coaker at every step o' the road, and little knowing that the poor blid was sleeping his last sleep in a grave in foreign parts to Ireland.

The very same evening she met Peter Hacker himself; and though he was a chap without much use for religion, yet, like a good few other godless men, he believed in a good bit more than he could understand, and hated to spill salt, or see a single pie, and wouldn't have cut his nails on a Friday for a king's ransom.

She told him that her old sweetheart, Nathan Coaker, was coming back, and that blood would be spilled, and that the wise woman didn't know for certain whether 'twas his blood or Nathan's. She wept a lot, and told him about Coaker, and what a strong, hard chap he was, and how he had the trick to ride over a woman's heart and win 'em even against their wills. And altogether she worked upon the mind of Peter Hacker so terrible, that he got into a proper sweat of fear and anger—but chiefly fear. And the next day—unknown to Mary—he rode up along to Walna, and had a tell with Charity Badge on his own account.

Peter began in his usual way with women. He blustered a lot, and talked very loud and stamped his foot and beat his leg with his riding-whip.

"What's all this here tomfoolery you've been telling my girl?" he says. "I wonder at you, Mrs. Badge, a lowering yourself for to do it—frightening an innocent female into fits. You ought to know better."

Of course Charity did know better, and she knowed Peter and his character inside out as well.

She looked at him, calm as calm, and smiled.

"I wish 'twas tomfoolery, Mr. Hacker. I wish from my heart that the things I see didn't happen; but they always do, if the parties ban't warned in time; though now and again, when a sensible creature comes to me and hears what's going to overtake 'em, they can often escape it—as we can escape a storm if we look up in the sky and know the signs of thunder and lightning soon enough."

"'Tis all stuff and rubbish, I tell you," he said, "and I won't have it! Fortune-telling be forbidden by law, and if I hear any more about you and your cards and your crystal, I'll inform against you."

"You'd better be quick and do it, then, master," she answers him, still mild and gentle, "for I'm very sorry to say there's that be going to happen to you, as will spoil your usefulness for a month of Sundays or longer; and that afore a fortnight's out. Of course, if you don't believe what I know too well to be the truth, then you'll go your rash way and meet it; but so sure as Christmas Day be Quarter Day, I'm right, and you'll do far wiser to look after your own affairs than to trouble about mine. And now I'll wish you good evening."

She made to go in, for Hacker was sitting on his horse at her very door; but that weren't enough for him. His cowardly heart was shaking a'ready.

"Don't you go," he said. "I'll onlight and hear more of this."

He dismounted and came in the house; and Charity Badge bade me go out of the kitchen, where I was to work, and leave 'em together, but I catched what came after through the keyhole.

"Now," he said. "It lies in a nutshell. My Mary was tokened in a sort of childish way to a man called Nathan Coaker —a horse-stealer or little better, and a devil of a rogue, anyway. But it seems you looked in your bit of glass and pretended to see——"

"Stop!" cried Charity, putting on her grand manner and making her eyes flash like forked lightning at the man. "How do you dare to talk about 'pretending' to me? Begone, you wretched creature! I'll neither list to you, nor help you now. Go to your death—and a good riddance. You to talk about 'pretending' to me!"

He caved in at that, and grumbled and growled, but she'd hear nought more from him till he'd said he was sorry, and that so humbly as he knowed how.

"Now you can go on again," she said, "but be civil, or I'll not lift a finger to aid you."

"'Tis like this," he went on. "It do look as if that man, Nathan Coaker, was coming back."

"That's so. I never seed the fellow myself, but his name certainly was Nathan Coaker, and Mary called him home in a minute from my picture in the crystal. They were certainly tokened, and if she's forgot it, he haven't; and such is the report I hear of him, that 'tis sure he'll overmaster such a man as you by force of arms. No woman can resist him. I guess he's made his fortune and be coming in triumph to marry her."

"She's going to marry me, however."

"So you think."

The man began to grow more and more cowed afore her cold, steady eyes, and the scorn in her voice.

"The strongest will win," he said.

"Yes," she answered him, "that's true without a doubt—so the cards showed."

"And what's stronger than money?" he axed.

"A man in a righteous rage," she replied; "and a charge of heavy shot with gunpowder behind 'em."

"Lord save us! You don't mean he'd lie in a hedge for me?"

"He'd do anything where his own promised woman was concerned," she said. "But 'tis more likely, from what I hear, that he'd meet you face to face in the open street, and hammer you to death for coming between him and her."

"She's my side."

"Now she may be, but wait till she sets eyes on him again. He's well knowed to be so handsome as Apollyon."

Peter Hacker got singing smaller and smaller then.

" 'Tis a thousand pities the wretched fellow can't be kept away."

" For your sake it is, without a doubt—a thousand pities," admitted Charity. " She loves you very well, and a good wife she'll make—and a thrifty—but she won't trust herself if that man's curly hair and blue eyes turn up here again."

" Is it to be done—can we keep him off—pay him off—bribe him—anything ? "

" Now you talk sense. There's very few things can't be done in this world, Mr. Hacker, if you get a determined man and a determined woman pulling the same way. Man's strength and woman's wit together—what's ever been known to stand against 'em ? "

" Help me, then," he said.

" Me ! You want me to help—with my ' tomfoolery ' ? "

She roasted him proper for a bit, then came to business.

" I can't work for nought, and since 'tis the whole of your future life that depends upon it, I reckon you'll be generous. If I succeed I shall look to you for thirty pound, Peter Hacker ; if I fail, I'll ax for nothing. Still, I do believe I may be able to get you out of this, though 'twill call for oceans of trouble."

He tried to haggle, but she'd none of that—wouldn't bate her offer by a shilling. So he came to it.

" Thirty pound I must have the day you marry Mary," she said. " And now tell me all you know about this rash, savage man, Nathan Coaker. The more I understand the better chance shall I have of keeping him off your throat."

With that Peter explained how t'other fellow was the young brother of Mrs. Sarah White ; and he went on to say that Sarah was one of his tenants ; but he didn't mention the row about Sarah's cottage.

Mrs. Badge then took up the story, and made it look as clear as daylight.

" My gracious ! " she said, " why now you can see how the crash be coming ! 'Tis a terrible poor look-out for you every way. Sarah's writ to him, of course, to say as you won't let her have the cottage your father faithfully promised to her husband,

and Coaker's coming over with threatenings and slaughters about that job. And then, as if that weren't enough, he'll find what a crow he's got to pluck with you on his own account about Mary."

"The more comes out, the more it looks as if he'd better be kept away," said Mr. Hacker.

"And the harder it looks to do it," added Charity. "You lie low, anyway. The next step is for me. I'll see Sarah and tell her that you've changed your mind about the cottage—to call it a cottage, for 'tis no better than a pig's lew house. You'll give it her, of course, for her life and the life of that man French, as she wants to marry. That's the first step."

"Why should I?"

"What a fool you are! Why, for two reasons I should think. Firstly, because your father promised her husband; secondly, because 'tis half the way to keeping Nathan Coaker in Ireland. If she lets him know as you be going to do the rightful thing, he'll have no more quarrel with you, since he don't know about you and Mary. Then, what you've got to do is to hurry on the match with her; and when you'm once married, 'tis all safe. Very like you'll not have to offer the man a penny after all."

"You'd best see Mrs. White to-morrow then," said Peter.

"I'll see her this very night," answered the wise woman. "In kicklish matters of this kind an hour may make all the difference for good or evil. To-night I'll tell her that the house is hers on condition that her brother Nathan don't come from Ireland this side o' Christmas; and she'll bless your name and do her best to keep him away altogether. In fact, I wouldn't be surprised if she succeeded, and it might even happen that when he comes to know of your marriage and hears that 'tis over and done, that he'll give up the thought of coming at all, and you'll get out of it with credit and a whole skin."

Peter thanked her a lot, and she was as good as her word, and went to see Widow White that very same evening.

She didn't put it to Sarah quite like she'd promised; but she explained that Mr. Hacker was quite a reasonable man in some ways, even where females were concerned, and that he had undertaken to let Sarah keep her house so long as she and

Mr. French should live. Which, of course, was all that Mrs. White or her Johnny cared about.

"Hacker naturally thinks that your brother is still living," explained Charity. "And mind you take mighty good care not to tell him 'tisn't so. The longer he supposes that Nathan is alive, the better for us all. And what you've got to say presently be this—that so soon as you told Nathan 'twas all right about the cottage, he changed his mind about coming to Postbridge for the present."

"'Twill be a lie," said Mrs. White.

"'Twill be a white lie, however," answered Charity; "and 'twill help a good many people out of a hobble and do harm to none; so I advise you to tell it."

And Sarah did tell it—with wonderful, far-reaching results, I'm sure; for it meant that she had her cottage for life; and that she had Johnny French for life also; and it meant that Mary married Peter Hacker afore the next Christmas and went honeymooning to London town for a week with the man; and it meant that, unbeknownst each to t'others, Sarah and Mary and Peter gived my mistress the money they promised her. So Charity Badge came out of the maze with flying colours, you might say, not to mention fifty golden pounds, all made out of her own head.

And many such like things she did, though never did they fetch such a dollop of money again.

No. XII
THE TORCH

No. XII

THE TORCH

In my opinion there's hardly an acre of Dartmoor as wouldn't set forth a good tale, if us could only go back along into time and get hold of it. Anyway, there's a 'mazing fine thing to be told about Vitifer Farm; and you don't want to go back far, neither, for it all happened but ten year ago.

Vitifer is one of the " tenement " farms and don't belong to the Duchy; and Furze Hill farm, which adjoins Vitifer, be likewise land handed down from father to son from generations forgot. The " tenements " are scattered over Dartmoor, mostly in the valleys of East and West Dart; but Vitifer and Furze Hill stood together half a mile distant from the famous Vitifer tin mine that lies in the wild ground west of Hameldon. And Joe Gregory farmed Vitifer when this fearful thing fell out, and his brother Amos Gregory was master at Furze Hill.

The Duchy had long desired the land, for 'tis Duchy's rule to snap up the tenement farms as they fall in the market, and indeed few will soon remain in private possession; but for the minute the two brothers—middle-aged bachelors both—held on where their forefathers had worked before them time out of mind, and it looked almost as though they was going to be the last of the ancient name to resist the over-lord of Dartmoor; for men come and men go; but Duchy lasts for ever and, no doubt, will have all it wants to the last rood afore many years be past.

One of the next generation, however, still stood for the Gregory race, and he was a nephew to Joe and Amos. A third brother they had, but him and his wife were dead, and their only son lived with Joe and was thought to be his heir. Ernest Gregory he was called, and few thought he'd make old bones, for the young man was pigeon-breasted and high-coloured and coughed a good bit when first he came up from the " in country " to the Moor.

Along with his uncle, however, he put on flesh and promised better. Fair and gentle he was—a quiet, timid sort of chap, who kept pretty much to himself and didn't neighbour with the young men and maidens. He was said to be vain behind his silence and to reckon himself a good deal cleverer than us Merripit people; but I never found him anything but well behaved and civil spoken to his elders, and I went so far sometimes as to ask his Uncle Amos why for he didn't like the man. Because the master of Furze Hill never did care about Ernest, though Joe Gregory, with whom the young fellow lived at Vitifer, thought very highly of him indeed.

And Amos confessed he hadn't got no deep cause to dislike his nephew.

"To be plain, 'tis a woman's reason and no more," admitted Amos. "Ernest have got a glide in his eye, poor chap, and God knows that's not a fault, and yet I never can abide that affliction and it would put me off an angel from heaven if the holy creature squinted."

It was a silly prejudice of the man, and in time I think he got it under and granted that you did ought to judge a person by their acts and not by their eyes; but human nature has its ingrained likes and dislikes, and I for one couldn't question Amos, because I hate a hunchback, and I wouldn't trust one of they humped people—man or woman—with anything that belonged to me. The broadest-minded of us have got a weak spot like that somewhere and hate some harmless thing if 'tis only a spider.

But, after he'd been along at Vitifer five years, I don't think a living soul felt anything but kindly to Ernest, and when it was rumoured that he'd got brave enough to go courting Sarah White from Postbridge, everybody wished him luck, including his uncles—especially Amos himself; for Joe's younger brother was very friendly to the Postbridge Whites, and them who thought they knew, always said how he'd offered for Jenny White twenty-five years before and might very like have won her if she hadn't loved the water-keeper on East Dart better and married him instead.

Then happened the wondrous mystery of Joe Gregory. 'Twas just before Christmas—rough stormy weather and not much doing on the high ground—when Joe set out early one morning for Exeter to see his lawyers. He'd done very well that year— better than Amos—and he was taking a matter of one hundred and fifty pounds in cash to Exeter for his man of business to invest for him. And Ernest drove him in to Ashburton, at cocklight of a stormy day, and was going in again that evening to meet his uncle and fetch him home.

All went well, and at the appointed time Joe's nephew set out once more with a light trap and a clever horse, after dark, to meet the evening train. And no more was heard till somewhere about ten o'clock of that night. Then Amos Gregory, just finishing his nightcap and knocking out his pipe to go to bed, uch to his astonishment heard somebody banging on the front door of Furze Hill. Guessing it was some night-foundered tramp, he cussed the wanderer to hell; but cussing was only an ornament in his speech, for a tenderer creature really never lived, and he wouldn't have turned a stray cat from his door that fierce night, let alone a human.

It weren't no tramp, however; it proved to be his nephew Ernest, and the young man was clad in his oilskins and dripping with the storm rain and so frightened as a rabbit.

In a word, he'd been to Ashburton and waited for the appointed train, only to find his uncle hadn't come back by it. And so he bided, till the last train of all, and still Joe hadn't turned up. So Ernest drove home, hoping to find a telegram had come meanwhile and been brought up from Merripit post office. But there weren't no telegram; and now he was properly feared and had come over to Amos to know what did ought to be done.

First thing to do, in the opinion of Amos, was to pour a good dollop of gin down Ernest's neck; then, when the shaking chap had got a bit of fight in him, he explained that till the morn they were powerless to take action.

"I know his lawyer, because Cousins and Slark be my lawyers also," said Amos; "and they always was the family men of business, so if us hear nought when the post office opens to-morrow, we'll send off a telegram to them; and if they've got nothing to say, then we must tell the police."

Ernest was a good bit down-daunted and said he felt cruel sure evil had over-got his uncle, and Amos didn't like it neither, for a more orderly man than Joe Gregory and one more steadfast in doing what he promised couldn't easily be found. However, they had to suffer till morning, and Ernest went back to Vitifer, which stood not quarter of a mile away.

Morning brought no letter nor yet telegram, so Amos went down to Merripit post office and sent a wire off to the Exeter lawyers axing for news of his brother; and he waited till an answer came down. It ran like this:

Mr. Gregory spent an hour with us yesterday and left at four o'clock to catch down train.
Cousins and Slark.

Well, that showed there was something wrong, and Amos felt he was up against it. He never let the grass grow under his feet, and in twenty minutes he was riding to Ashburton, to catch a train for Exeter. And afore he went, he directed Ernest to tell the police that his uncle was missing. So hue and cry began from that morning, and the centre of search was Exeter, because from there came the last sure news of the man. The lawyers made it clear that Joe was all right when he left them. He'd handed over his money to be invested, and he'd put a codicil to his will, which, of course, the lawyers didn't divulge to Amos. Then he'd gone off very cheerful and hearty to buy a few things afore he catched his train. But from that moment not a whisper of Joe Gregory could be heard. He wasn't a noticeable sort of chap, being small with an everyday old face and everyday grey whiskers; and nobody to the railway stations at Exeter or Totnes, where he would change for the Ashburton line, had seen him to their knowledge. Yet in the course of the next few days, when his disappearance had got in the papers, three separate people testified as they'd met Joe that evening, and Ernest Gregory was able to prove they must have seen right. The first was a tobacconist's assistant at Exeter, who came forward and said a little, countrified man had bought two wooden pipes from him and a two-ounce packet of shag tobacco; and he said the little man wore a billycock hat with a jay's blue wing feather in it. And a barmaid at Newton Abbot testified that she'd served just such a man at the station after the train from Exeter had come in, about five-thirty, and afore it went out. She minded the jay's feather in his hat, because she'd asked the customer what it was, and he'd told her. And lastly a porter up at Moretonhampstead said that a small chap answering to the description had got out of the Newton train to Moreton, which arrived at Moreton at fifteen minutes after six. But he'd marked no jay's feather in the man's hat and only just noticed him, being a stranger, as went out of the station with half a dozen other travellers and gave up his ticket with the rest. The tickets was checked, and sure enough, there were two from Exeter to Moreton; but while Ernest could prove the jay's feather to be in his uncle's hat, neither he nor anybody else could give any reason why Joe should have gone to Moreton instead of coming home. He might have left the train for a drink at Newton, where there was time for him to do so; but he would have gone back to it no doubt in the ordinary course. Asked if he came in alone for his drink, the barmaid said he did so and was prepared to swear that nobody spoke to him in the bar but herself. And he'd gone again afore the down train left. But at Totnes, where Joe was known by sight and where he ought to have changed for Ashburton, none had seen him.

The police followed the Moreton clue, but nobody there reported sight of Joe on the night he disappeared. He'd got a friend or two at Moreton; but not one had fallen in with him since the autumn ram fair, when he was over there with his nephew for the day.

The law done all in its power; the down lines were searched from Newton, and Amos Gregory offered a reward of fifty pounds for any news of his lost brother; but not a speck, or sign, of Joe came to light. A month passed and the nine days' wonder began to die down a bit.

I met Amos about then, and we was both on horseback riding to Ashburton, and he told me that he was bound for the lawyers, to make inquiry of how the law stood in the matter and what he ought to do about Vitifer Farm.

"My nephew Ernest, is carrying on there," he told me, "and he's a good farmer enough and can be trusted to do all that's right; but there's no money to be touched and I must find out if they'll tell me what have got to be done and how the law stands."

He was a lot cut up, for him and his brother had always been very good friends; and he was troubled for his nephew also, because Ernest had lost his nerve a good deal over the tragedy.

"He's taking on very bad and can't get over it," said Amos to me. "The natural weakness of his character have come out under this shock, and the poor chap be like a fowl running about with its head off. He never had more wits than please God he should have, and this great disaster finds him unmanned. He will have it his uncle's alive. He's heard of men losing their memory and getting into wrong trains and so on. But I tell him that with all the noise that's been made over the country, if Joe was living, though he might be as mad as a hatter, 'tis certain by now we should have wind of him."

"Certain sure," I said. "He's a goner without a doubt, and 'twill take a miracle ever to get to the bottom of this."

I was reminded of them words a fortnight later, for it did take a miracle to find the shocking truth. In fact you may say it took two. And one without the other might just as well not have happened. And 'tis no good saying the days of miracles be passed, because they ban't.

I heard later that the lawyers let Amos read his brother's will and got a power of attorney for him to act and carry on. And the will left Vitifer Farm to Amos, on the condition that he would keep on his nephew Ernest. It was four year old; and the codicil, that Joe wrote the day he disappeared, ordained that when Amos died, Vitifer shouldn't be sold to Duchy, but handed down to the next generation of the Gregorys in the shape of Ernest.

Well, Amos had no quarrel with that, and when he went home, he asked his nephew if he'd known about the codicil, and he said he had not. And when he learned of his uncle's kind thought for him, he broke down and wept like a child, till Amos had to speak rough and tell him to keep a stiff upper lip and bear himself more manly.

"If you be going to behave like a girl over this fearful loss, I shan't have no use for you at Vitifer," Amos warned the young chap. "You must face this very sad and terrible come-along-of-it same as I be doing. And you must show me what you're good for, else I may do something you won't like. This tragedy reminds me, Ernest," he said, "that I haven't made my own wil yet, and as you be my next-of-kin, if your poor uncle have gone home, that means you'll inherit Furze Hill also in course of time and be able to run a ring fence round both places. But that remains to be seen; and if you are going to show that you haven't got manhood enough to face the ups and downs of life, then I shall turn elsewhere for one to follow me and young Adam White, my godson, may hap to be the man."

He gave his nephew a bit more advice and told him he'd best to go on courting the maiden, Sarah White, to distract his mind.

."For you're the sort," said Amos, "that be better with a strong-willed woman at your elbow in my opinion, and if Sally takes you, I shall be glad of it."

So Ernest bucked up a bit from that day forth, and no doubt the fact that he was to have Vitifer in the course of nature, decided Sarah, for she agreed to wed the young man ten days afterwards, and Amos was pleased, and decided that the wedding should fall out next Easter.

Ernest Gregory, as we all marked, was a changed man from that hour; for though he was built to feel trouble very keen, he hadn't the intellects to feel it very deep, and in the glory of winning Sarah, he beamed forth again like the sun from a cloud. And nobody blamed him, because, whether your heart be large or small, a dead uncle, however good he was, can't be expected to come between a man and the joy of a live sweetheart, who has said "Yes" to him.

II

Then came a night of stars, and once again Amos Gregory was shook up to his heels by somebody running in hot haste with news just as the farmer was about to go to bed. And once more it was his nephew, Ernest, who brought the tale.

"I've found a wondrous pit in the rough ground beyond Four Acre Field," he said. "I came upon it this afternoon, rabbiting, and but for the blessing of God, should have fallen in, for the top's worn away and some big stones have fallen in. 'Tis just off the path in that clitter of stone beside the stile."

The young man was panting and so excited that his words tripped each other; but his uncle didn't see for the minute why he should be, and spoke according.

"My father always thought there was a shaft hole there," answered Amos, "and very likely there may be, and time have worn it to the light, for Vitifer Mine used to run out into a lot of passages that be deserted now, and there's the famous adit in Smallcumbe Goyle, half a mile away, to the west, long deserted now; and when I was a child, me and my brothers often played in the mouth of it. The place was blocked years ago by a fall from the roof. But why for you want to run to me with this story at such an hour, Ernest, I can't well say. Us ought to be abed, and Sarah will soon larn you to keep better hours, I reckon. You're a lot too excitable and I could wish it altered."

But the man's nephew explained. "That ain't all, Uncle Amos," he went on, "for I found Uncle Joe's hat alongside the place! There it lies still and little the worse—blue jay feather and all. But I dursn't touch it for fear of the law, and seeing it just after I'd found the hole, filled me with fear and terror. Because it looks cruel as if Uncle had pretty near got home that fatal night, and coming across by the field path in the dark, got in the rough and went down the pit."

Well, Amos had reached for his boots you may be sure before Ernest was to the end of his tale, and in five minutes he'd put on his coat and gone out with Ernest to see the spot.

Their eyes soon got used to the starlight, and by the time they reached the field called Four Acre, Amos was seeing pretty clear. In one corner where a field path ran from a stile down the side, was a stony hillock dotted with blackthorns and briars and all overgrown with nettles, and in the midst of it, sure enough, time and weather had broke open a hole as went down into the bowels of the earth beneath. And beside this hole, little the worse for five weeks in the open, lay Joe Gregory's billycock hat.

Amos fetched a box of matches out of his pocket, struck one and looked at the hat. Then he peered down into the black pit alongside, and, as he did so, he felt a heavy push from behind, and he was gone—falling down into darkness and death afore he knew what had happened. And in that awful moment, such a terrible strange thing be man's mind, it weren't fear of death and judgment, nor yet horror of the smash that must happen when he got to the bottom, that gripped Gregory's brain : it was just a feeling of wild anger against himself, that he'd ever been such a fool as to trust a man with a glide in his eye !

In the fraction of time as passed, while he was falling, his wits moved like lightning, and he saw, not only what had happened, but why it had happened. He saw that Ernest Gregory knew all about Joe and had probably done him in five weeks ago ; and he saw likewise that now it was his turn to be murdered. Then Vitifer and Furze Hill would both belong to the young man. All this Amos saw ; and he felt also a dreadful, conquering desire to tell the people what had happened and be revenged ; and he told himself that his ghost should come to Merripit if he had to break out of hell to come, and give his friends no rest till they was laid upon the track of his nephew.

All that worked through his brain in an instant moment, like things happen in a dream, and then he was brought up sudden and fell so light that he knew he weren't dead yet, but heard something crack at the same moment. And then Amos discovered he was on a rotten landing-stage of old timber, with the shaft hole above him and a head, outlined against the stars, looking down, and another hole extending below. He was, in fact, catched half-way to his doom and hung there with the devil above and the unknown deep below and hung up on the mouldering wood. He heard Ernest laugh then, and the sound was such as none had ever heard from him before—more like a beast's noise than a man's. Then his head disappeared and Amos was just wondering what next, when his nephew came to the hole again and dropped a great stone. It shot past the wretched chap where he hung, just touching his elbow, and then Amos, seeing he was to be stoned to make sure, called upon God to save him alive. He pressed back against the pit side, while the crumbling timber gave under him and threatened to let him down any moment, but the action saved his life, for the time being, for as he moved, down came another stone and then another. Where the joists of the stage went in, however, was a bit of cover for the unfortunate chap—just enough to keep him clear of the danger from above, and there he stuck, pressed to the rock like a lichen, with great stones going by so close that they curled his hair. All was black as pitch and the young devil up over had no thought that his poor uncle was still alive. Amos uttered no sound, and presently, his work done as he thought, Ernest began the next job and Gregory heard him making all snug overhead. Soon the ray of starlight was blotted out and the pit mouth blocked up with timber first and stones afterwards; and Amos doubted not that his young relation had made the spot look as usual and blocked it so as nothing less than the trump of Doom would ever unseal it again.

And even if that weren't so, he knew he could never climb up the five and twenty feet or more he'd fallen. Indeed, at that moment the poor chap heartily wished he was at the bottom so dead as a hammer and battered to pulp and out of his misery. For what remained? Nought but a hideous end long drawn out. In fact he felt exceeding sorry for himself, as well he might; but then his nature came to the rescue, and he told himself that where there was life there was hope; and he turned over the situation with his usual pluck and judgment and axed himself if there was anything left that he might do, to put up a fight against such cruel odds.

And he found there was but one thing alone. He couldn't go up and he felt only too sure the only part of him as would ever get out of that living grave was his immortal soul, when the end came; but he reckoned it might be possible to get down. The only other course was to bide where he was, wait till morning, and then lift his voice and bawl in hope some fellow creature might hear and succour. But as the only fellow being like to hear him was his nephew, there didn't seem much promise to that. He waited another half hour till he knew his murderer was certainly gone home ; then he lighted matches and with the aid of the last two left in his box scanned the sides of the pit under him. They were rough hewn, and given light he reckoned he could go down by 'em with a bit of luck and the Lord to guide his feet. Then he considered how far it might be to the bottom, and dropped a piece of stone or two, and was a good bit heartened to find the distance weren't so very tremendous. In fact he judged himself to be about half-way down and reckoned that another thirty feet or thereabout would get him to the end. He took off his coat then and flung it down ; and next he started, with his heart in his mouth, to do or die.

Amos Gregory promised himself that nought but death waited for him down beneath, and he was right enough for that matter. How he got down without breaking his neck he never could tell, but the pit sloped outward from below and he managed to find foothold and fingerhold as he sank gingerly lower and lower. A thousand times he thought he was gone. Then he did fall in good truth, for a wedge of granite came out in his hand ; but to his great thankfulness, he hadn't got to slither and struggle for more than a matter of another dozen feet, and then he came down on his own coat what he'd dropped before him. So there he was, only scratched and torn a bit, and like a toad in a hole, he sat for a bit on his coat and panted and breathed foul air. 'Twas dark as a wolf's mouth, of course, and he didn't know from Adam what dangers lay around him ; but he couldn't bide still long and so rose up and began to grope with feet and hands. He kicked a few of the big stones that Ernest Gregory had thrown down, as he thought atop of him ; and then he found the bottom of the hole was bigger than he guessed. And then he kicked a soft object and a great wonder happened. Kneeling to see what it might be, he put forth his hand, touched a clay-cold, sodden lump of something, and found a sudden, steady blaze of light flash out of it. He drew back and the light went out. Then he touched again and the light answered.

By this time Amos had catched another light in his brain-pan and knowed too bitter well what he'd found. He groped into the garments of that poor clay and found the light that he'd

P

set going was hid in a dead man's breast pocket. Then he got hold of it, drew out an electric torch and turned it on the withered corpse of his elder brother. There lay Joe and the small dried-up carcase of him weren't much the worse seemingly in that cold, dry place; but Amos shivered and went goose-flesh down his spine, for half the poor little man's face was eat away by some unknown beast.

Joe's brother sat down then with his brains swimming in his skull, and for a bit he was too horrified to do ought but shiver and sweat; and then his wits steadied down and he saw that what was so awful in itself yet carried in its horror just that ray of hope he wanted now to push him on.

His instinct was always terrible strong for self-preservation, and his thoughts leapt forward; and he saw that if a fox had bit poor dead Joe, the creature must have come from somewheres. Of course a fox can go where a man cannot, yet that foxes homed here meant hope for Amos; and there also was the blessed torch he'd took from his dead brother's breast.

He nerved himself and felt all over the poor corpse and found Joe's purse and his tobacco pouch and the two pipes he was reported to have bought at Exeter; and doubtless he'd bought the electric torch also, for Amos knew that his brother possessed no such thing afore. But there it was: he'd been tempted to buy the toy, and though it couldn't bring him back to life, there was just a dog's chance it might save his brother's. Amos knew the thing wouldn't last very long alight, so he husbanded it careful and only turned it on when his hands couldn't tell him what he wanted to know.

At first it seemed as though there weren't no way out; but with the help of the light, he found at last a little, low tunnel that opened out of the hole; and then he found another opposite to it. And the one he reckoned must run up under Vitifer into the thickness of the hill; while t'other pointed south. Then, thinking upon the lay of the land, Amos reckoned the second might be most like to lead to the air. And yet his heart sank a minute later, for he guessed—rightly as it proved—that the south tunnel was that which opened into a cave at Smallcumbe Goyle, near half a mile down under. A place it was where he'd often played his games as a child; but that ancient mine adit was well known to be choked by a heavy fall of rock fifty yards from the mouth, so it didn't look very hopeful he'd win through. However, his instinct told him the sole chance lay there; for t'other channel, if pursued, could only lead to the heart of the hill. He set out according and after travelling twenty yards with bent head, found the roof of the tunnel lift and went on pretty steady without adventures for a few hundred yards. 'Twas very evil air and he doubted if he'd keep his head much longer; but with the torch light to guide his feet, he staggered forward conscious only of one thing, and that was a great and growing pain in his elbow. That's where the first stone had grazed him that his nephew had thrown down the pit, and he stopped and found he was cut to the bone and bleeding a lot. The loss vexed him worse than the pain, for he knew very well you can't lose blood without losing strength, and he couldn't tell yet whether it might not be within his strength to save him at the other end. So he slit a piece off the tail of his shirt and tied it above his elbow so tight as he was able. Then he held on, but knew too well he was getting spent. For a man well over fifty year can't spend a night of that sort and find himself none the worse for it.

A bit farther forward there was a little more to breathe, and as the tunnel dropped, he felt the air sweeter. And that put a pinch more hope into him again. It was up and down with him and his mind in a torment, but at last he tried not to think at all, and just let his instinct to fight for life hold him and concentrated all his mind and muscle upon it. Yet one thought persisted in his worst moments: and that was, that if he didn't come through, his nephew wouldn't be hanged, but enjoy the two farms for his natural life; and the picture of that vexed Amos so terrible that without doubt 'twas as useful to help him as a bottle of strong waters would have been.

On he went, and then he had a shock, for the torch was very near spent and began to grow dimmer; so he put it out to save the dying rays against when he might need them. And he slowed down and rested for half an hour, then refreshed, he pushed slowly on again.

And things happened just as he expected they would do; for after another spell, he was brought up short and he found the way blocked and knew that he stood a hundred feet and no more from the mouth of the tunnel in a grass-grown valley bottom among the rocks outside. But he might as well have been ten miles away, and too well he knew it. The air was sweet here, for where foxes can run, air can also go; but outlet there was none for him, though somewhere in the mass of stone he doubted not there was a fox-way. He turned on the torch then and shifted a good few big stones and moved more; but he saw in half an hour the job was beyond his powers and that if he'd been Goliath of Gath he couldn't have broke down that curtain of granite single-handed.

He'd found a pool of water and got a drink and he'd satisfied his mind that his elbow bled no more, and that was all the cheer he had, for now his torch went out for good and with its last gleam he'd looked at his watch and seen that it was half after two in the morning. Night or day, however, promised to be all the same for Amos now, and he couldn't tell whether daylight would penetrate the fall of stone when it came, or if the rock was too heavy to allow of it. And in any case a gleam of morning wouldn't help him, for the Goyle was two good miles from Merripit village, and a month might well pass before any man went that way. Nor would Amos be the wiser if a regiment of soldiers was marching outside. So it looked as if chance had only put off the evil hour, and he sat down on a stone and chewed a bit of tobacco and felt he was up against his end at last. Weariness and chill as he grew cold acted upon the man, and afore he knew it he drew up his feet, rested his head on his sound arm, and fell into heavy sleep. For hours he slumbered and woke so stiff as a log. But the sleep had served him well and he found his mind active and his limbs rested and his belly crying for food.

He poked about and at last saw something dim that thrust out of the dark on the ground, and then it got brighter, and he marked low down, no higher than his knee, a blue ghost of light shooting through some cleft among the stones. It waxed until he could put down his watch and read the hands by it. And he found it was past six o'clock.

He set to work at the rocks again presently, but surrounded by darkness he didn't know where to begin and knew that a hungry man, with nought but his two hands, could make no great impression on all that stone; but he turned where the ray came through and putting his head to the earth, found there was a narrow channel out to the daylight, and wished he could take shape of a badger and so get through.

Time dragged and hope waned. But the water proved a source of strength, and Amos knew a man can hold out a long time if water ban't denied. His life passed through his mind with all its ups and downs, and he found time to be thankful even in all his trouble that he was a bachelor without wife or child to mourn him. And then his thoughts ran on to the great mystery there would be and the hunt after him; and he saw very clear indeed that all would go just as it done before, and the police would never find a trace, and Ernest Gregory would weep his eyes out of his head very near and offer a reward so large that everybody would say he was an angel barring the wings.

Amos was dwelling on what his nephew would get in the next world, to make up for his fun in this one, and marvelling in his simple mind that the wicked could flourish like the green bay tree and nothing be done against 'em by Providence, when that happened to fill his mind very full of his own affairs again.

He was sitting with his eyes on the shaft of daylight under the stones, when suddenly it went out and for a moment disappeared. But then, like a cork out of a bottle, something emerged, and Amos saw a long red thing sneak through and drop, panting, on its side not three yards from him. And well he knew what it was, even if the reek hadn't told him. 'Twas a hunted fox that had saved its brush—not for the first time belike—in the old tin mine working, and that meant more to the man than a sack of diamonds just then. He moved and the fox, little thinking to find an enemy on that side of the barrier, jumped to his feet and galloped up the passage so hard as he could pelt; while Amos strained his ears to the hole and prepared to lift his voice and have the yell of his life for salvation when the moment arrived.

How long the fox had stood afore hounds he couldn't tell; but long or short, they'd run him to the rocks for certain, and then the prisoned man would hear 'em and try to make the hunters hear him if he could. Hounds met at Dart Meet that day, and Gregory doubted not they'd found a fox as was had took 'em up East Dart and then away to the Vitifer mine district, where he knew he was safe.

And in ten minutes he heard hounds and in five minutes more they was got within a few yards of him, yelping and nosing t'other side of the granite. He guessed the huntsman would soon be with 'em at the cave mouth and presently gave tongue down the road the fox had come, and after shouting thrice with all his breath, waited, and sure enough heard an answering shout.

Yes, he'd been heard screaming for his life, and presently the men outside drew off the hounds and was able to get into conversation with Amos and larn the rights of his fearful story.

It was only a question of time after that and the field gave up hunting a fox to save a man. Labourers were sent for, and the rocks attacked in good earnest; and the huntsman did a very clever thing, for he sent his fox terrier through the hole to Amos with a packet of sandwiches tied on his back. Presently the little dog went in again with a bottle of cordial as one of the hunters gladly gave for the purpose, for Amos Gregory was well known for a good sport, and the field felt terrible glad as they'd been called to save him.

As soon as he was in communication with the outer world, Amos had ordered one thing to be done before all else, and it was done. So long before he'd got free, for it took five hours of desperate hard work to get to him, the police had done their bit elsewhere and arrested Ernest Gregory for the murder of his Uncle Joe. He was spreading muck on Four Acres Field at the time and called on God to strike the constables dead for doing such a shameful deed as to suspect him.

'Twas all in the newspapers next day, of course, and all men agreed that never was such an escape from death afore. In fact, my friend Amos was one of the wonders of the Dartmoor world for a long time afterwards. He never got back the full use of his elbow, but weren't a penny the worse any other way in a month and quite well enough to testify afore the law about all his adventures had showed him.

And Ernest turned out one of they vain murderers who be quite content to go down to history on the debit side so long as he's famous, if only for sin. He explained that Joe Gregory had always intended to come home from Exeter by way of Moreton, and that he had done so, and that Ernest had met him there and reckoned that particular wild, black night very well suited for putting the old man away. He knew all about the codicil to Joe's will, and having found the mine shaft months afore, used it as we know how. He'd took Joe to see it on getting home, and knocked him in, just as he'd treated Amos after. And 'twas all done for the land, which had become his god; and when Amos told his nephew he'd made no will, he was so good as signing his own death warrant.

They tried to fetch him in insane; but it didn't work with the jury nor yet the judge, and Ernest Gregory was hanged for his sins to Exeter gaol; and Sarah White, who had meant to wed him, felt terrible glad it happened before and not after the wedding.

As for Vitifer and Furze Hill, now both the property of Amos Gregory, no doubt Duchy will get 'em after all some day. In fact, Duchy always wins in the long run, as them mostly do who can afford to wait.

Our old parson preached a fine sermon on the affair after Ernest Gregory had gone to his reward; for he showed how by the wonderful invention of his Maker, Joe Gregory, though dead, yet was allowed to save his brother's life and so proclaim the wonder of God to sinful man. And no doubt all right-thinking people believed him.

Anyway, Amos set great store upon the electric torch ever after and it hangs above his mantelshelf to this day. And henceforth he always took off his hat to a fox whenever he seed one; for he was a very grateful sort of man and never forgot a kindness.

No. XIII
' SPIDER '

No. XIII

'SPIDER'

I

SURELY few things be sillier than the way we let human nature surprise us. For my part 'tis only the expected that ever astonishes me, for men and women have grown so terrible tricky and jumpy and irregular nowadays, along of better education and one thing and another, that you didn't ought to expect anything but the unexpected from 'em. And I never do.

So when Jenny Pardoe took Nicky White I dare say I was the only party in Little Silver that didn't raise an upstore and cackle about it, because to the common mind it was a proper shock, while to me, in my far-seeing way, I knew that, just because it was the last thing on earth you might have thought Jenny would do, it might be looked for pretty confident. She could have had the pick of the basket, for there was a good few snug men took by her nice figure and blue eyes and fine plucky nature; but no: she turned 'em all down and fell in love with Nicky White, or 'Spider,' as the man was called by all that knew him, that being the only possible name for the creature.

Under-sized, excitable and small-minded was 'Spider.' He had breadth and strength of body, but no more intellects than please God he wanted. He was so black as if he'd been soaked in a peat bog—black hair, black eyes, black moustache and black beard. A short, noisy man with long arms and hair so thick as soot on 'em. He owned Beech Cot on Merripit Hill when his mother died, and there he took Jenny after they was wed; and the people called 'em Beauty and the Beast.

Not that there was anything right-down beastly about Nicky but his spidery appearance. He would be kind to childer and never picked a quarrel with nobody—too cowardly for that;

but he was ugly as they make 'em and a sulky fashion of man. He had a silly, sensitive nature and a suspicious bent of mind. Such a man, with a wife as pretty as a June morning, was like to put a bit of a strain upon her; and he did, no doubt; for Nicky found himself cruel jealous of mankind in general where Jenny was concerned, and though there weren't no shadow of reason for it, he kept her mighty close and didn't like to think of her gossiping with the neighbours when he was away to work. At first she was rather pleased with this side of her husband, thinking jealousy a good advertisement, because it showed how properly he loved her; and there's no doubt no ugly little man ever had a more faithful and adoring wife. She thought the world of him and always said he was wonderful clever and much undervalued and good for far more important work and bigger money than ever he'd reached to. But that was her love blinding the woman, because in truth Spider had terrible poor thinking parts, and to cut peat, or cut fern, or lend a hand with a dry-built wall, or such-like heavy work was pretty much all as he could be trusted to do. And none the worse for that, of course. There's lots of work for good fools in the world; and there's lots of good fools to do it, if only the knaves would let 'em alone.

Well, all went proper enough with the Whites till Solomon Chuff came to Vitifer Mine as foreman, and he got to know 'em, and Jenny liked the man because he put her in mind of her dead father. He was ten years older than Spider—a big, handsome, clever chap with no vices in him; but there's no doubt he did like Jenny and found her suit him amazing well; and such was his innocence of all evil that once or twice he offered Spider a chance to growl. Once, for example, he over-got Jenny in the road by night and gave her a lift home in his trap. An innocent deed in all conscience, but Nicky didn't think so; for jealousy working in a silly man soon unseats his wits.

I pointed out to Spider, who was soon rampaging about him behind Chuff's back, that he had nought to fear. Because if the miner had been crooked, he'd have took care to give Jenny's husband no call for alarm.

" 'Tis granted," I said, " that any wife can hoodwink any husband if she wants to do so. No woman's such a fool but she's equal to that. In your case, however, you've got a partner that would sooner die and drop into her coffin than do anything to bring a frown to her husband's face, or a pang to his heart; while as for Solomon Chuff, he's far ways off the sort of man you think him, a more decent and God-fearing chapel member you'll not find."

But wisdom couldn't live with Spider. He was made to flout it and go his own sheep-headed way. He hadn't the pluck to stand up to Chuff and explain his grievances and tell the man he'd kill him if ever he crossed his threshold again, or ought honest and open like that. Instead he sulked and plotted awful things quite beyond his powers to perform; and then finally the crash came six months after he'd glumped and glowered over his silly fancies.

Spider went fishing one Saturday afternoon when the Dart was in spate and the weather fierce and wild. He'd been wild and fierce himself for a week, as his wife told after; but she didn't trouble about his vagaries and never loved him better than when he went off to catch some trout for her that dark afternoon in March. But he didn't return, and when she came down after dark to her aunt, Maria Pardoe, the washerwoman at Little Silver, and made a fearful stir about the missing man, the people felt sorry for her, and a dozen chaps went down the river to find Spider and fetch him along. His rod they found, and his basket and his bottle of lob-worms on the bank above a deep pool, but they didn't see a hair of the man himself; and when the next day came and a proper police search was started, nothing appeared, and it seemed terrible clear that Jenny's husband was a goner.

Some thought he'd just fallen in by chance and been swept to his death in the flood; while others, knowing the fool he was, whispered that he'd took his silly life along of fears concerning Solomon Chuff. But for my part I never thought so, because Spider hadn't got the courage to shorten his own thread. He was the sort that threaten to do it if they lose a halfpenny; but they don't perform. I reckoned he'd slipped in the bad light and gone under with none to save, and fallen in the river and been drowned like many another spider afore him.

Months passed and Jenny was counted a widow; but though she mourned like one and wore her black, she never could feel quite sure about her state; and when Bill Westaway, the miller's son, began to push into her company, she gave him to understand 'twas far too soon for any thoughts in his direction. In fact you might say she worshipped her husband's memory as her most cherished possession, and now he was gone, she never wearied of his virtues, and wept at the mention of his name. She'd had two years of him before he went, and there weren't no family and nothing to remind her of him but her own faithful heart. Never a worthless imp won a better woman.

And then—after a full year was told—happened the next thing. I well mind the morning Jenny come over to me, where I was digging a bit of manure into my garden against seed planting. A March day it was, with a soft mist on the moor and the plovers crying behind it, like kittens that want their mother.

"Might I have a tell, Mr. Bates?" she said.

"You might," I answered, "and I'll rest my back and light my pipe while you do so."

She was on the way to her aunt's wash-house, where she worked Mondays.

"'Tis like this," she said. "I've had a very strange, secret sort of a letter, Mr. Bates. It's signed 'Well Wisher,' and I believe it's true. Thank God I'm sure if it is."

She handed me the letter and I read it. There weren't much to it so far as the length, but it meant a powerful lot for Jenny. It ran like this:

Dear Mrs. White, your husband's working to Meldon Quarry, so don't you marry nobody else. Well Wisher.

"Say you believe it," begged the woman, when I handed her letter back to her.

"Whether 'tis true or not can quickly be proved," I answered. "And if it's true, then Spider's foolisher and wickeder than I thought him."

"I don't care how wicked he is so long as he's alive," she said.

"His one excuse for leaving you was to be drownded in the Dart, and if he ain't drownded, he's done a damn shameful thing to desert you," I told her. "However, you can put it to the proof. The world is full of little, black, ugly, hairy men like your husband, so you needn't be too hopeful; but I do believe it's true. Of course somebody may have seen his ghost; and to go and wander about at Meldon is just a silly thing his ghost might do; but I believe he's there—the fool."

"Where's Meldon Quarry?" she asked, and I told her.

"Beside Meldon Viaduct, on the railroad over Okehampton way. And what the mischief will you say to the wretch if you do find him?"

"Be very, very angry," answered Jenny—in a voice like a sucking dove.

"I'm sorry for Bill Westaway," I said. "He'd have made a much finer husband for you."

But she shook her head impatiently.

"I hate him!" she vowed. "I couldn't say for why, exactly; but there's something about him——"

"All's fair in love," I told her.

"I only love Nicky and I shall go to Meldon Quarry and not leave it again till he be found," she promised. "And don't tell Mr. Westaway, please. He'd be properly furious if he thought my dear husband wasn't drownded after all."

And at that moment if the miller's son didn't come along himself. A very tidy-looking chap, and a good worker, and a likely sort of man by all accounts. They left me and walked up the street together; and I heard afterwards what they talked about.

"How much longer are you going to hold off?" he asked. "You know I won't let you marry anybody on God's earth but me."

Jenny hid the great hopes in her mind, for she doubted if she could trust Will with the news.

"How can I marry anybody until I know Nicky is dead?" she inquired of the man, as she often had before.

"If he's alive, then that makes him a low-down villain, and you ought never to think of the creature again. If he's alive, he's happy without you. Happy without you—think of that! But of course he's not alive."

"Until we know the solemn, certain truth about him I'm for no other man," she told him; and her words seemed to give Will a notion.

"'The truth about him': that's an idea," he said.

"It is now a year since he went to fish and vanished off the earth," went on Jenny. "I've sometimes thought that the people didn't search half so carefully for the dear chap as what they might."

"I did, I'll swear. I hunted like an otter for the man."

"You never loved my husband," she said, shaking her head, and he granted it.

"Certainly I never did. Weren't likely I could love the man who was your husband. But I tried to find Spider, and I'll try again—yes, faith! I'll try again harder than ever. He's in the river somewheres—what be left of him. The rames* of the man must be in the water round about where he was fishing."

"What's the use of talking cruel things like that?"

"Every use. Why, if I was to find enough to swear by, you could give him Christian burial," said Will, who knew how to touch her—the cunning blade. "Think of that—a proper funeral for him and a proper gravestone in the churchyard. What would you give me if I was to fetch him ashore after all?"

Jenny White felt exceedingly safe with her promises now. She'd got a woman's conviction, which be stronger than a man's reason every time, that Spider was alive and kicking, and had run away for some fantastic jealousy or other foolishness. For the little man was always in extremes. She felt that once she faced him, she'd soon conquer and have him home in triumph very likely; and so she didn't much care what she said to Will that morning. Besides, the thought of giving the man a job that would keep him out of her way, for a week perhaps, rather pleased her.

"I'll give you anything I've got to give if you bring my poor

---

* Rames = Skeleton.

Nicky's bones to light," she said. "But it's impossible after all this time."

Will Westaway's mind was in full working order by now.

"Nought's impossible to a man that loves a woman like what I love you," he said. "How was the poor blade dressed the day he went to his death? Can you call home what he'd got on?"

"Every stitch down to his socks," she answered. "He'd got his old billycock hat and his moleskin trousers and a flannel shirt—dark blue—and a red-wool muffler what I knitted him myself and made him wear because it was a cruel cold afternoon. And his socks was ginger-coloured. They was boughten socks from Mrs. Carslake's shop of all sorts. He was cranky all that day and using awful crooked words to me. I believe he knew he weren't coming back."

"By God, he shall come back—what's left of him," swore Will. "If it takes me ten year, I'll go on till I find the skelington of your late husband or enough to prove he's a dead 'un. He shall be found, if only to show you what my love's worth, Jenny."

"Looking for the little man's bones in Dart would be like seeking a dead mouse in a haystack," she said.

"Difficult, I grant, but nothing to the reward you've promised."

"Well," she told him, "you can have me, such as I am, if you find Nicky."

Then she left William, and he turned over what she'd said. He was cunning and simple both, was Bill Westaway. He believed by now that Jenny really did begin to care a lot for him, and was giving him a chance in her own way to make good.

"An old billycock hat and a bit of red-wool muffler, the tail of a blue shirt, a pair of ginger-coloured socks," he thought. "It don't sound beyond the power of a witty man like me. But she'll want more than that. Us must find a bone or two as a doctor could swear by."

Full of dark, devilish ideas, the young man went his way; and Jenny got down the hill and walked in her aunt Maria Pardoe's wash-house as usual.

But she weren't herself by no means, and the first thing she done was to tear some frill-de-dills belonging to the parson's wife. Then she had another accident and so she went to Maria —the kindest woman on earth—and told her aunt she weren't feeling very clever this morning and thought she'd better go home. " 'Tis just a year since Nicky was took, as we all know," said Maria, " and no doubt you'm feeling wisht about it, my dear. But you must cut a loss like what your betters be often called to do. You must take another, Jenny, and be large-minded, and remember that there's better fish in the river than ever came out."

" Is Nicky in the river ? " asked Mrs. White. " I'm powerful certain he ban't, Aunt Maria."

" He's there," said the old woman, cheerfully. " Don't you worry about your first. He'll rise at the Trump along of all of us. His Maker won't forget even Nicky. And meantime he's just so peaceful under water as he would be in the Yard. And when you think of the fiery nature of the man, what is there better than peace you could wish him ? "

So Jenny went home and her great idea grew upon her, till by noon she'd built up her resolves and made ready for journeying.

And the very next day she was off and her house locked up, and a bit of paper with writing on it fixed up on the door.

Jenny White gone away for a bit. Please be kind to her yellow cat.

II

A good deal under the weather and terrible sorry for herself, Jenny set out to fetch over to Okehampton and see if her husband was alive or not. And if he was, it looked harder than ever to understand why for he'd left her. There weren't but one explanation as she could see, and that didn't make her feel no brighter. He'd done a thing only a madman would have done, which being so, he must be mad. She shed a good many tears on her way to find the man when she reached that conclusion ; but Nicky mad was better than no Nicky at all in her opinion, and such was her faithful love for the ugly little monkey that she held on and prayed to God in the train all the way from

Tavistock to Okehampton that Nicky might yet be saved alive and be brought back to his right mind. Because Jenny knew folk went mad and then recovered. So she was pretty cheerful again afore she alighted off the train at Okehampton; and then she hired a trap down to the 'White Hart' hotel, and drove out to Meldon Quarry with a fine trust in her Maker. She left the trap in the vale and climbed over a fence and began to look about her.

'Twas a great big place with scores of men to work nigh a mighty railway bridge of steel that be thrown over the river valley and looks no more than a thread seen up in the sky from below. And then, just when she began to feel it was a pretty big task to find her husband among that dollop of navvies and quarrymen, if she didn't run right on top of him! He was the first man of the lot she saw, and the shock took her in the breathing parts and very near dropped her. But she soon found that she'd have to keep all her wits if she wanted to get Nicky back, and the line she took from the first showed her a fierce battle of wills lay afore 'em.

It was going round a corner into the mouth of the quarries that she ran upon Spider wheeling a barrow; and she saw he was but little changed, save that he looked a good bit dirtier and wilder than of old. His hair was longer than ever and his eyes shone so black as sloes; and to Jenny's mind there was a touch of stark madness in 'em without doubt. He was strong and agile seemingly, and he began to gibber and cuss and chatter like an ape the moment he catched sight of her. He dropped the barrow and stared, and his jaw dropped and then closed up again. He drew up to his full height, which weren't above five foot, five inches, and he screamed with rage and began his talk with several words I ban't going to write down for anybody. Then he axed her how in the devil's name she dared to find him out and stand afore him.

"What do you mean, you vile woman?" he screamed. "Who told you I was here? I'll tear his heart out when I know who 'twas—and yours also—you hateful hell-cat!"

"Alive! Alive, thank God! They told me true," she cried. "Oh, Nicky!"

"Not alive to you," he answered. "I'm dead to you for evermore, so you can be gone again, so soon as you mind to. I know all about you and your goings on, and I ordain to strike at my appointed time and no sooner. And them as told you I was here shall suffer in their bones for it! So you clear out, or I'll pitch you over the quarry with these hands."

He picked up his barrow handles to push past her; but she was three inches taller than him and so strong as a pony; and she knew when you be along with a madman you've got to stand firm.

"Put that down and listen to me, Nicky," she said. "I ain't come all this way and spent eight shillings on a railway ticket and a horse and trap to be turned down without hearing my voice. Listen you shall—it's life and death for me, if not for you. I got a 'nonymous letter from a well wisher saying you was here and that's why I be come."

He heaped curses on her head and made horrible faces at her. He threatened to murder her on the spot if she went an inch nearer, and he picked up a great stone to do it with. In fact you'd have said he weren't at all the sort of man for a woman to fret at losing. But woman's taste in man be like other mysteries, and 'tis no good trying to explain why a nice, comely she such as his wife had any more use for this black zany.

"Devil—beast!" he yelped at her. "For two pins I'd strangle you! How have you got the front to dare to breathe the same air with the man you've outraged and ruined?"

"Do as you please and strangle me and welcome, Nicky; but listen first. Us'll have everything in order if you please. First read that. Somebody here—I don't know from Adam who 'twas—wrote to tell me you were working to Meldon; and that's how I've found you."

He read the letter and grew calmer.

"As to that," he said, "I've told a good few stonemen of my fearful misfortunes and what I meant to do; and one of 'em has gone back on me and given my hiding-place away to you; and if I knew which it was, I'd skin the man alive. But I'll find out."

"So much for that then," answered his wife, "and the next

thing be to know why you are in a hiding-place and what you're hiding from. And if I was you, I'd come home this instant moment and explain after you get back."

"Home!" he screamed. "You say 'home!' A nice home! D'you think I don't know all—every tricky wicked item of your plots and your wickedness? D'you think I don't know you be going to marry Solomon Chuff? You stare, you foul slut; but I know, and that's what I'm waiting for. So soon as the man have took you, then I was coming back to turn you out of my house—my house, you understand! I was only waiting for that, and when Chuff thinks he's settled in my shoes, I'll be on to him like a flame of fire, and he'll call on the hills to cover him. And I won't take you back—don't think it. I'm done with you for evermore and all other beasts of women."

"Aw Jimmery!" cried his wife. "I'm hearing things! And where did you larn these fine lies if I ban't axing too much?"

"From a friend," he said. "I've got one good and faithful friend left at Postbridge, and thanks to him, I've had the bitter truth these many days."

"Would it surprise you to hear, Nicky, that Solomon Chuff's tokened to Miller Ley's oldest daughter? They be going to wed at Easter, and 'twas Alice Ley herself that told me about it a month ago and I wished her joy."

"Liar! I know better, and Bill Westaway knows better. Yes, you may gape your hateful eyes out of your head; but Bill Westaway's my friend; and he's straight; and he's took good care to keep me in touch with the facts ever since I came here—so now then! You was after Chuff from the minute he went to Vitifer Tin Mine, and I knew it. I weren't blind to the man and I soon saw my revenge—fearful though it was."

"A funny sort of revenge," said Jenny, smiling at him. "I'm afraid, my poor little man, your revenge have come back on your own silly head. You've seen Bill Westaway, have you?"

"Yes, I have. And you needn't think to bluff it off. Every three months since I went away he's been over here to tell me how my vengeance was working."

"He knew all about your plot then, and that you weren't in the river?"

"He did so. A likely thing a man like me would drown hisself for a woman like you. And terrible sorry he felt to bring me the fatal news of what you was up to, though well I knew you would be. Nought astonished me. I knew you'd wait a year, to save your shameful face, and then take Chuff."

"What a world!" said Jenny. "What dark, hookem-snivey creatures be in it—men most times. Do you know who's been pestering me to marry him ever since the people all thought you'd fallen in the river and was drownded, Nicky? Not Mr. Chuff, but Billy Westaway himself. He's your rival, my dear, and none other. Fifty times has that man called on me to take him."

"You cunning liar! He hates women worse than I do."

"D'you know where he is this minute? Down on Dart pretending to hunt for your bones. God's my judge, Nicholas White, if I ain't telling you the truth."

The little wretch stared at her, and saw truth in her eyes, and felt all his idiotic vengeance slipping away from him. He didn't want to believe in her and made another struggle.

"What rummage be you talking, woman? Do you think you can sloke me off with this stuff? Westaway's my friend through thick and thin. Be you mad, or me?"

"Neither one nor t'other," she answered. "I thought to find you mad naturally; but I'm not the sort to shirk my duty, whatever you are. For better, for worse I took you, and I'd meant, if I found you cracked, to put you away nice and comfortable in a proper asylum, where they'd look after you, as became an unfortunate man with good friends. But you're not mad, only deceived by a damned rascal. Drop that rock and come here and listen to me."

He obeyed her and crept a foot or two nearer.

"What's happened be this," she said. "The Almighty have punished us for loving each other too well. I've worshipped you and, till Solomon Chuff came along, you worshipped me. And God wouldn't stand for such wickedness on our part, so He threw dust in your eyes and led you out into the wilderness—to home with a lot of navvies and be deceived by a rare rascal. And you've had your dose by the look of you; and I've had mine; and what I've suffered you'll never know, I assure you."

He went whiter than a dog's tooth behind his black hair, and his eyes bulged on her. He crept a bit nearer and she held out her hand. But the little loony had got his pride yet.

"I ban't so sure," he said. "No doubt you've come with a tale; but you'll have to hear me first. Your tongue be running a thought too smooth I reckon. How do I know this is truth? Why should I believe you afore Bill? He's sworn on his oath that Chuff spends half his time along with you and the banns be called. He's come, as I tell you, off and on, to let me know everything, and never a good word for you."

"You ought to break his neck," said Jenny. "However, you ain't heard all yet. It may interest you to know that at last I've promised to marry—not Chuff—he's old enough to be my father—but Bill himself."

"And you've come here to tell me that?"

Nicky looked round for his stone again.

"No, I have not. I've come firstly to forgive you, which be a lot more than you deserve, and secondly to take you home."

"'Tis for me to forgive you I reckon; and why for should I?"

"I've worn black for a year and prayed for your soul and eaten the bread of tears and lived like the widow-woman I thought I was—just lived in the memory of our beautiful life together," she says. "That's all you've got to forgive, Nicky. And it didn't ought to be partickler hard I should think. Poison—poison—that's what you've been taking—poison—sucking it down from Bill Westaway, like a little child sucks cream."

"And you tell me you're going to marry the man—or think you are? What's that mean?"

Spider had come right alongside of her now.

"On one condition I shall certainly marry him, so you needn't pull no more faces. I told him I'd take him if he found all that was left *of you in the river*! And so I will."

"But I ban't in the Dart! I ban't in the Dart! I'm alive!" cried Nicky—as if she didn't know it.

"Working along with these quarry men have made you dull seemingly," she answered. "It is true no doubt that you ban't in the Dart; but that's no reason why Billy Westaway shouldn't find you there. He's quite clever enough for that. He's a cunning, deep rogue, and I'll lay my life he'll find you there. He's separated us for a whole bitter year, to gain his own wicked ends, and if you can't see what he's done you must be mad after all."

"And what if I refuse to come back?" he asked, his monkey face still working.

"Then I'll marry Bill—rascal though he is. When I look into the past and think how he used to tell me you were running after the girls behind my back! But did I believe him? No! I boxed his ears and told him where the liars go. I didn't run away and hide from my lawful husband."

Nicky took it all in very slow.

"I'll have such a fearful vengeance on that dog as never was heard about!" he swore. "Strike me blind if I don't! I'll strangle him with these hands afore the nation."

"You can tell about that later," she said. "Meantime you'd best forget your kit and come home this minute. You've grown cruel rough and wild seemingly. You want me after you."

"I shall calm in fullness of time," he told her, "and no doubt be the same as ever I was before this fearful affair happened. I never thought to take off my clothes, nor yet wash again. I've been like a savage animal with such troubles as I've suffered; but now, thank the watching God, my woes be very near passed seemingly, and I've got my honour and my pride and a wife and a home also."

"Come back to 'em then!" begged Jenny, and the little creature put his spider arms around her and pressed her to his shirt.

"You must certainly wash again, and the sooner the better," she said; then she kissed his hairy muzzle and patted his head and thanked the Lord for all His blessings. As for Spider, he pawed her and called upon heaven and wept out of his dirty eyes.

"It is almost too much," he said; "but mark me, I'll never rest no more till I've took my revenge on that anointed devil from hell and torn his throat out!" Knowing the nature of the man, however, Jenny didn't fret too much about that. They went afore the master of the works presently, and being a human sort of chap, he took a sporting view of the situation and let Spider go along with his wife; which he did do. He had certainly suffered a good bit one way and another, owing to his own weak-minded foolishness, and found himself meek as a worm afore Jenny and terrible thankful to be in sight of better times.

"I wanted to die, too," his silly wife assured him; "but Providence knew better and saw the end from the beginning."

"Providence shan't be forgot," promised Nicky. "I'll turn over a new leaf and even go to chapel I shouldn't wonder —after I've done in William Westaway."

III

They spent that night at Plymouth, and she made Nicky scrap his clothes and get a new fit out; and the next day she took him home. No doubt her yellow cat was terrible pleased to see the pair of 'em; but the home-coming had its funny side too, for none marked them arrive—'twas after dark when they did so—and they'd only just finished their meal, when come heavy footsteps up the path, and Jenny well knew the sound of 'em.

"'Tis Bill Westaway!" she said. "He don't know as I've been away and no doubt he's found what he's pretending to search for. Slip in here, afore I let him come in, then you'll hear all about yourself."

There was a cupboard one side of the kitchen fireplace, and being quite big enough to take in Spider, he crept there, and his wife put home the door after him, but left a little space so as he could hear. And then she went to the cottage door and let in the visitor. 'Twas William sure enough, and his face was long and melancholy.

"A cruel time I've had—more in the river than out of it," he said. "I'm bruised and battered and be bad in my breathing parts also along of exposure and the wet. I dare say I've shortened my life a good bit ; but all that was nothing when I thought of you, Jenny. And now I'm terrible afraid you must face the worst. I've made a beginning, I'm sorry to say." He drew a parcel from under his arm and laid out afore her the wreck of a water-sodden billycock hat, a rag of a dark-blue flannel shirt and one ginger-coloured sock in a pretty ruinous state.

"What d'you make of these here mournful relics ?" he asked. "Without doubt they once belonged to your Spider, and where I found 'em I'm afraid his poor little bones ain't far off."

"They be even nearer than you think, William Westaway," she said. "In fact, I've found 'em myself."

"Found 'em !" he gasped out, glazing with his shifty eyes at her and a miz-maze of wonder on his face.

"Found 'em—not in the Dart neither ; but at Meldon Quarry. Nicky is alive and well, and you know it, and you always knew it. And your day of reckoning be near ! "

She paused. You might have thought she'd expect for her husband to leap out of the cupboard, but he didn't ; he bided close where he was, like a hare in its form ; and she knew he would.

Of course Bill Westaway felt a good bit disappointed. He cussed Spider up hill and down dale and poured a torrent of rude words upon him.

"That know-nought, black swine come back ! And you put him afore the likes of me ! You don't deserve a decent man," he finished up. "And the patience and trouble I've took, thinking you was worth it ! "

"Go !" she said. "You're a wicked, bare-faced scamp, and God, He'll reward you. You did ought to be driven out of Little Silver by the dogs, and no right-thinking person ever let you over their drexels * no more."

---

* Drexels = Thresholds.

"I'm punished enough," he told her. "Good-bye, my silly dear! A thousand pities you've took that little worm back. You'd have grown very fond of me in time. I'm worth a wagon-load of such rubbish as him."

He lit his pipe, cussed a bit more, hoping Spider would front him, and then went away, banging the gate off its hinges very near ; and after he was well clear of the premises Nicky bounced out of his cupboard full of brimstone and thunder.

"Lock the door," he said, " or I'll be after him and strangle him with these hands!"

"I most feared you'd have blazed out and faced the wretch," said Jenny—to please the little man.

"I managed to hold in. I drew out my knife however ; but I put it back again. I hadn't got the heart to spoil the night of my home-coming. His turn ain't far off. His thread's spun. Nothing short of his death be any good to me —not now."

"Us'll forget the scoundrel till to-morrow, then," said Mrs. White.

It was six months later and summer on the wane, when I met a fisherman on the river—a gent I knew—and made him laugh a good bit with the tale of they people.

"And what did Spider do after all, Mr. Bates?" inquired the fisher, when I came to the end of the story, and I answered him in a parable like.

"When the weasel sucked the robin's eggs, sir, the robin and his wife was properly mad about it and swore as they'd be fearfully revenged upon him."

"And what did they do?" axed the gentleman.

"What could they do?" I axed him back.

"Nothing."

"That's exactly what they did do ; and that's exactly what Nicky White done—nothing. Once—in the street a bit after he'd come home—Will Westaway turned round and saw Spider making hideous faces at him behind his back. So he walked across the road and smacked the little man's earhole and pulled his beard. Nought happened, however."

"And what became of William Westaway?"

"Well, most of us was rather sorry for him. He'd took a lot of trouble to queer Spider's pitch and put up a mighty clever fight for Jenny, you see. But the woman liked her little black beetle best. In fact she adores him to this day. Billy married a very fine girl from Princetown. But I reckon he never felt so properly in love with her as what he did with Mrs. White."

No. XIV
THE WOODSTACK

No. XIV

THE WOODSTACK

As butler at Oakshotts I was a busy man no doubt, with a mighty good master who knew he'd got a treasure. Because wine and tobacco be second nature to me, and though very sparing in the use of both, I have great natural gifts and a sort of steadfast and unfailing judgment for the best. And as master be fond of saying in his amusing way, the best is always good enough for him, so Sir Walter Oakshott of Oakshotts trusted in me, with great credit to himself and applause from his guests. Never was such an open-handed man, and being a widower at fifty, with no mind just then to try again, he let his sociable instincts run over for his friends, and Oakshotts, as I sometimes said, was more like an hotel than a country house. For he had his gardening pals come to see his amazing foreign rhododendrons in spring, and his fishermen pals for his lakes and river-banks in summer; while so soon as September came, it was sportsmen and guns and dogs till the end of the shooting season.

So I was a busy man and also a prosperous, because money cleaves to money and Sir Walter's friends were mostly well-to-do, though few so rich as him; and the gentlemen were experienced and knew a butler when they met one.

But few be too occupied for romance to over-get 'em sooner or later, and at forty I fell in love—a tiresome thing at that age and not to have been expected from a bachelor-minded man same as me. And if I'd had the second sight and been able to see where the fatal passion was going to take me, I'd have kept my eyes off Jenny Owlet very careful indeed.

But so it was, though fifteen years separated us there's little doubt Jenny loved me very well afore Tom Bond appeared. Because I'd never loved before I saw her, and even an elderly man —and a butler's always elderly by virtue of his calling—has a charm to the female mind if she knows he's never loved before. In me Jenny saw a well-set-up and personable party, inclined a thought to a full body, but smart and active, clean-shaven and spotlessly clean every way, with brown eyes and a serious disposition, yet a nice taste for a seemly bit of fun. My hair was black and kept sleek and short, of course, and my voice was slow and deep, and my natural way of approaching all women most dignified, whether they belonged to the kitchen or the drawing-room. And, of course, she well knew I was a snug man and her worldly fortune would be made if she came to me. That was what I had to offer, while for her part she was a high-spirited thing and good as gold, aged twenty-five, with a cheerful nature and a great art for taking what pleasure life had to offer the second kitchen-maid at Oakshotts, which weren't very much. But she never groused about her hard career, or was sorry for herself, or anything like that. I liked her character and I liked her good sense and I much liked her nice and musical voice; and if she'd been educated, she'd have shone among the highest by reason of her back answers, which I never knew equalled. Not that she had any chances in that direction with me, because I'm not a man to let my inferiors joke with me, though none knows how to put 'em in their place quicker than I do.

Her eyes were betwixt blue and grey and sometimes favoured one colour and sometimes t'other, and her hair was a light brown and her figure inclined to the slim. But she was very near about five foot eight—two inches shorter than me—and of an amazing activity and enjoying most perfect health. Her home was in Little Silver, which is our village; and only poverty and the need for work had took her out of it. There she tended her widowed father, and he had such a passion for the girl, her being his only one, that 'twas only the shadow of the Union Workhouse ever steeled him to part from her. But she saw him oftener than her day out and would many a time run like a lapwing the mile to his cottage, so as he should have a glimpse of her. And it was her wages that helped the man to carry on. He hated her working at Oakshotts and prayed ceaselessly to her to come back and starve along with him, for he was a very unreasonable fashion of man—a dog-like man with one idea and one worship and one religion, you may say. In fact he lived for Jenny alone, and when I came to be acquaint with him, I feared it was to be war to the knife between us. He always proved queer and difficult, and nought but my great love for Jenny would have made me tolerate a man like Joshua Owlet for a moment.

You couldn't absolutely say there was a screw loose in him, because to love your only child with all right and proper devotion is in the order of nature; but to come between a daughter and her future mate, when the mate was a man like me, seemed weak-minded, to say no more. A very selfish man in fact, and the thought of Jenny having a home of her own away from him, though to any decent father a right and proper thing to happen, got Joshua Owlet in a rage, and I had to exercise unbounded patience. He was a small-brained man, and that sort is the most obstinate.

"Such a woman be bound to wed, Mr. Owlet," I told him, "and lucky for you in your humble way of life that she's fallen in with one that can make her a home worthy of her and lift her up in the land. And if you love her so fierce, surely the first thing you did ought to feel is that, when she takes me, your mind will be at rest about her for evermore. I ain't retiring yet and, be it as it will, I'm Devonshire, and the home I determine upon won't be very far ways off, and she'll be within call and you'll find yourself welcome under my roof in reason."

He scratched in his grey beard and looked at me out of his shifty eyes, and if looks could have killed he'd have struck me dead, for he was a malicious sort of man and a pretty good hater. Owlet wore rags for choice and he picked up a living making clothes-pegs and weaving osier baskets. That was his mean fashion of life, and he was allowed to get his material down in Oakshotts swamps, where the river overflowed and the woodcock and snipe offered sport in winter. But the keepers hated Owlet poking about, because they said he took more than withies from the osier beds.

Well, the man most steadfastly refused to sanction the match and held off and cussed and said he was Jenny's duty and she didn't ought to dream of leaving him under any conditions.

Of course he held no power over her and at heart she never liked him very much, because he'd served her mother bad and she remembered it. But she told me straight that I was first, father or no father, and that she'd come to me when I was ready to take her. So I could afford to feel no fear from Joshua and went my own way and dwelt on a clever scheme by which I'd bide along with Sir Walter after marriage and see my wife uplifted in the establishment—to help the housekeeper or something like that. For well I knew my master would pleasure me a long way before he'd lose me. I'd served him steadfast and we'd faced death together in the Great War.

And so I settled down in my usual large and patient spirit and just kept friendly touch with Jenny's father and no more. Nor did Jenny say much upon the future when she was home, and so, no doubt, Joshua got to hope he'd have his way in the long run.

And then came Tom Bond upon the scene of action and the fearful affair of the woodstack began to take shape. We wanted a new first footman, and he offered, and his credentials looked so right that Sir Walter, in his careless way, didn't bother about 'em, seeing by his photograph that Tom was a good-looking man and hearing he stood six feet two inches. And certainly, after his arrival, nobody thought no more of his character, for a cleverer and more capable chap you couldn't wish to meet. He knew his job from A to Z, and I will say here and now that, merely regarded as a first footman, Tom was never beat in my experience. He had an art to understand and anticipate my wishes and a skill to fall into my ways that gave me very great satisfaction, and he pleased the gentlemen also and shone in the servants' hall. In fact I seldom liked a young man better, and what followed within six months of his arrival came as a fearful shock upon me, because by that time I'd grown to feel uncommon friendly to the wretch.

He was amazing good-looking, with curly hair and blue eyes and very fine teeth. And he was one of those men that win the women by their nice manners and careful choice of words. You never heard him speak anything unbecoming, and he was just as civil to the humblest as he was to the housekeeper herself. A care-free man seemingly, with his life before him and such gifts that he might be expected to make a pretty good thing of it. An orphan, too, or so he said.

Thirty-two he claimed to be, but I judged him to be a bit more in reality.

Then came the fatal cloud. Knowing that I was engaged to Jenny, he took good care to keep the right side of her on my account, but all too soon there dawned the making of the future tragedy and he was pleasuring her for her own sake. He hid his games from me, of course, and it was an easy thing to do, because I stood above any suspicion with regard to Jenny; but a time came when he didn't hide his games from her, and it was only when I began to see queer signs about her I couldn't read that any uneasiness overgot me. I do think most honest that she didn't know what was happening to her for a long time, because she loved me, or thought she did; but little by little her old gladsome way along with me wilted and I found her wits wandering. She'd be dreaming instead of listening to my discourse, and then she'd come back to herself and squeeze hold of my hand, or kiss me, and ask me to say what I'd just said over again. I passed it off a lot of times, and then on the quiet had a tell with her father, thinking, maybe, if there was anything biting her, he might know it.

But he said little. He only scowled and glowered and wriggled his eyebrows like a monkey—a nasty trick he had.

" If there's trouble on her mind," said Joshua, " you may lay your life it's the thought of deserting a lonely father. And if conscience works in her, as I hope to God it will, then you'll find yourself down and out yet, William Morris."

That's how he talked to me; but my great gift of patience never deserted me with Owlet, and seeing he knew nothing about any real disquiet in his daughter's head, I left it at that and hoped I was mistook.

Mighty soon I found that I was not, however, and then, in the hour for my daily constitutional, which I never missed, rain or shine, I turned over the situation and resolved to approach Jenny on the subject and invite a clean breast of it.

There was a woodman's path ran on the high ground behind

Oakshotts, and here I seldom failed to take an hour's walk daily for the sake of health. Up and down I'd go under the trees in the lonely woods, and mark the signs of nature and rest my mind from the business of the house. And sometimes Jenny would come along with me, but oftener I went alone, because our regular afternoon out gave me the opportunity for her company and she couldn't often break loose other times.

There was an ancient woodstack on the path hid deep in undergrowth of laurels and spruce fir, and not seldom in summer I'd smoke a pipe with my back against it ; but oftener I'd tramp up and down past it, where it heaved up beside the narrow way. They was always going to pull it down, but there never rose no call for wood and it was let bide year after year—a very picturesque and ancient object.

During an autumn day it was that I went there, with the larches turned to gold and the leaf flying from the oaks and shining copper-red on the beech trees. And I resolved once for all to challenge Jenny upon her troubles, because if her future husband couldn't throw no light on 'em and scour 'em away, he must be less than the man I took him for.

I'd about spent my hour and was turning back to the house half a mile below when Jenny herself came along, well knowing where I was ; and so I wasted no words, but prepared to strike while the thought of her set uppermost in my mind. She spoke first, however, and much surprised me. 'Twas her way of breaking into the matter did so, and she well knew that what she had to tell would let the cat out of the bag.

" William," she said, " I couldn't bear for you to hear the thing what's happened except from me, and I want for you to be merciful to all concerned."

She was excited and her hair waving in the autumn wind so brown as the falling leaves. Her eyes were wild also, and her mouth down-drawn, and a good bit of misery looked out of her face.

" I'm known for a merciful man where mercy may be called for, my lovely dear," I said to her. " Us'll walk up and down my path once more since you've come. I've long known there was a lot on your mind and went so far as to ask your father what it might be; but he only said 'twas your conscience up against you leaving him."

" 'Tis my conscience all right," she answered, " but not like that—a long sight more crueller than that. Tom Bond has gone to see father this afternoon and—oh, William, I wish I was dead!"

I kept my nerve, for that was the only hope in her present frame of mind.

" 'Tis a very ill-convenient thing for my future wife to wish she was dead," I told her; " and why for has Tom gone to see your father? Mr. Owlet ain't the sort of man to find a gay young spark like Tom much to his taste."

"You must listen," she said, "and God forgive me for saying what I'm going to say, but I can't live a lie no more, William, and Tom can't live a lie no more. He loves me and I love him. I thought I loved you, and do love you most sure and true and never better than now; but I don't love you like I love him."

Then she poured it all out—how they'd found their real selves in each other and so on—and I couldn't make up my mind on the instant whether she spoke true, or whether she only thought she did. Being a proud sort of man, I very well knew that there'd be no great fuss and splutter on my side in any case, nor yet no silly attempts to keep her if her heart was gone; but she appeared so excited and so properly frantic and so torn in half between what she felt for Tom Bond and what she felt for me, that I perceived how I must go steady and larn a lot more about the facts before I stood down. There was my self-respect, of course, but there was also my deep affection for the girl. What did amaze me was that I'd never seen the thing unfolding under my eyes, and that none of the staff had called my attention to it. But none had—man or woman—and when, afterwards, I asked one or two of the elder ones if they'd marked any improprieties I ought to know about, all said they had not. So that was another feather in Tom Bond's cap in a manner of speaking, for he'd made amazing sure of his ground and got himself safe planted in Jenny's affections without giving one sign, even to my eyes, that he was up to any wickedness.

I knew he was clever, but shouldn't have thought anybody

could be so clever as that with the woman of my choice. And I knew, only too well, that Jenny must have been amazing clever also. I calmed her down and showed no spark of anger and didn't say a hard word against Bond; but that night, after dinner, I bade him come in my pantry and tell me what he'd been doing. Because a lot turned in my mind on the way he was going to state the case, and I weren't in no yielding mood to him. Words flowed from the man, like feathers off a goose, and under his regrets and shame, and all the rest of it, was a sort of a hidden note of triumph, which I didn't like at all, because it showed he was contemptuous of me at heart and knew he'd got the whip-hand.

"It's this way, Mr. Morris," he said. "I have nothing much to tell you that will excuse what's happened. I knew you were engaged to her and all that; and God's my judge, I never dreamed to come between; but nature's stronger than the strongest, and I hadn't been here six months before I knew it was life or death between me and Jenny. I fought it down and so did she, and we suffered a terrible lot more than you'll ever know or guess; but such things happen every day and true love never did run smooth. But the truth of what has happened you can see on her face, and nought will ever change her again. And I'm the sun to your moon if you'll excuse my saying so. And the triumph to have won such a woman is all lost for me, because I know a man like you—so straight and honest—will never understand such a thing and find it hard to pardon. It will darken our lives, no doubt, that she made such a fatal mistake and thought she loved you and made you think the same; but you're old enough to know that girls make that mistake every day of their lives, and think love's come to 'em before it has, and only know the difference when the true and only man appears afore 'em."

He ran on like that, and I marked that his old, straight glance was gone. There was a new expression in his eyes and a sort of suggestion that he was tired of the subject and only concerned to save his face and let me out so quick as might be. He spoke like a conqueror, in fact, and I well knew he didn't care a farthing for my feelings under his pretence that he did.

But I weren't going to let him out quite so easy. I'd seen war, which Tom Bond had not, for I'd been my master's batman at the front and was known for a brave man, though not a warrior like Sir Walter. So I weren't going to be swept aside as a thing of no account in the matter, and I meant to know a lot more about Bond himself before I went out of the game and handed Jenny over.

When he had done I spoke and went on polishing while I did so :

"A man who would have run into this bad work open-eyed is a man who'll need a power of thinking about," I said to him. "On your own showing you've played a very dirty and devious trick to win this woman, or try to do so, and it lets light on a side of your character I'd overlooked because, no doubt, you was parlous quick to hide it. You knew Jenny Owlet had ordained to marry me at her own wish and desire, and, knowing that, you made love to her and was sloking her affection away, while all the time I befriended you and praised you and set store upon you. And that's both ends and the middle of it. And no call to bleat about nature, because nature's a heathen thing, and you well knew it was no time to yield to any temptations that would make you a knave if you did yield to 'em. And I'm still minded to think the woman would be a lot happier and safer with me than ever she'd find herself with a man that could do what you've done. And that I say though I may be 'the moon to your sun.'

"So for the present, till I've had more truck with her and got to the bottom of her feelings and put reason and decency afore her, I'll ask you to behave and keep off her. She's engaged to marry me at this minute, whatever the pair of you think to the contrary, and I hold her to that undertaking until I am well satisfied it would be better for her if I broke it. So now you watch out, or you'll find yourself in a tighter place than you ever was before."

I threatened on purpose, to see how he'd take it ; and I found he took it ugly.

He showed his beautiful teeth and his brow came down and his eyes flashed.

"You'll fire me, I suppose?" he said. "That's the reward of being honest and straight; and much good that will do you. You won't win her back, because she's gone, and well you know it; and now you're going to bully me and rob me of my job."

"Go," I answered the man, "and don't be a fool. If you've lived along with me for near a year, you well know I bully none. I shan't fire you; but I order this and no more or less: keep off her till I'm satisfied about you and satisfied about her. And keep off her father likewise. Joshua Owlet has got a screw loose where his daughter is concerned and it won't advance nothing if you go to him. Now be off."

He made no answer, but I pointed to the door and he cleared out.

We were busy at the time and the house full of gentlemen, for it was half through October and shooting in full swing. So I left it at that for a bit and avoided Jenny also till her afternoon out; and then I told her we'd walk together and drink tea at the Wheatsheaf in Little Silver. Which we did do, and I explained the position and bade her hold off Tom until she heard me on the subject again. She was a lot cut up about it and poured scorn on herself and appeared very wishful to please me in the matter; but there wasn't no more love-making, of course; and to make Jenny understand the gulf that now separated us, I let her pay for her own tea. I loved her still most ardent, but I meant for everything to be done decent and in order; and so far as I am able to see, both of 'em fell in with my wishes and waited for my future commands.

Then a most amazing thing fell out, and Jenny, who had spent an afternoon with her father, told me he was very wishful to see me. So I called on the man and heard news that astonished me a good bit.

Joshua Owlet was changed to the roots! He told me a story that chimed very close with my own wishes, and for that reason I was tardy to believe it; but he gave me chapter and verse, and when I heard my own life was got in danger, I did believe it as the safest course to pursue.

"That Bond is a rogue, William," Joshua began, and he was terrible excited from the start off.

"I'm inclined to agree with you," I answered, "for he's done a dirty thing and, so far as I can tell, he's worked very artful to get Jenny away from me, which no honest man would have set out to do."

"That's nothing," he answered. "The girl has been a fool and still is; but the point is this. While she was all for him, Bond felt the going good; but now, along of your high-minded action and the way you've took it, and the way he's took it, and what I've said, she's in two minds yet. Love him she did and love him she do and don't deny it; but she begins to see, as well she may, that for her lifelong salvation, if she must wed, she'd have a safer and a better time with you than Bond."

Well, I was a good deal surprised to hear Joshua talk so reasonable, and what he said next astonished me still more.

"That's so far to the good," I answered, "for I care a lot too much for the maiden to stand between her and her real welfare. But, apart from her, I've always suspicioned Tom Bond was too good for this world till this happened. Men ain't so perfect as him, and when I heard he'd got round Jenny, I began to fear there was more to the young man than meets the eye."

"A plucky sight more," declared Owlet. "You can leave him for a minute. I'll come to him—the wicked rascal. But first I want for you to know that I'd a darned sight sooner see my daughter married to you than him, or any other man; and though I hate like hell for her to leave me, I ordain, since it's got to be, that you have her and none other. And none else ever shall."

I couldn't believe my ears, of course, but he was terribly in earnest. He tore at his beard as his manner was, and his eyes flashed, and I couldn't tell for my life whether he was speaking truth or was lying to me.

"So much for that then," I said, "and I'm very glad to hear you take that view, for it was time you saw sense in the matter. But I don't wed Jenny if she don't want to wed me—not to please you, or nobody. And that brings us to Tom Bond. At this moment I'm in a difficulty, because seeking, where I counted to learn more about him, I've been headed off. His credentials was all they should be, and Sir Walter didn't trouble to verify 'em ; and asking him for 'em a few days since, I was a good bit put about to hear that master couldn't find 'em. But he dared me to say there was anything wrong with Bond, because he thinks the world of the man and wouldn't have him away on no account whatever."

" I'll lay my life the blackguard stole those credentials poking about where he didn't ought," said Joshua ; but I answered 'twas little likely.

" The master be almost sure to have destroyed 'em, for he's got a mania for tearing up in a hurry," I explained, " and he'll often do so and lament too late."

" I hope he did, then, and I'll tell you why," said Owlet to me. " And, come to think of it, I guess he did, for Bond is terrible anxious and worried and like a rat in a trap. He knows you are on his track and he knows that if those credentials exist and you can put hand to 'em you'll mighty soon find they was forged. So don't you whisper they can't be found."

" And how do you know they was forged ? " I asked.

" Because he told me so," answered Joshua. " He came here about Jenny and pitched a tale and I listened, and presently I found the man was far different from what he makes out at Oakshotts. I did a bit of play-acting myself, William, and led him on, and though he was cautious as a rat, I made him think after a bit I was a wrong 'un myself and got his confidence."

" And how did you do that ? " I asked. " And why ? "

" I did it by holding out against you and saying I'd sooner my gal had him than you ; and why I did it was because I had dark suspicions. And you can thank God I had. When he found I was up against Oakshotts and didn't care for nobody there and took a lawless view of life, he came across with it. He's a bad lot and have done time, and he's here for no good whatsoever to Oakshotts. But he's worse than hot stuff, William. He's a dangerous criminal, and he's going to put you out of his path pretty soon as if you was no more than a carrion crow, unless you climb down about my daughter."

" Is he ? " I said. " And how does he intend to set about it ? "

" I've called you here to tell you," answered Owlet. " Only yesterday he let out his plans and I pretended to applaud 'em.

Nobody's easier to wipe out than you, owing to your regular habits, and on Wednesday next, which is his afternoon off, he'll lie behind a hedge for you and do you in. That's as sure as death."

I was a good bit amused to hear this tale.

"And what hedge ? " I asked.

"He'll shoot you," said Owlet, "and when you go for your walk, you won't come back. And he'll have his alibi all right and never be suspected, for that matter. He means to get you from the woodstack and be gone like a flash of lightning. I got it out of him by pretending that nothing would suit me better than your death ; and I'm telling you, so as you shall either be the hunter instead of the hunted, if you're brave enough for such a job, or else give him up to justice instanter on my word. He's got a army revolver and that he'll use if you don't take the first step yourself."

I looked at Joshua and felt a lot puzzled about his yarn. Fear I did not feel, because them that was in the War know it not in peace. But for a moment my mind was took off Bond by Owlet himself, and I couldn't somehow feel his story had the ring of truth about it. In fact I told him so, and he swore a barrow-load of oaths that it was only too true.

"I've told you," he said, "and I've worked for you in this matter, Morris, and hid myself and hoodwinked the wily devil till he believed I was with him heart and soul. But if you don't believe me I can do nought. All I say is that the man is well aware how only you stand between him and Jenny, and he'll do you in next Wednesday so sure as you're born, if you don't watch out."

"Never heard anything so interesting, Joshua," I said, "but whether I believe you or not, I can't be sure. However, fear nought. If I could get through the War, I ain't likely to go down afore this damned rogue. And forewarned is forearmed. I'll keep my weather eye lifting on Wednesday, be sure of that much."

"Have you got a revolver ? " he asked.

"I've got my old war revolver," I said, "and it will be in my pocket when I go out for my health."

"I hope your health won't suffer, then," he told me.

I left him after that and went home. Jenny was friendly enough and Tom Bond was so meek and mild that butter wouldn't have melted in his mouth. So the time passed till Wednesday and the footman was off for his afternoon out; and at my usual hour, forbidding Jenny to seek me that afternoon, I went my way. We were quiet for the minute with a week between guns at Oakshotts. A still evening with the reds in the sky and frost promising. My thoughts were difficult, because the more I turned over what Owlet had told me, the more mad it sounded; but I couldn't get any line on Bond and I couldn't get any line on Jenny, though I had a fancy she was pretty miserable and inclining a bit more towards me. For that walk, however, I concentrated on self-preservation, because if the man really thought to slay me, 'twas up to me to get in first, of course. So I went mighty wary when I came to the trees, and being blessed with amazing good long sight, used it. And I also pricked my ears and had my gun in my pocket and my hand upon it. A shot I heard, but it was dull and far off and didn't sound no ways different from the usual shots you always heard in Oakshotts. Then, after going without any event for half a mile or more, I saw the woodstack ahead on my way, and that minded me of Owlet's warning and the chance it might be true. A very handy place for any man to lie in wait for an enemy on the woodman's path; so I stopped, crept off into the undergrowth and reckoned to come up behind the stack, so as if there was to be any surprises, I'd give 'em. But the surprise was mine notwithstanding. I stalked the stack as cautious as though it had been an elephant, and crept up inch by inch through the laurels with my blood warm and my senses very much alive and my revolver at full cock. And at last I was parted from the danger-point by no more than a screen of leaves. But not a soul I saw, and I was just pushing out with a good bit of relief in my mind, when my eyes fell on the ground and I marked a man lying so still as a snake behind the pile with his head not a yard from the path that ran alongside of it! He was waiting and watching; but he'd not heard me; so there lay Tom Bond sure enough, looking for me to come along; and there stood I behind him not ten yards distant. The dusk was coming down by now and the wind sighing in the naked branches overhead, and I didn't see no use in wasting time. I couldn't have wished to get him in a more awkward position for himself; so I covered him with my revolver and I stepped out quick as lightning, and afore he could move, my muzzle was at his ear.

"Now, you damned scoundrel," I said, "the boot is on the other leg, I reckon!"

But not a muscle of the man twitched, and then I got the horror of my life, for Tom Bond was dead. He lay flat on his face with his hands stretched afore him, and a revolver, the daps of mine, had fallen from his hand and dropped a foot away from it. And, looking close, I saw a big dabble of blood about him, that had come from his body and his mouth.

'Twas a very ugly situation for me, and nobody saw that quicker than what I did; but I kept my nerve and didn't lift a finger to the man after I was satisfied that not a spark of life remained in him. I said to myself as I ran home that all I could do was to tell naked truth and hope for the best, though at that moment I couldn't fail to see the truth as I told it was bound to look a thought fanciful to the unbiased eye. But I went straight to Sir Walter, and gave him word for word, leaving out no item of the story and putting my revolver on his desk for him to guard after he'd heard all.

He was a lot shocked, of course, and awful sorry to lose Tom Bond; but he believed every word I told him and knew the facts must be exactly as I revealed 'em. Then he sent post-haste for the police and a doctor, and I took 'em to the scene, and men fetched a hurdle and the body of Bond was brought down to the garage and treated with all due respect. The doctor examined him then and found he'd been shot through the back at tolerable close range; and the ball had gone through heart and lung and killed him instantly. 'Twas dark by now, and Dr. James said as how he'd be back with another surgeon next morning. But one mighty strange thing increased my difficulties, because, when we came to hunt for it, the weapon I marked a foot from the dead man's hand was there no longer. And that meant two things. It meant, to me, that somebody had been beside Bond after I left him; and it meant to the police a tidy big question as to whether my word could be depended upon. Nought was done until the next day and then the inquest was arranged for and a police inspector spent a long time in my company and finished by telling me straight that I was in a tolerable tight place. We knew each other as friends in Little Silver, but the inspector—Bassett he was called—felt terrible disposed to arrest me, and only when Sir Walter went bail I wouldn't run away did he abstain from getting a warrant.

To Joshua Owlet, of course, they went; but there a shocking thing happened, for the man swore I was lying and that he knew nought about the affair and that he had never warned me nor nothing like that. He said how Bond had come to him with his tale about loving Jenny, and he'd only told him same as he'd told me, that Jenny's duty would lie with her father and he didn't wish her to marry anybody. So it looked as if the only one who knew the truth must be the dead man, and he was gone beyond recall. They found he'd been shot by an army revolver with a ball of the usual pattern, and more they didn't know; and when Sir Walter pointed out that my revolver was loaded in all chambers and hadn't been fired, all the police said was I'd had plenty of time to fire it and clean it and load it again afore I gave it to him.

And the next thing that happened to me was that I was locked up, tried afore the justices and committed for trial at the Assizes for the murder of Tom Bond.

Of course nobody who knew me believed such a fearful thing, but seeing how it stood and how the details looked to the public, I didn't blame any for doubting except Joshua Owlet; and even in my nasty fix I couldn't but admire the devilish craft of that man. Of course I knew from the first he'd done the trick; and more I knew, because I'd seen his far-reaching reasons and his cunning, to use Bond against me and so plot that we should wipe out each other and leave Jenny free. I could see it all; and when Sir Walter had one of the big swells from Scotland Yard to investigate the murder from the beginning, and when that man heard all I'd got to say, he saw it too.

A mean little build of chap, but properly bursting with intellect, was Detective-Inspector Bates; and after hearing Sir Walter and after hearing me, he never felt no doubt himself about my innocence.

" 'Tis like this," I said. " You can see what Owlet did. He told me Bond meant to take my life ; and no doubt he told Bond I meant to take his life ; and the difference was this : Bond did mean to shoot me that afternoon, doubtless believing that if he didn't, I'd be the death of him later. He could get me when he liked. But I never meant to do more than prove he was a rascal, or satisfy myself that he was not. For the rest, and as to details, only Owlet can tell 'em ; but it's very clear to me he did what they say I did. He knew where Bond was going to lie for me, and he was there hid afore Bond came and slew him and left him so as it should be shown, as it has been shown, that I slew him. Very like he watched the whole thing and was hid at my elbow somewhere when I found Bond ; and then, after I'd gone, he got Bond's revolver and took it away so as I should be catched in a lie and prove the only one that was armed. And more than that : he may have lent Bond the revolver himself."

I think the Detective-Inspector felt very pleased with my view ; and there was another good point for me, because, afore they buried him, they took the dead man's fingerprints and found he'd been in prison before. In fact he was a bad 'un—a juvenile adult that had served two years for three burglaries ; and so Owlet had told me a bit of truth mixed up with his lies. But of course poor Bond might have meant to run straight after he fell in love with Jenny, till Owlet tackled him and encouraged him to try and murder me. Nobody will ever know what his game at Oakshotts was, for he died before he'd played it. Anyway, he was gone, and all that mattered to me remained to get my neck out of the noose if it could be done.

And it was done, though more by the act of God than any particular cleverness of man. But, primed with what I'd told him, Mr. Bates got up Owlet's sleeve and, little by little, wormed out the truth. And Owlet, who'd been on the razor edge over the job for a good bit with a mind tottering, lost his nerve at last and gave himself away. He'd got in some queer fashion to believe Bates was his friend and on his side, for these deep detective chaps have a way often to show friendship to them they most suspect ; and so it happened ; for Joshua let it out at last, finding the other knew very near as much about it as he did. And then the darbies were on him, and soon after they were off me.

He'd done it with a madman's cleverness, to free his girl and get her back ; and he went to a criminal lunatic asylum for his bit of work and bides there yet. And as for Jenny, I left the rest to her and didn't lift a finger to draw her to me no more. She came, however, and felt the Lord had saved not only me alive, but her also.

For three year we worked at Oakshotts after that, as man and wife ; and then I took my pension and went into Little Silver to live. Because Sir Walter got it into his head to marry again before it was too late, and his new lady never liked me so well as he did. He'd applauded me far too much to her, and 'tis always a fatal fact in human nature, that if you hear a fellow-creature praised up to the sky, your mind takes an instant set against 'em.

No. XV
THE NIGHT-HAWK

No. XVI

THE NIGHT-HAWK

I

THERE'S no doubt that a man's opinions change with his business, because the point of view's just everything. What be good to you is what you want to happen and think ought to happen ; and if it don't happen, then you'm a bit fretful about it, and reckon there's a screw loose somewhere in the order of things. For instance, I be a gamekeeper to-day, and I take a view of fish and birds according ; but once on a time I was a fly-by-night young rip of a poacher, and had a very different idea about feathers and fins.

"A fish be no more the bank-owner's fish than the water in the river be his water ! " That's what I used to say. "Because a salmon—he's a sea-fish, and free as air and his own master. Same with a bird. How do I know whether 'twas Squire Tom, or Squire Dick, or Squire Harry as reared a pheasant I happen to knock over on a moony night ? Birds will fly, as Nature meant 'em ; and, again, it may be just a wild bird, as never came out of no boughten egg at all, but belonged to the country, like his father and his grandfather afore him. And so 'tis common property, same as the land did ought to be, and if I be clever enough to catch 'un and kill 'un—why, so much the better for me ! All for free trade you see I was. And in a poacher that must be the point of view. But time and chance play all manner of funny pranks with a man; and time and chance it were that turned me from this dangerous walk of life into what I be now. The way of it was simple enough, in a manner of speaking, yet I'm sure no such thing happened afore, or be like to hap again.

Woodcotes was a very great estate on the brink o' Dartmoor. In fact, the covers crept up the hills as far as the fierce winds would let 'em ; and they was cold woods up over—cold and rocky and better liked by the foxes than the pheasants. But the birds done very well half a mile lower down, and the river that run through Woodcotes carried a lot of salmon at the proper time. A ten-pound fish was no wonder, and more'n one twenty-pounder have left it in my memory.

I was twenty-five on the night this tale begins—twenty-five year old, and a proper night-hawk of a chap, as loved the hours of darkness and gloried in the shedding of blood. Sport was in my veins, so to say, handed down from father to son, for my grandfather had been a gamekeeper, and my father a water-bailiff, and my uncle—my father's brother—a huntsman. That was the line of life I'd thirsted for, or even to go for a jockey. But Nature weren't of the same mind. I growed six foot tall afore I was seventeen—my mother's family was all whackers—and so riding was out of the question, and I went on the land and worked behind the horses instead of on 'em.

Well, the river ran very suent through the water-meadows below my village, and there was wonnerful fine stickles and reaches for trout, and proper deep pools for salmon. And on a fine night in June, with the moonlight bright as day, I was down beside it a bit after one o'clock, busy about a little matter of night-lines. I meant to make an experiment, too, because I'd read in a book how the salmon will come up to stare if you hold a bright light over 'em. They'll goggle up at you and get dazed by the light, and then you can spear 'em as easy as picking blackberries. 'Twas news to me, but a thing very well to know if true, and I got a bull's-eye lantern to prove it.

Through a hayfield—half cut, 'twas—I went, where the moon throwed a shadow beside each uplifted pook, and the air was heavy with the scent, and a corncrake somewhere was making a noise like sharpening a scythe. A few trout were rising at the night moths, but nothing moved of any account in the open, and I pushed forward where the hayfield ended at the edge of the woods. There, just fifty yards inside the trees, was one of the properest pools on the river; and, having set my night-lines for a trout or two higher up, I came down to the salmon pool, spear in hand, and lit my lantern and got on a rock in the mid-channel, where 'twas clear and still, with nought but the oily twist and twirl of the currents running deep beneath me.

I felt so bold as a lion that night, for Squire Champernowne, of Woodcotes, had died at dawn, and the countryside was all in a commotion, and I knowed, what with talking and drinking in the pubs and running about all day, that not a keeper would be to work after dark. A very good man had been the Squire, though peppery and uncertain in his temper, and quick to take offence, but honest and well-liked by all who worked for him. 'Twas one of they tragical moments, long expected but none the less exciting, when death came, and I felt certain sure that I should have the river to myself till morning.

But I was wrong. Looking upstream by good chance afore I got to work, I saw a man in the meadow moonlight. There he was, making for the woods. He was following the path I followed, and in five minutes I saw that he'd be on the river-bank within ten yards of me. Of course, I thought the chap was after me and had tracked me down. It astonished me a good bit to mark him, and I saw he was a tall, slim man, much lighter than me, though very near the same height. He didn't tally with my knowledge of any of the Woodcotes keepers, so I felt better and hoped as it might be a stranger, or a lunatic, or somebody as wouldn't be feeling any interest in me. But I had to shift, of course, so I nipped off my rock and went under the bank where the ivy fell over at the tail of the salmon pool. 'Twas a deep, sandy-bottomed reach, with the bank dipping in steeply o' one side and a shelving, pebbly ridge the other. The river narrowed at the bottom of the pool and fell over a fall. So there I went, and looked through the ivy unseen and watched my gentleman along the river-path.

He came, and the light of the moon shone on him between two trees, so that I could mark who 'twas; and then I seed the man of all others in the world I'd least have counted to see. For there, if you please, went young Mister Cranston Champernowne, the nephew of the dead man, and thought to be heir to Woodcotes! For Squire never married, but he had a good few nephews, and two was his special favourites: this one and his brother, young Lawrence Champernowne. They were the sons of General Sir Arthur Champernowne, a famous fighter who'd got the Victoria Cross in India, and carried half the alphabet after his name.

Well, there stood the young youth, and even in the owl-light I could see he was a bit troubled of spirit. He looked about him, moved nervously, and then fetched something out of his pocket. 'Twas black and shining, and I felt pretty sure 'twas a bottle; but I only had time to catch one glimpse of it, for he lifted his arm and flung it in the pool. It flashed and was gone, and then, before the moony circles on the water had got to the bank, the man was off. He walked crooked and shaky, and something told me as the young fellow had done terrible wrong and felt it.

Whatever 'twas he'd hid, it lay now in the deepest part of the river, and that, no doubt, he knew. But I knowed more. The bottom where his bottle was lying happened to be fine sand with a clear lift to the little beach; and so, given a proper tool, 'twas easy enough to rake over the river-bed and fetch up anything of any size on that smooth surface.

Of course, my first thought was to fetch that bottle out of the water; but then a cold shiver went through me, and I told myself to mind my own business and leave Cranston Champernowne to mind his. Yet somehow I couldn't do that. There was a sporting side to it, and a man like me wasn't the sort to sit down tamely afore such a great adventure. So I said to myself: " I'll have that bottle ! "

My wits ran quick in them days, as was natural to a night-hawk, and I only waited till the young chap was off through the woods, and then nipped back into the grass field, fetched a haymaker's rake, made fast a brave stone to 'un, got my night-lines up, and soon lowered down the rake over the spot where the bottle went in. At the second drag I got him, and there, sure enough, was the thing that Mister Champernowne had throwed in the pool. But it weren't a bottle by no means. Instead, I found a black, tin, waterproof canister a foot long; and, working at it, the lid soon came off. Inside was one piece of paper and no more. That was all the canister hid; and the next thing I done was to light up my lantern and see what wonderful matter it could be as the young man was at such pains to do away with so careful. For Woodcotes House was two mile from the river, and Cranston Champernowne had been at all this trouble, you see, on the very day of his uncle's death.

Well, I soon found out all about it, for the thing was simple enough. The paper was a will, or, as I heard long after, a thing called a codicil—a contrivance what you add to a will. And it revoked and denied everything as the dead man had wrote before. In a few words the paper swept away Squire Champernowne's former wills and testaments, and left Woodcotes to Lawrence Champernowne, the son of General Sir Arthur and the brother of the chap as had just flung the paper in the river.

So there 'twas, and even a slower-witted man than me might have read the riddle in a moment. No doubt young Mister Cranston thought himself the heir, and reckoned 'twas all cut and dried. Then, rummaging here and there after his uncle was gone, he'd come upon this facer and found himself left in the cold. The paper was dated two year back, and signed by two names of women-servants at Woodcotes.

Well, I soon came to myself afore this great discovery, and though, no doubt, the right and natural thing for me to have done, as a sporting sort of blade always open to the main chance, would have been to go to Lawrence Champernowne or his father, yet I hesitated; because, though I held a poacher's ideas about game and such like, I wasn't different from other folk in other matters. I'd got religion from my mother, for she taught me the love of God, and father, the water-bailiff, he taught me the fear of God likewise; and if you've got them two things properly balanced in your intellects, you can't go far wrong. And at that moment the feeling in my mind was not to be on the make. No, I swear to you I only felt sorry for the young chap as had done this terrible deed. I was troubled for him, and considered very like the temptation was too great, that he'd just fallen into it in a natural fit of rage at his disappointment, and that presently, when he came to his senses, he'd bitterly mourn such a hookem-snivey deed. For, of course, Champernownes were great folk, high above any small or mean actions, and with the fame of the family always set up afore them. Yes, I thought it all out, and saw his mind working, and felt so sure as death that a time would come when he would regret the act and feel he'd ruined his life. " He'll return here some day afore 'tis too late, and seek to fetch up the paper," I thought. And with that I was just going to fling the canister back in the pool when a better idea took hold on me. I'd make it easier and quicker for the man, and even now, while he was smarting and doubtless battling with his better nature, I'd help him in secret to do the right thing. He'd think it was a miracle, too, for, of course, I wasn't going to give myself away over the business. And no doubt, if the young fellow saw a miracle worked on his behalf, he'd turn from his wickedness and repent.

In a word, my purpose was to put the paper back in his path again, afore he got home ; and not only that, but I meant to speak a word or two—just a voice he should hear out of the night. I might save his soul, and, whether or no, 'twas a sporting idea to try to do so. So I set to work, and even in them exciting moments I thought what strange messengers the Lord do choose to run His Almighty errands.

I knowed the way the young chap had to go, and how long 'twould take. Two miles from the river lay Woodcotes, and, by following over a hill and dropping down t'other side, I could get in his track again and be at the edge of the home gardens where he'd come out. I saved half a mile going that way, and would be able to get there long afore him.

Of course, all this went through my head a lot quicker than I set it down. Like a flash came my determination, and I acted on it, and ran through the night and headed him off, and hid in a rhododendron bush just by the main drive, where he'd leave the woods on his way home. And right in his path, where his feet must go, I'd put the tin canister. 'Twas dry again, and flashed in the moonlight so bright that he couldn't miss it nohow.

Still as a mouse I waited for him, and just over my head hooted an owl. " Hoo-hoo-hoo ! Hoo-hoo-hoo-hoo ! " he shouted out ; and another, long ways off, answered to him.

What should I say ? was the question in my mind while I waited for Mr. Champernowne. And first I thought I'd say nothing at all; but then I reckoned 'twould be more solemn and like a miracle if I did. I minded a thing my father used to speak when I was a li'l one. He'd tell it out very serious, and being poetry made it still more so. " Don't you do it, else you'll rue it ! " That's what my father used to tell me a score of times a day, when I was a boy, and the words somehow came in my mind that night. Therefore I resolved to speak 'em and make 'em sound so mysterious as I could, just when the young fellow found the canister.

It all went very well—in fact, a lot better than I'd hoped for, chance favoured me in a very peculiar way, and the Dowl hisself couldn't have planned a greater or more startling surprise for Cranston Champernowne. Along he came presently, with his head down and his shoulders up. Like a haunted creature he crept from the woods ; his face was white, and misery stared out of it. Presently he looked upward at the moon, while he walked along like an old, tired man. And when I see his face, I was terrible glad I'd took such a lot of trouble for him, because 'twas properly ravaged with suffering. He came to the canister, and the owl was hollering for all he was worth, and the matter fell out like this. First Mister Champernowne catched sight of the canister and stood still, as if the sight had froze him ; then the bird shouted, and I had to wait for him to shut up afore I had my say.

" Hoo-hoo-hoo ! Hoo-hoo-hoo-hoo ! " went the owl. Then, the moment he stopped, I spoke, very loud and slow.

" Don't you do it, or else you'll rue it ! " I said.

And the young man gazed up into the air and very near fell down in a fit, I believe, for he 'peared to think he'd heard but one voice, and that the owl was telling to him ! I'm sure it must have been like that with him, for he cried aloud and he lifted up his hands, and he shook like a reed in the river.

" Good God in Heaven, what's this ? Am I mad ? " he says. Then the owl was frightened, and slipped away silent on open wing, and the young man stood still staring and panting. He put his hands over his face to wipe away the canister, for 'twas clear that he didn't believe the thing was real ; but when he looked again, there it lay, glittering like a star—the very item he'd thrown in the deepest part of the river not an hour afore! Then he crept towards it very slow, as if 'twas a snake; and he bent and touched it and found it to be a real thing and not a dream. With that he picked it up and strained his ears to listen; and I could see the sweat shining on the face of 'un and the breath of the man puffing in a mist on the night air. He stood all doubtful for a little, while I bided so still that not a leaf moved; then he went on his way, like a creature sick or drunk, and he passed into the gardens and disappeared from sight.

I waited till he was properly gone, and after that I got back in the woods and returned to the river. Always a neat and tidy man—as poachers mostly are—I took the hayrake back to the field and wound up my lines. Then I went home, for 'twas peep of day by now, and I felt I'd done a very proper night's work, and wondered if there'd ever be anything to show for it.

Well, there wasn't—in fact, it looked much as if I'd done a miracle for nothing. Days passed by. Squire Champernowne got buried with a proper flare-up, and we heard that Mr. Cranston Champernowne was heir to Woodcotes and the farms and all. And next time I was out and about on the river according to my custom, I heard the owl hollering, and I said to the owl: "You and me had our trouble for nought, my old dear, for 'tis very clear he wouldn't listen to us. He was a hard case and a bad lot, and 'tis no good honest folk like you and me putting a man into the straight road if he won't bide in it."

And the owl—he goes—"Hoo-hoo-hoo!"—laughing like.

II

Two full years passed afore the end of my tale. The new Squire did very wisely, and was highly thought upon. He ruled well, for he had an old head on young shoulders, and he was a good landlord and a patient, sensible, and kind-hearted chap. He got engaged to be married also, and seemed so bright and cheerful as need be, and good friends with his brother Lawrence, and popular with high and low. Yet right well I knowed there was a cruel canker at his heart, for no well-born man could do the thing he'd done and not smart to his dying day and feel all his prosperity was poison. Not to mention the terrible shock as he had got from me on the night after his uncle's death.

I felt sure, somehow, as the truth would come out, and that I should hear more about that coorious evening. And so I did, but 'twas in a manner very different from what I guessed or expected. In a word, to be quite honest about it, I got into smart trouble myself one night—in October 'twas, and a brave year for pheasants. The chaps at Woodcotes outwitted me for the fust time in their lives, and cut short my little games. They set a trap for me, and I got catched. There's no need to dwell upon the details, but I found myself surrounded by six of 'em, and knowing very well that, if I showed fight, 'twould only be a long sight worse for me in the end, I threw up the sponge, gived 'em my air-gun—a wonderful weapon I'd got from a gipsy—and let 'em take me. I was red-handed by ill-fortune, which, indeed, they had meant me to be. In fact, they waited just where they knowed I was going to be busy, having fust throwed me off the scent very clever by letting one of their number tell a pack o' lies to a woman friend of mine in a public-house the night afore. She told me what a keeper had told her, and I believed it, and this was the result.

There weren't no lock-up within five miles, and so the men took me to Woodcotes till morning; and very pleased they was, and very proud of themselves, for I'd been a thorn in their hands for a good bit. And I said nought, understanding such matters, and knowing that every word you speak at such a time will be used against you.

And then we got to Woodcotes, and I had to speak, for though 'twas three in the morning or a bit later, young Squire, knowing about the thing, hadn't gone to bed. He commanded 'em to bring me afore him, and I came in, handcuffed, to his libery, and there he sat with a good fire and a book. And a very beautiful satin smoking-jacket he wore, and the room smelled of rich cigars. I blinked, coming in out of the dark, and he told the keepers to go till he'd had a talk along with me. And then he dressed me down properly, but not till his men was t'other side of the door.

He knowed all about my family and its success in the world, and its fame in all to do with sport, and he said that 'twas a crying sin and shame that such as me should break away and be a black sheep and get into trouble like this.

" 'Tis a common theft, and nothing more nor less," he said. " You've been warned more than once, and you knew right well that, if you persisted, this would be the end of it."

Well, I made ready for a dig back, of course, and was going to surprise the man; but somehow he spoke so kind and generous and 'peared to be so properly sorry for me, that I struck another note. I thought I saw a chance of getting on his blind side and being let off, so I kept away from such a ticklish subject as the canister. Instead, I spoke very earnest of my hopes for the future, and promised faithful as I'd try to see the matter of pheasants and such like from his point of view. And I told him that I was tokened to a good girl—same as he was—and that 'twould break her very heart if I got a month, and very likely make her throw me over and wreck my life, and so on. I worked myself up into a proper heat, and pleaded all I knew with the man. I implored him to put mercy before justice for once, and assured him that 'twould pay him a thousandfold to let me off. I was contrite, and allowed that no doubt my views on the subject of game might be altogether mistaken. I took his word for it that he was right and I was wrong. In fact, I never talked so clever in all my life afore; but at the end it was that the really thrilling thing fell out. For then, just to make a good wind-up like, I called home my father's oft-spoken words, and said to the man the very same speech that I'd said to him more'n two years afore, when I was hid in the rhododendron bush.

" Don't you do it, or else you'll rue it ! " I said. And then I stopped, and my heart stopped too, I'll swear, for in an instant moment I saw that Squire remembered when and where he'd heard that warning afore. He turned a awful sort o' green colour, and started from his chair. Then he fell back in it again and stared upon me as if I was a spectrum rose out of a grave.

He couldn't speak for a bit, but presently he linked up my voice with the past, and squared it out and came to his senses. But he didn't twist, nor turn, nor quail afore me. In fact, when he recovered a bit, he was a good deal more interested than frightened.

"Those words!" he said. "Could it be—is it possible that you——"

"God's my judge, Squire Champernowne, that I didn't mean to touch on that," I answered. "'Twas dead and buried in my heart, and the kind words you have said to me would have made me keep it there for evermore. I ban't your judge, though you be going to be mine, and I didn't speak them words in no sense to threaten, and I didn't speak 'em to remind you as you'd ever heard 'em before. 'Twas just because the words be solemn poetry," I said. "'Twas just because of that I used 'em, and for no other reason."

He nodded and considered.

"Tell me," he answered in a simple, quiet way—"tell me everything you know about that night from the beginning."

And so I did. I hid nought and explained all, even down to my feelings in the matter, and my wish, man to man, to give him another chance for to do right. And I never see a male creature so much moved as Squire was when I telled the tale.

"I thought it was a miracle," he said very quietly, after I'd finished. Then, after a pause: "Yes, and so it was a miracle, and this is a miracle, too!"

Then he had his say.

"I would sooner have had this happen than anything in the world," he declared. "First, the mystery has been cleared up for me, and, secondly, the mystery can be cleared up for you. You did me the best turn that living man could have done for me—you put me right with myself. You'll stare at that, but it's true. I had done a crooked thing that night; but I did a straight one the next morning, for I was strong again by that time. The lawyer came then, and I showed him the codicil, which had come into my hands quite by chance the day before when I was searching for another paper. But he only laughed at it. My late uncle was a man of strong temper, a gusty, fiery man of moods and whims. His passions were like storms—he would forget them when they had swept over him. More than once in his life had he committed the gravest actions in a rage and entirely forgotten them afterwards, until he was reminded, by unpleasant results, of the things that he had done. 'Your uncle,' said the lawyer to me, 'well understood his own peculiarities, and was aware, long before his end came, that there existed evidences of his past ungovernable temper in the shape of unjust additions to his will and hasty alterations now regretted. Six months ago, when you were abroad, I visited him and made a will for him that revoked and annulled all that preceded it. You are the heir and the only heir.' So it appeared. And now I must ask you to see the proofs of what I tell you, for I shall not be at peace until you have done so. They are with my lawyers, and if you come to see me a week hence, they shall be here for you to read."

The young man was fussy, you see, and very tender about his honour, and didn't think I'd believe him. But, of course, I did.

"A week hence I shall be in klink, Squire," I said, and moved my handcuffs, just to remind him of the state of things. And then he had the head-keeper in and set me free. 'Twas a case of one good turn deserving another, no doubt; and though the young man never forgave himself for his one slip, he forgave me for my many, and a month from that day I went as third keeper to Woodcotes. And I never regretted it, I do assure you, nor more didn't he. I'm head-keeper now, and growing terrible old, and he's been dead these many years, but I'm hopeful and wishful to meet him again afore long, for he was a sportsman and more than a good master to me.